ROOM AT THE TOP

JOHN GERARD BRAINE was born in Bradford, Yorkshire in 1922. He sprang to immediate fame in 1957 with the publication of his first novel, *Room at the Top*, which was a critical success and a major bestseller in England and America and was adapted for the screen in an Oscar-winning 1959 film starring Simone Signoret and Laurence Harvey. Braine's second novel, *The Vodi* (1959), met with mixed reviews and disappointing sales, but was his favourite of his own works. His next book, *Life at the Top* (1962), a sequel to *Room at the Top*, sold well and was filmed in 1965.

Braine, who was commonly associated with what the British media dubbed the "Angry Young Men" movement of working-class writers disenchanted with the traditional British class system, continued writing until his death in 1986, though at the time of this publication, all his works were out of print. Recently, there has been renewed interest in Braine's work, with Valancourt's reissues of *Room at the Top* and *The Vodi*, and a 2012 BBC miniseries adaptation of *Room at the Top*.

JANINE UTELL is Associate Professor and Chair of English at Widener University, where she teaches 19th and 20th century British literature. She is the author of *James Joyce and the Revolt of Love: Marriage, Adultery, Desire* (Palgrave Macmillan, 2010).

Cover: The cover reproduces the jacket art of the first British edition by John Minton (1917-1957). Minton was an acclaimed artist who illustrated a number of books and dust jackets, often for publisher John Lehmann, who like Minton was gay. Suffering from depression and alcohol abuse, and feeling himself increasingly outside the abstract art movement that prevailed at the time, Minton committed suicide in January 1957, shortly before the release of *Room at the Top* in March.

By John Braine

Room at the Top (1957)*

The Vodi (1959)*

Life at the Top (1962)

The Jealous God (1964)

The Crying Game (1968)

Stay With Me Till Morning (1970)

The Queen of a Distant Country (1972)

Writing a Novel (1974)

The Pious Agent (1975)

Waiting for Sheila (1976)

Finger of Fire (1977)

J. B. Priestley (1978)

One and Last Love (1981)

The Two of Us (1984)

These Golden Days (1985)

* Available from Valancourt Books

JOHN BRAINE

ROOM AT THE TOP

With a new introduction by
JANINE UTELL

VALANCOURT BOOKS

Room at the Top by John Braine
First published London: Eyre and Spottiswoode, 1957
First Valancourt Books edition 2013

The publisher is grateful to the Royal College of Art for
permission to reproduce the original cover illustration by
John Minton and to Mark Terry of Facsimile Dust Jackets,
LLC for providing the reproduction used for this edition.

Published by Valancourt Books, Kansas City, Missouri
Publisher & Editor: JAMES D. JENKINS
20th Century Series Editor: SIMON STERN, University of Toronto
http://www.valancourtbooks.com

Library of Congress Cataloging-in-Publication Data

Braine, John.
  Room at the top / by John Braine ; with a new introduction by
Janine Utell. – First Valancourt Books edition.
    pages ; cm. – (20th century series)
  ISBN 978-1-939140-33-3 *(acid free paper)*
1. Working class – England – Fiction. I. Title.
PR6052.R265R66 2013
823'.914–dc23

                        2013008116

Also available as an electronic book.
Set in Dante MT 11/13.5

INTRODUCTION

JOE LAMPTON has been called an angry young man, a ruthless adventurer, an exploiter of women with a sexual drive matched only by his ambition to acquire money and status. He is a have-not who claws his way to the top, and on the way he loses his soul. Yet it is in his success—and his loss—that he becomes almost sympathetic, relaying his story in an unvarnished, authentic voice that draws the reader in even when Joe is at his most repellent. We get just enough of his soul to be sorry when it's gone.

Our first glimpse of Joe has him on the train from Dufton, a working-class town patterned on northern industrial cities in Yorkshire huddled in the rough landscape of the Pennines, "where the snow seemed to turn black almost before it hit the ground." He's headed to Warley, where he will make his fortune. He is hungover but bright with anticipation for his new job, new lodgings, new life. A singular characteristic of Joe, his intensely observed reflections on class markers and status symbols, is immediately established. Upon arriving at his lodgings, significantly located in a neighborhood at the top of the hill in Warley, where the hedges are manicured, the houses are large, and the expensive cars line the streets "in a kind of ostentatious litter," he notes: "The hall smelled of beeswax and fruit. . . . It looked almost too good to be true, like an illustration from *Homes and Gardens*." These kinds of observations define Joe and how he positions himself in the world; he notes furnishings, clothes, cars, even women's haircuts, and judges them according to how they connote class, taste, and status. And he wants it all, with a burning acquisitiveness that takes in material goods, social position, and, of course, women.

The detailed realism of Joe's world, the unmediated rawness of his voice, is one of the strengths of *Room at the Top*, John Braine's first and by far most successful novel. A sensation upon its publication by the reputable house Eyre and Spottiswoode in 1957, it was one of the initiators and exemplars of the Angry Young Men movement in Britain; its equally successful film adaptation, released in 1959, inaugurated the British "New Wave" in cinema. The novel sold 35,000 copies in its first year at a time when the usual numbers expected for a first novel hovered around 5,000; it was serialized (abridged and expurgated) in the *Daily Express* and sold many more thousands of copies in a book club edition. With the deal from Romulus Films and the paperback edition from Penguin, sales of Braine's novel leapt to almost 300,000 copies by the end of 1957. The novel made him a celebrity both in the UK and in America, and critics heralded him as an important, even revolutionary, new voice in British fiction.

The contemporary reception of *Room at the Top* was almost overwhelmingly positive. While some found the book to be brutal and lacking in literary art, these qualities were precisely the ones that most critics found to be praiseworthy. The *Times Literary Supplement* said that "an extraordinary vitality pulses" through the novel; in the *Evening Standard* Richard Lester wrote, "If you want to know the way in which the young products of the Welfare State are feeling and reacting, 'Room at the Top' will tell you." Reviews in the United States were even more effusive. Charles Rolo in *The Atlantic* said that Braine "has gifts which could carry him far—humor and vitality, an unsmutty forthrightness in handling erotic love, and a capacity to project with passionate sharpness the hungers of youth." In the *New York Times*, James Stern singled out the "eye for significant detail" and the "economy and unaffectedness of the prose."

These were a hallmark of the Angry Young Men movement from the mid-1950s to the early 1960s, acknowledged by many to have begun with the publication of *Room at the Top*, along with John Osborne's play *Look Back in Anger* (put on by the English Stage Company in 1956, and directed by Tony Richardson; both of these would be influential in flourishing the Angry Young Men, particularly on screen in adaptations of plays and novels). Not exactly a movement, the phrase "Angry Young Men" was coined by journalists and taken up by the media to characterize a loosely defined but still major shift in English literary culture. Its qualities were an emphasis on working-class life in the industrial provinces, usually the North of England; a vaguely leftist politics and a rejection of the Establishment; an unvarnished response to postwar life under austerity and the emergence of the Welfare State. An important precursor would be *Scenes from Provincial Life*, a 1950 novel by William Cooper (pen name of Harry Summerfield Hoff), considered by postwar writers and critics to be a crucial influence on the Angry Young Men. The writers associated with the group—Osborne, Braine, John Wain, Kingsley Amis, Alan Sillitoe, Arnold Wesker, and Shelagh Delaney (the only woman)—came from working-class or lower middle-class backgrounds and had either not been to university or had attended a newer, provincial "red-brick" institution (Birmingham, Leeds, Sheffield, Manchester, etc.; the sort of place satirized in Kingsley Amis's *Lucky Jim*). Thus a key feature of this instance in the British writing scene is a push away from Establishment literary culture notable for aesthetic experimentation grounded in Modernism and centered in London and Oxbridge. The novels and plays of the Angry Young Men are identifiable less by a coherent set of principles or practices and more so by their themes and style: sexual frankness, social realism, discontentment, a desire for escape, a straightforward, vigorous, colloquial prose style.

The Joe Lampton we meet at the beginning of *Room at the Top* is narrating the main events of the story ten years after they occur, in 1957. When we first see him retrospectively on that train in 1947, he has spent the war as an RAF man holed up in a prisoner of war camp called Stalag 1000. Both his parents have been killed by the only bomb to fall on Dufton, and he decides to escape that grimy, soot-stained town; if he stays he has nothing to look forward to but more deprivation and greasy evenings at the pub. Joe opens his story flashing back with affection (and a little bit of scorn) towards the young man starting a new life in Warley: "I looked well enough that morning [on the train] ten years ago; I hadn't then begun to acquire a middle-aged spread and – whether it sounds sentimental or not – I had a sort of eagerness and lack of disillusion. . . . My face is, not innocent exactly, but *unused*. I mean unused by sex, by money, by making friends and influencing people, hardly touched by any of the muck one's forced to wade through to get what one wants." The Carnegie-esque language is sarcastic, and deliberate. Joe narrates his story from that place at the top he tried so hard to reach; now that he "always wears the best," he cannot help but think about how he got there and how the journey sullied him.

At the same time, the reader cannot necessarily blame Joe for wanting to escape austerity, rationing, an uncertain economic future, and the squalor of working class life: all of the hardships of the immediate postwar environment. England, especially in the North, saw difficult times in the 1930s and 1940s; the "Great Slump" following World War One led to families on the dole, strikes, and massive unemployment. Deprivation and difficulty continued with the Second World War and a program of widespread and systemic rationing, part of Home Front policies meant to strengthen the nation's resources in the face of the exigencies of war. Even after the war, the Labour Government, put into place in 1945 and led by Clement Atlee, struggled to get the nation back on a path to prosperity; Labour sought to create a new society built on reforms that came to be known collectively as the Welfare State. Founded on the work of the Beveridge Report (1942), these reforms created universal education and health care, social security, and nationalized industry. Braine's novel shows a world in transition, with Joe Lampton embodying change. He carries the shadow of war with him, he wants to escape the past and reject the Establishment that made life dismal, but he looks forward to the possibility of prosperity and opportunity. He sees a world exhausted by war and poverty, and responds with an almost virile drive to claim some of the new affluence for himself.

Upon arriving in Warley, Joe takes his job as an accountant for the City Council (he'd taught himself bookkeeping while a prisoner of war), joins the local theater group (the Thespians), and sets his sights on the daughter of one of the wealthiest men in town. Susan is young, innocent, and beautiful: the perfect instrument for Joe's designs. However, his plans and his love life are complicated by the adulterous liaison he develops with Alice, the wife of a successful Warley businessman. Much of the novel turns on this dichotomous tension in Joe's world; he has authentic friendship and love with Alice, but his plans hinge on hypergamy, on marrying up and using Susan as his way to the top. Incidentally, the concerns around increased mobility for the working classes, particularly as they relate to marriage, manifest themselves throughout sociologically informed journalism at the time of Braine's writing; *Room at the Top* was often cited as a case study, and Braine himself intervened in these debates. For example, in 1957 Geoffrey Gorer published an article entitled "The Perils of Hypergamy" in the *New Statesman* in which he claimed that increased tensions between the lower and middle classes were inevitable given attempts by lower class men to rise through pursuit of middle class women and the class attainments and status that would go along with such a move. Anxieties around sex and masculinity are clear in such writings, as one sees in a 1958 piece by Frank Hilton from *Encounter*, where he says, "Our underdogs are on the move today. Remember they are ambitious, intelligent, and they come from nowhere. They have no inhibitions." In a letter to the editor, Braine responded by calling Hilton "sentimental."

John Braine took great pains to differentiate himself from his protagonist; in his book on fiction, *Writing a Novel*, he claims, "The way that it's done is to make your hero someone else." Nevertheless, parallels resound, from the background of the two men to the brash embracing of ambition and all its prizes. Braine was born in Bradford, the pattern for Dufton and Warley, in 1922; he left formal education after grammar school, served in the Royal Navy in 1942-43 (a stint cut short due to tuberculosis), and worked as a librarian until *Room at the Top* brought him financial success. While celebrity seemed to come overnight, in fact Braine had been working on the novel since 1951, under the title *Born Favourite*, and it had gone through a round of rejections. He told the story of the book's origin in a scene similar to one early in the novel: "I saw a man sitting in a big shiny car. He'd driven up to the edge of some waste ground, near some houses and factories, and was just sitting there looking across at them. It seemed to me there must have been a lot that led up to that moment." In an oft-cited anecdote, one that similarly echoes Joe Lampton, Braine responded to the success of the book thus: "What I want to do is drive through

Bradford in a Rolls Royce with two naked women on either side of me covered in jewels."

Throughout the novel Joe, in much the same way, equates sexual conquest with success; ultimately this is the means by which his corruption and failed moral compass is revealed to himself, and to us. Angry Young Men fiction might be seen to trace its social realist roots to Victorian-era "condition of England" novels such as Benjamin Disraeli's *Sybil, or, The Two Nations* (1845) or Elizabeth Gaskell's *North and South* (1855); we might even see Joe Lampton as a descendant of the brute-hero of Gaskell's novel, John Thornton. These men from the North are powerful in contrast to effete intellectuals, driven by ambition, and not afraid of change. However, where Gaskell saw her Thornton as somewhat necessary for reinvigorating England and he himself as noble, authentic, and capturing a sort of ideal masculinity, Joe is the dark side of that predatory drive. Scenes between Joe and Alice capture his charm and lustfulness; they also show his awareness that he is not his best self: she calls him a "beautiful uncomplicated brute," and he relishes the naturalness of their "loving friendship." Alice makes Joe realize, retrospectively, that she made him of a "higher quality, if one accepts that a human being is meant to have certain emotions, to be affected strongly by all that happens to him, to live *among* the people around him." An instance of erotic jealousy is what prompts this reflection, as Joe realizes that feelings are what make him human, and of a higher caliber; but these sensibilities do not survive the tragedy that occurs to Alice when Joe finally chooses Susan, a job with her father, and the life of what he once called "Zombies"—people who have chosen not to care, not to live lives of feeling but only of material gain and ease.

It was the sexual explicitness, and the ways it is used to comment on Joe's lack of a moral compass, that earned the film, carrying the tagline "A Savage Story of Lust and Ambition," its X Certificate from the British Board of Film Censors. An important crosscurrent with the Angry Young Men scene was the emergence of the British New Wave in cinema, sparked by the adaptation of *Room at the Top*. Made by the Wolfe brothers of Romulus Films, directed by Jack Clayton, the adaptation was envisioned as a serious artistic endeavor that actually wound up being, like the novel, a runaway success. *Room at the Top* sparked a wave of book-to-film projects coming from Angry Young Men writers: Osborne's *Look Back in Anger* (1959) followed shortly after, starring Richard Burton, and met with similar popularity; Alan Sillitoe's *Saturday Night and Sunday Morning* (1960), Delaney's *A Taste of Honey* (1961), David Storey's *This Sporting Life* (1963) all found their way to the screen. Studios like Romulus and Woodfall employed directors including Tony Richardson, Karel Reisz, and John Schlesinger—all influenced by the Free Cinema school of documentary filmmaking—to adapt Angry Young Men works. Like the literary texts themselves, these films changed the landscape of British cinema, including a spike in X Certificates from just two in 1955 to 17 in 1960. The major themes of *Room at the Top*, like the book, are class and sex, loss of innocence and the ways moral integrity and conscience are complicated, even diminished, by a consumerist culture run rampant. Joe is a materialist in every sense of the word: he expends his energies—physical, intellectual, moral—in pursuit of material goods and comfort, and he sees people either as obstacles to be overcome or bodies to be used.

A new adaptation, produced by the BBC in 2012, indicates ongoing interest in *Room at the Top*. Despite its specific grounding in a historical moment fading further into memory—the gradual emergence out of austerity into affluence immediately following the Second World War—Braine's novel continues to speak to readers, and bears new readings and new re-imaginings. It resonates with an audience reeling from socioeconomic upheaval in a late capitalist society and the ethical challenges it raises. In the words of William Wordsworth: "Getting and spending we lay waste our powers. . . . We have given our hearts away, a sordid boon!" *Room at the Top* asks difficult moral questions about what it means to live in a society of increasing affluence, about the gap between the haves and have-nots. It offers a hard look at what consumer culture does to our sense of individuality, our ability to be real and authentic in a manufactured world.

Braine's muscular prose, and the challenging but ultimately poignant figure of Joe Lampton, make *Room at the Top* a powerful read. Despite Braine's disavowal of the overtly literary, his creation has the power to make us feel even as he himself acknowledges he no longer can. Using a particularly apt metaphor—an American car—Joe reflects: "I could have been a different person. What has happened to my emotions is as fantastic as what happens to steel in an American car; steel should always be true to its own nature, always have a certain angularity and heaviness and not be plastic and lacquered; and the basic feelings should be angular and heavy too. I suppose that I had my chance to be a real person." Something human is lost when social reality shifts in favor of attainment and ambition; material progress comes to wreck basic values. Joe's tragedy is that he weighs the human cost of his ambition, both for himself and for those he loves, and then follows his own worst impulses, sanctioned by a grasping and acquisitive society that forgives his choices even when he can no longer forgive himself.

JANINE UTELL
Widener University

May 6, 2013

ROOM AT THE TOP

To Pat

One

I came to Warley on a wet September morning with the sky the grey of Guiseley sandstone. I was alone in the compartment. I remember saying to myself: "No more zombies, Joe, no more zombies."

My stomach was rumbling with hunger and the drinks of the night before had left a buzzing in my head and a carbonated-water sensation in my nostrils. On that particular morning even these discomforts added to my pleasure. I was a dissipated traveller – dissipated in a gentlemanly sort of way, looking forward to the hot bath, the hair-of-the-dog, the black coffee and the snooze in the silk dressing-gown.

My clothes were my Sunday best: a light grey suit that had cost fourteen guineas, a plain grey tie, plain grey socks, and brown shoes. The shoes were the most expensive I'd ever possessed, with a deep, rich, nearly black lustre. My trench-coat and my hat, though, weren't up to the same standard; the coat, after only three months, was badly wrinkled and smelled of rubber, and the hat was faintly discoloured with hair-oil and pinched to a sharp point in front.

Later I learned, among other things, never to buy cheap raincoats, to punch the dents out of my hat before I put it away, and not to have my clothes match too exactly in shade and colour. But I looked well enough that morning ten years ago; I hadn't then begun to acquire a middle-aged spread and – whether it sounds sentimental or not – I had a sort of eagerness and lack of disillusion which more than made up for the coat and hat and the ensemble like a uniform. The other evening I found a photo of myself taken shortly after I came to live at Warley. My hair is plastered into a skullcap, my collar doesn't fit, and the knot of my tie, held in place by a hideous pin shaped like a dagger, is far too small. That doesn't matter. For my face is, not innocent exactly, but *unused*. I mean unused by sex, by money, by making friends and influencing people, hardly touched by any of the muck one's forced to wade through to get what one wants.

This was the face that Mrs. Thompson saw. I'd arranged my lodgings through an advertisement in the *Warley Courier* and hadn't actually seen her yet. But even without the maroon coat and copy of the *Queen* she'd said I'd recognise her by, I knew immediately who she was; she was exactly what I'd imagined from her thick white handmade writing-paper and her near-copper-plate with its Greek e's.

She was waiting by the ticket-barrier. I gave up my ticket and turned to her. "Mrs. Thompson?"

She smiled. She had a pale, composed face and dark hair turning grey. The smile was perhaps the result of long practice; she hardly moved her mouth. It came from her eyes, an expression of personal friendliness, not the usual social grimace. "You're Joe Lampton," she said. "I hope you had a pleasant journey." She stood looking at me with a disconcerting steadiness. I suddenly remembered that I should offer my hand.

"I'm glad to meet you," I said, meaning the words. She had cool dry hands and returned my clasp firmly. We went out over a covered footbridge which vibrated as a train went underneath, and then through a long echoing subway. I always feel hemmed-in and lost in railway stations and for a moment I was overcome by depression and the buzzing in my head became an ache.

When we were outside I felt better; the rain had diminished to a drizzle and the air tasted fresh and clean with that special smell, like good bread-and-butter, which means that open country is near at hand. The station was at the centre of the eastern quarter of Warley. The effect was as if all the industries of the town had been crammed into one spot. Later I discovered that this segregation was Council policy; if anyone wanted to set up a mill or factory in Warley, it was the east or nowhere.

"This isn't the prettiest part of Warley," Mrs. Thompson said, waving her hand in a gesture which included a big mill, a fish-and-chip shop, and a seedy-looking Commercial Hotel. "It's always like this around stations, I don't know why. Cedric has some theory about it. But, you know, it's rather fascinating. There's a positive maze of streets behind the hotel. . . ."

"Is it far to Eagle Road?" I asked. "We could get a taxi." There were half-a-dozen of them in the station yard, their drivers all apparently frozen at their steering-wheels.

"That's a good idea," she said. "I feel quite sorry for those poor men." She laughed. "I've never seen any of those taxis in use; they just wait here, day by day and year by year, for fares who never come. I sometimes wonder how they live."

When we were in the taxi she gave me another long look. It was searching but not embarrassing, as cool and dry but as friendly and firm as her handshake; I had the impression of having passed some test. "I'll call you Mr. Lampton if you like," she said, "but I'd rather call you Joe." She spoke without a trace of awkwardness or flirtatiousness; she had now, her attitude implied, settled the whole matter. "And my name is Joan," she added.

"That'll be fine, Joan," I said. And from then on I always used her Christian name; though, oddly enough, I never thought of her as anything else but Mrs. Thompson.

"This is St. Clair Road," she said as the taxi turned up a long steep hill. "We live at the top. It's always T'Top in Warley, though, with a capital T. My husband has some theory about that, too. . . ."

She spoke very well, I noticed; she had a low but clear voice, with no hint either of the over-buxom vowels of Yorkshire or the plum-in-the-mouth of the Home Counties. I congratulated myself on my good fortune; all too easily she might have been the usual sort of landlady, smelling of washing-soda and baking-powder, my lodgings might easily have been one of those scruffy little houses by the station – from one Dufton to another. Instead I was going to the Top, into a world that even from my first brief glimpses filled me with excitement: big houses with drives and orchards and manicured hedges, a preparatory school to which the boys would soon return from adventures in Brittany and Brazil and India or at the very least an old castle in Cornwall, expensive cars – Bentleys, Lagondas, Daimlers, Jaguars – parked everywhere in a kind of ostentatious litter as if the district had dropped them at random as

evidences of its wealth; and, above all, the wind coming from the
moors and the woods on the far horizon.

What impressed me most was Cyprus Avenue. It was broad
and straight, and lined with cypresses. The street where I lived in
Dufton was called Oak Crescent; it didn't curve one inch and there
wasn't even a bush along it. Cyprus Avenue became at that instant
a symbol of Warley – it was as if all my life I'd been eating sawdust
and thinking it was bread.

Mrs. Thompson put her hand on my knee. I caught a whiff of
eau-de-cologne, the best kind, discreet and aseptic. "We're home,
Joe," she said. The house was semi-detached; I'd hoped it wouldn't
be. But it was a decent size and built of an expensive-looking
biscuit limestone and there was a garage. The paintwork gleamed
with newness, the lawn had the texture of moleskin; it was a house
that had always had the best of care. Except, strangely enough, for
the garage, with its peeling, blistered paint and cracked window.

"Cedric uses it for his oddments," Mrs. Thompson said. She
had an uncanny way of answering questions one hadn't asked. "It
needs attention but we never seem to get round to it. We disposed
of the car when Maurice died. It was his really; we hadn't the heart
to use it somehow."

She opened the door. "He was in the Forces?" I asked.

"A pilot in the RAF. Killed in a silly accident in Canada. He was
just twenty-one."

The hall smelled of beeswax and fruit and there was a large
copper vase of mimosa on a small oak table. Against the cream-
painted walls I could see the faint reflection of the mimosa and the
vase, chrome-yellow and near-gold; it looked almost too good to
be true, like an illustration from *Homes and Gardens*.

I helped Mrs. Thompson take off her coat. For a woman of,
I estimated, at least forty-five, she possessed a good figure, with
a small waist and no tendency either to bulges or to stringiness.
It was easy to imagine her as a young woman, though she made
no attempt to disguise her age. I looked at her, however, without
the least flicker of desire; I never wished at any time to make love
to Mrs. Thompson, though I certainly wouldn't, to be perfectly
frank, have thrown her out of my bed.

She looked at me again with that peculiarly steady gaze. "You're very like him," she murmured. Then she straightened her back, as if recalling herself. "I'm sorry, Joe. I'm forgetting my duties. I'll show you your room."

My room at Eagle Road was the first room of my own in the real sense of the word. I don't count my cubicle in the N.C.O.'s quarters at Compton Bassett because I hardly ever used it except for sleeping; and I always had the feeling that it had been made impersonal by the very number of others there before me, living on the verge of departure to another station or death. Nor do I count my room at my Aunt Emily's; it was strictly a bedroom. I suppose that I might have bought some furniture and had an electric fire installed, but neither my uncle nor my aunt would have understood the desire for privacy. To them a bedroom was a room with a bed – a brass-railed one with a flock mattress in my case – and a wardrobe and a hard-backed chair, and its one purpose was sleep. You read and wrote and talked and listened to the wireless in the living-room. It was as if the names of rooms were taken quite literally.

Now, following Mrs. Thompson into *my room*, I was moving into a different world. "It's marvellous," I said, feeling the inadequacy of the words and yet not wanting to appear too impressed; after all, I hadn't been living in the slums. I looked at it with incredulous delight: wallpaper vertically striped in beige and silver, a bay window extending for almost the whole length of the room with fitted cushions along it, a divan bed that looked like a divan and not like a bed with its depressing daylight intimations of sleep and sickness, two armchairs, and a dressing-table, wardrobe, and writing-table all in the same pale satiny wood. On the cream-painted bookcase was a bowl of anemones and there was a fire burning in the grate, leaving an aromatic smell, faintly acid and faintly flower-like, which I knew but couldn't quite place.

"Applewood," Mrs. Thompson said. "Thanks to the coal shortage we're becoming connoisseurs. There's an electric fire but I thought a real one would be more cheerful on a miserable day like this."

There were three small pictures hanging on the far wall: *The Harbour at Arles*, a Breughel skating scene, and Manet's *Olympe*.

"Especially chosen in your honour," Mrs. Thompson said. "Medici reproductions. We have quite a picture library – you just slip in new ones when you become tired of them."

"I like the skaters," I said, meaning I liked it best. It wasn't true; even as I said it I was looking at Olympe, white, plump, and coldly self-possessed. But my upbringing held me back; I couldn't bring myself to admit to a woman that I liked a nude.

Until that day I'd never really looked at a picture. I knew, for instance, that there were three water-colours in Aunt Emily's living-room, but outside the house I couldn't even remember their subjects. I'm normally observant and I'd used the living-room daily for over two years; it was simply that in Dufton pictures were pieces of furniture, they weren't *meant* to be looked at. The Medicis quite definitely were. They belonged to a pattern of gracious living; to my surprise the worn phrase straight from the women's magazines accurately conveyed the atmosphere of the room – it was as if a ready-made suit fitted perfectly.

"I expect you'd like a wash," Mrs. Thompson said. "The bathroom's to the right and the usual offices next to it." She took a bunch of keys from the dressing-table. "Your keys, Joe, before I forget. Front door, this room, wardrobe, bureau, and Heaven knows what these two are for but I'll remember presently. There'll be some coffee in half-an-hour, by the way. Or would you prefer tea?"

I said that coffee would suit me splendidly (I would much rather have had tea but I had an instinctive feeling that it wasn't quite correct at that hour). When she'd left the room I opened my suitcase and unfolded my dressing-gown. I'd never had one before; Aunt Emily thought not only that they were an extravagance (an overcoat would serve their purpose) but that they were the livery of idleness and decadence. As I looked at it I seemed to hear her voice. "I'd sooner see someone naked," she'd say. "Working people look daft in dressing-gowns, like street-women lounging about the house too idle to wash their faces. . . . Spend your money on something sensible, lad." I smiled; there was certainly nothing sensible about the garment. Its material was, I remember, a very thin rayon and the shop assistant had used the term shot silk, which meant that, according to the light, it looked either garish or drab. The stitching was poor and after one washing it became a shapeless rag. It was a typical example of the stuff turned out for a buyer's market in the early postwar period and I rather think that I was drunk when I bought it.

For all that, it gave me far more pleasure than the dressing-gown I have now, which was bought from Sulka's in Bond Street. Not that I don't like the Sulka; it's the best, and I always wear the best. But sometimes I feel uncomfortably aware that I'm forced to be a living proof of the firm's prosperity, a sort of sandwich-board man. I've no desire to be ill-dressed; but I hate the knowledge that I daren't be ill-dressed if I want to. I bought the cheap rayon garment to please myself; I bought the expensive silk garment because always to wear clothes of that quality is an unwritten term of my contract. And I shall never be able to recapture that sensation of leisure and opulence and sophistication which came over me that first afternoon in Warley when I took off my jacket and collar and went into the bathroom wearing a real dressing-gown.

The bathroom was the sort you'd expect to find in any middle-class home – green tiles, green enamel, chromium towel-rails, a big mirror with toothmug and toothbrush holders, a steel cabinet, a flush-sided bath with a shower attachment, a steel cabinet, and a light operated by a cord instead of a switch. It was immaculately clean, smelling faintly of scented soap and freshly laundered towels: it was nothing except a bathroom, it had been designed as a bathroom.

The bathroom I'd used the night before I came to Warley had been adapted from a bedroom. At the time the houses in Oak Crescent were built it wasn't considered that the working-classes needed baths. It was a small room with pitch-pine flooring (if you weren't careful you could pick up a nasty splinter) and brown wallpaper blotchy with splashes. Towels were kept in the cistern cupboard, which was generally full of drying undergarments. On the windowsill were a razor, a stick of shaving-soap, a tube of toothpaste, and a dingy mess of toothbrushes, used razor-blades, face-cloths, and no less than three cups with broken handles which were supposed to be used as shaving-mugs but, obviously, from their encrusting of dust, never had been.

I'm not going to pretend that I spent all my time at Aunt Emily's in a state of outraged sensibility. Charles and I used to make it a point of honour not to be squeamish about anything; we didn't want to be like the grocery manager at the top of Oak Crescent who was perpetually professing his great regard for cleanliness and his disgust at other people's lack of it. Charles often used to mimic him – "Soap and water's cheap enough, goodness knows. A person doesn't have to be *rich* to be clean. I wouldn't be without my *bath* for anything . . ." He talked of baths as if there was something commendable about the mere fact of immersing one's body in water. As Charles said, he made you want to yell at the top of your voice that you kept coal in your bath and only washed when you began to itch.

For all that, I was beginning to find certain details of living in Dufton a bit too sordid to be funny. I was very fond of Aunt Emily and Uncle Dick and even their two sons, Tom and Sydney, thirteen and fourteen respectively, noisy and clumsy and clueless, heading straight for the mills and apparently perfectly happy about it. I even had a slight feeling of guilt about leaving Dufton, because I knew that the monthly eight pounds which I gave her had been a great help to her. But I couldn't stay in her world any longer. Already, drying my face and hands on a large soft towel, looking out of the corner of my eye at the dressing-gown hanging behind the door (I used to watch that garment as if I were frightened it would run away) and breathing the room's odour of perfume and cleanliness, I had a footing in a very different world.

I went back to my room and changed my collar and brushed my hair. Looking at myself in the mirror, I suddenly felt entirely alone. I had a childish longing for the ugly rooms and streets where to be hungry or lost wasn't possible; for the familiar faces which might bore or irritate but never hurt or betray. I don't suppose that homesickness can entirely be avoided; but I had all mine in one concentrated dose of a few seconds that first day, and I never suffered from it again.

I looked out of the window. The back garden was surprisingly large. It was bordered by a privet hedge and there was a big apple-tree at the far end. There were two cherry-trees next to it; I remembered my father telling me once that cherry-trees can't flourish by themselves. "They have to be wed afore they're fruitful," he'd added, innocently pleased at the image. Father had never possessed a garden of his own, only a plot at the municipal allotments. No apple-trees, no cherry-trees, no lawn, no privet hedge . . .

I straightened my tie and went downstairs to the drawing-room. I'd hardly been there five minutes when Mrs. Thompson came in with the coffee. She brought it on a silver tray; I wondered how much money was coming into the house. She'd told me in her letter that her husband taught English at the Grammar School; but that didn't seem sufficient to explain their standard of living. It wasn't only the tray and coffee-pot which impressed me – they might, after all, have been wedding presents – but the cups and milk-jug and sugar-basin. They were thin and translucent and enamelled in clear primary colours – red, blue, yellow, orange – and I knew that they were expensive because of their lack of ornament and the deep glow of the enamel. I've an instinct like a water-diviner's where money's concerned; I was certain that I was in the presence of at least a thousand a year. When I noticed the matter-of-fact way in which Mrs. Thompson handled the coffee-set, without a trace of that expression of mingled pride and anxiety which most women assume on bringing out good china, I increased the amount by five hundred.

"We've never had a lodger before," she said as she handed me my coffee. Her voice paused perceptibly at the word *lodger* as if considering and rejecting all the euphemisms – paying guest, young gentleman to stay with us, and so on. "But I've suffered from land-ladies myself in my younger days. I do want you to understand, Joe, that your room's entirely your own. And you must bring your friends any time you like." She hesitated. "If ever you feel lonely – it's always a little strange at first, living in a new place – you'll be very welcome down here. Is this the first time you've been away from home? Apart from the Forces, I mean?"

"It is and it isn't. My father and mother were killed during the War and I've been living at my Aunt Emily's." I was going to pronounce Aunt with a broad a but decided not to attempt it yet.

"What sort of a place is Dufton exactly?"

"A lot of mills. And a chemical factory. And a Grammar School and a war memorial and a river that runs different colours each day. And a cinema and fourteen pubs. That's really all one can say about it."

"You haven't a theatre then?"

"The Nonconformists work their way through Abe Heywood's catalogue each winter. I used to go into Manchester if I wanted to see a show. There isn't anything in Dufton."

To Charles and me it was always Dead Dufton and the councillors and chief officials and anyone we didn't approve of were called zombies. At first we used to number them; "Zombie Number Three," Charles would say, referring to his boss, the Librarian, "made a joke today. It's pathetic when they pretend to be alive, n'est-ce pas?" When Number Ten was reached, it became difficult to remember whom we meant, so we adopted another system. "The Fat Zombie's been watering the beer again," I'd remark as the landlord of the Dufton Horseman waddled by in a new worsted suit. "He didn't come by that new shroud honestly." And there was the Washable Zombie, the grocery manager who was always talking about baths, and the Smiling Zombie, who ran a clothing club and a moneylender's. There were many others; we knew a great deal about the people of Dufton. Much more, for instance, than the Adulterous Zombie and the Childloving Zombie, two of the town's most prominent citizens, realised; if they had, we shouldn't have kept our jobs very long.

"We have a very good Little Theatre in Warley," Mrs. Thompson said. "The Warley Thespians – silly name really. You must come to our next social evening, Joe. They'll snap you up – men are scarce."

I raised my eyebrows.

"Male actors, I should have said." She smiled. "Though handsome young bachelors are greatly in demand too. Have you done any acting?"

"A little at camp concerts. But I didn't have much spare time at Dufton. And to tell you the truth, I didn't much fancy *Careless Cyril Comes A Cropper* and *Peggy's Prize-Packet*."

"You've made those up," she said, appearing rather pleased with me on that account. "Though I admit they've got the Heywood flavour."

"It was Charles actually," I said. "My friend Charles Lufford. We've known each other since we were children."

"You're very fond of him, aren't you?"

"We're as close as brothers. A great deal closer than most brothers." I remembered Charles' plump face with its absurdly large hornrimmed spectacles and its mixed expression of innocence and bawdy cheerfulness; I used to say that he looked like a parson on the razzle. "There's nothing in Dufton, Joe. Leave it before you become a zombie too . . ." I could hear his deep, rather beery voice so distinctly that he might have been in the same room. "When you go to Warley, Joe, there'll be no more zombies. Remember that. *No more zombies.*"

"You'll miss him," Mrs. Thompson said.

"Yes. I'll get over it, though—" I paused, not quite knowing how to express myself.

"I think men's friendships are much deeper than women's," Mrs. Thompson said. "But not so possessive, they never stand in each other's way." She didn't say that she knew what I meant; but the effect was as if she had; with her usual efficiency she saved me the embarrassment of explaining that I wasn't heartbroken about leaving Charles but that I wasn't totally unaffected by it either.

The clock struck the half-hour and Mrs. Thompson said that she'd better attend to the chicken. When she'd left the room I lit a cigarette and walked over to the mantelpiece. Hanging over it was a large framed photograph of a young man in RAF uniform with the white air-crew slip in his cap. He had dark thick hair, a full mouth held very firmly, and heavy eyebrows. He was smiling with his eyes – Mrs. Thompson's trick. He was good looking; he was also charming, a quality which doesn't often come through in photographs.

Charm was a favourite object of discussion between Charles and myself; we had the notion that if only we could learn how to use it our careers would be much benefited. The possession of charm wasn't in itself a guarantee of success, but it seemed to follow ambition like a pilot fish. It wasn't a highly esteemed quality in Dufton, though. Bluntness was the fashion; as Charles said, everyone behaved as if they were under contract to live up to the tradition of the outspoken Yorkshireman with a heart of gold underneath a rough exterior. The worst of it was, he'd add, that underneath the rough exterior their hearts were as base and vicious as anyone's from the Suave and Treacherous South. Not, I think, that they were entirely to be blamed; there wasn't much room for gracious living in Dufton. The young man in the photograph (obviously Mrs. Thompson's son who'd been killed during the war) had been given from birth the necessary background for charm. It's astounding how often golden hearts and silver spoons in the mouth go together.

I was a little surprised that Mrs. Thompson should so prominently display the picture of her dead son; I wouldn't have thought that she could have borne to be reminded of him. Then I remembered something that Charles had said: "Zombies always pass away or cross the Great Divide or go into the sunset. And they *lose* people like a parcel or a glove. And they can't bear to talk of It or to be reminded of It. They're dead already, that's why."

Mrs. Thompson wasn't a zombie; she'd be able to look at her dead son without hysteria. The room hadn't the necessary atmosphere for hysteria anyway. It was a drawing-room furnished in what seemed to me to be very good taste with Sheraton-type furniture, thin-legged and graceful but not spindly or fragile, and pale yellow and cream wallpaper in an arrangement of colour rather than a pattern. There was a radiogram and a big open bookcase and a grand piano; the piano top was bare, a sure sign that it was used as a musical instrument and not an auxiliary mantelpiece. The white bearskin rug on the parquet floor was, I suppose, strictly Metro-Goldwyn-Mayer, but it fitted in, added a necessary touch of frivolity, even a faint sexiness like scented cachous.

I looked at Maurice's photograph again. It reminded me of someone I knew. I was irritated with myself for not remembering; it was as if a catalogue card had been misplaced of a book which I knew was in stock. It seemed very important that I should recall the likeness; but the harder I tried the more neutral and anony-

mous his face became. I gave up the attempt and went upstairs to
unpack.

Two

C edric Thompson stood a good three inches above me, and
I'm five foot eleven in my socks. He was very thin, though.
I don't think that he could have weighed much more than ten
stone. He had a very deep, rumbling voice – it seemed too powerful for his body. His suit, a clerical grey worsted, had that close,
heavy weave, that elasticity disciplined only by first-rate tailoring,
which isn't bought for very much under thirty guineas; but there
was chalk-dust on the right sleeve and both the middle and the
top buttons of his jacket were fastened, pulling it out of shape.
And his red-and-blue Fair Isle cardigan and brown checked shirt,
though smart enough in themselves, didn't go with the suit. My
impression wasn't so much that he was wearing the wrong clothes
because he thought that they looked nice, but that he just put on
whatever was nearest to hand.

"I'm so glad that you're not a teacher," he said. "They never
seem real somehow . . . An accountant's is a sensible yet glamorous occupation. *He made Homer sound like balance sheets and balance
sheets like Homer . . .*"

"I saw it in London," I said.

"Oh, *theatregoing's* all right. It's reading that you should beware
of. Healthy young men shouldn't read. They finish by becoming
broken-winded ushers."

We were sitting in the dining-room having lunch. Cedric was at
the head of the table carving the chicken but he'd forgotten what
he was doing and his carving-knife was still poised in the air.

"Cedric," said Mrs. Thompson firmly, "stop practising your Literary Society paper on Joe and give him some chicken. He's been
travelling since six this morning." She smiled. "With that knife
flourished so menacingly it looks more as if you intended to eat
him than give him something to eat."

We all burst out laughing. It was one of those remarks which aren't funny in black and white but irresistibly comic in actuality; our shared laughter had the effect of drawing me into their circle.

As Cedric was spooning out some mashed potatoes for me, Mrs. Thompson stopped him. "Oh dear, I'd forgotten. Joe, you do like onions, don't you?"

"They're my favourite vegetable."

"Splendid. These are my speciality – potatoes seethed in milk with chopped onions."

"All virtuous and handsome and intelligent men like onions," Cedric said. "But only paragons among women like onions." He forgot to serve the potatoes. "It was when I first discovered that Joan liked them that I decided to marry her. We used to go for long walks in the Dales and live on onions and cheese washed down with mild-and-bitter."

Mrs. Thompson's eyes sparkled and she began to giggle. "Remember what Father said? He thought we smelt so strongly that we'd *have* to marry each other because no-one else would take us."

We all burst into laughter again.

When we took our coffee into the drawing-room and I was lighting a cigarette for Mrs. Thompson I found out whom Maurice reminded me of. Cedric suddenly stopped in the middle of what he was saying and looked at me as if he'd just noticed that I had three eyes.

"How could I have failed to see it?" he asked me angrily. "Don't move, Joe." He circled me as if inspecting a sculpture. "You have fair hair, that's what misled me. I wouldn't have believed it . . . the same eyes, the same bone structure, the same expression—"

"I noticed it straightaway," Mrs. Thompson said. "He's the image of Maurice."

I looked at the photograph above the mantelpiece and saw my own face for the first time. It shook me for a moment: I was jerked into that zone of unreality one would inhabit for seconds at a time in the RAF, watching a Wimpey scarcely a wing-tip away disintegrate into rather gaudy green and orange flames, knowing that the men inside, with whom one had been drinking a few hours ago, were being fried in their own fat like bacon.

"I'm sorry, Joe," Mrs. Thompson said. "Talking about you as if you weren't there – do forgive us." She put her hand on mine. "You know, we miss him very much at times. But we haven't built a kind of shrine to him, we're not *always* thinking of him. And we don't mind being reminded of him – that sounds mixed but you know what I mean."

"I feel like that about Father and Mother," I said to my own surprise.

Cedric was looking at me anxiously. He had a bony gentle face with bushy eyebrows and thinning black hair. "I'm an insensitive, crass, boorish, ill-mannered old fool," he said. "I do apologise if I embarrassed you, Joe."

"I'm not embarrassed," I said, and smiled at him. There was a silence, but not an uncomfortable one. We'd engaged top gear, as it were; the three of us were together in the best relationship possible to a young man and a middle-aged couple. We were on a basis of intimacy – if the Sunday papers haven't dirtied the word beyond use – because they were the sort of people with whom one couldn't live on any other basis. I had enough sense, though, to be aware that I mustn't presume too much upon the intimacy, that though we were in top gear the journey had only just begun.

After Cedric had returned to school I went to my room to lie down. I hadn't slept well the night before and, having eaten a heavy lunch, was agreeably drowsy. I took off my shoes and jacket, put on my dressing-gown (more for effect than for warmth) and settled down on the divan.

I didn't drop off straightaway but lingered deliberately on the borders of sleep, the taste of chicken and lemon pie and Turkish coffee still on my tongue, speculating what they'd be like at the Town Hall and particularly what kind of a boss Hoylake the Treasurer would be. I didn't begin work till Monday and today was Friday so there was plenty of time for investigation . . . The rain had stopped; it was very quiet in the house and I could hear Mrs. Thompson in the kitchen downstairs. It didn't disturb me, it didn't hold me back from the long smooth slope down which I was gliding into sleep; it was as if every sound – the wood fire's friendly crackling, the tinkle of crockery, the splash of running water – were invented especially for my pleasure.

Three

I awoke at three, wondering for a moment where I was. Outside the sun was shining, pale but warm, the colour of Demerara rum. There was a blackbird perched on the cherry-tree, sleek and glistening as if it had been bathed in oil, its beak the same clear primary yellow as the cup I'd drunk my coffee from that morning. It started singing as I looked out of the window, ending each phrase abruptly as if out of breath, a curiously amateur effect.

Mrs. Thompson was rolling some pastry when I went downstairs. The kitchen was large and clean and bright with an electric oven which had a control panel like a bomber's. All the canisters, one felt certain, contained exactly what their labels stated, all the knives would be sharp, all the implements, from egg-whisk to orange-squeezer, in perfect working order. And yet the room was as gay as Mrs. Thompson's flowered apron, it would, just as it was, have served as a film set for any middle-class comedy. It didn't make one feel an intruder, there were no squalid little secrets like stopped-up sinks and dirty dishcloths.

"I'm off to do some shopping, Joan," I said. "Is there anything I can bring back for you?"

"Nothing, thanks," she said. "You'll find most of the best shops round the market-place. The Modley 'bus will take you there – the stop's at the bottom of the road. Going back, it's on the half-hour from the bus-station. The Food Office is at the Town Hall, by the way. Aren't I a mine of information?" She unwrapped a piece of cheese and began to grate it.

"What's that going to be?" I asked.

"You'll find out at six o'clock," she said. "I hope it's going to be perfectly delicious, but I won't promise anything, mind." She

looked at me with a cool tenderness. "It's nice to have two men to
look after again."

I went out into Eagle Road. The Thompsons' house, wasn't, I
perceived on further inspection, quite at the top either of Eagle
Road or Warley; the topmost building of the road was a block of
flats in ferro-concrete and glass with the glass predominating, and
St. Clair Road, from which Eagle Road branched off, continued
upwards for at least a quarter of a mile.

The houses were a mixed bag, in every style from mullion and
half-timber to what, from its white walls and dark green roof and
profusion of ironwork, I took to be Spanish. No doubt it would
all have been a nightmare to anyone with any understanding of
architecture; but I didn't look at it æsthetically. I saw it against
the background of Dufton, the back-to-back houses, the outside
privies, the smoke which caught the throat and dirtied clean linen
in a couple of hours, the sense of being always involved in a charade
upon Hard Times. What pleased me about Eagle Road was the
clean paintwork and stonework, the garage for each house, the taste
of prosperity as smooth and nourishing as egg-nog. Anyone who
lives on a private income in Bath will consider me a crass brute; but
anyone who lives in a place like Dufton will understand the sensation of release and lightness, of having more than one's fair share
of oxygen, which I experienced that September afternoon.

The Town Hall was a queer mixture of Gothic and Palladian,
with battlements and turrets and pillars and two stone lions. It was
rather like Dufton's – like a hundred others, for that matter. As
soon as I passed the front door I recognised the municipal smell of
radiators, disinfectant, and floor polish; having been away from it
for two days I'd forgotten how depressing it could be – the smell of
security and servitude, Charles used to call it.

The Food Office was like Dufton's too – the long counter, the
trestle tables, the rows of filing-boxes, the bright posters appealing for blood, for safety on the roads, for volunteers for the Army.
And though it was part of the Town Hall it had its own smell, the
unmistakable Government smell halfway between a teashop and a
stationer's.

It was empty except for two girls behind the counter. The elder, a plump girl with black eyes, attended to me. "You're coming to work at the Treasurer's, aren't you?" she asked. "I saw your picture in the *Courier*. It doesn't do you justice, though. Does it, Beryl?"

"He's smashing," said Beryl. She stared at me impudently. She had unformed babyish features and no perceptible breasts but there was about her a disturbingly raw provocativeness as if, along with her School Certificate, she'd passed some examination on the subject of the opposite sex.

"I'm even more smashing when you get to know me better," I said. "I've hidden charms . . ." They giggled.

"You're very naughty—" Beryl was beginning when a middle-aged man carrying a sheaf of cards like the Holy Grail walked into the room, and the atmosphere of flirtatiousness and self-aware femininity as young and silly and pretty as kittens was instantly dispelled. There was enough left over, though, to linger with me pleasantly for the rest of the day; I carried the traces out with me like face-powder on the lapel.

After I'd finished my shopping I went into Snow Park. It wasn't as one expects a municipal park to be, an open space set aside from the pattern of ordinary living, existing in a kind of quarantine; it seemed to mingle with the town. The River Merton loops the southern half of Warley; the park stood between the river and Warley Forest, narrowing at Market Square as if to let the forest come nearer, so that the narrow cobbled streets round the market all seemed to end in running water and trees.

I sat on a bench by the river and took out the *Warley Courier*. Looking at the Merton – so clear that I could distinguish the colours of the stones on its bed – I thought of the dirty harlequin of a river which ran, if that's the word to apply to a body of water as sluggish as pus, through the black streets of Dufton. The Merton was full from the day's rain and running strongly but in a backwater about a hundred yards from where I was sitting I noticed something even more important than clarity; that pale green film of algae which means that water's clean enough for fish to live in. I felt a bitter envy towards the two small boys walking along the path with their mother at that moment: they would grow up beside a river where they could swim and boat and fish. The Langdon at Dufton could and frequently did drown people; and that was the only characteristic of a river which it possessed.

The bench was on a little rise sloping down to the river; from that vantage point the park broadened out again past Market Square, so that it was in two halves, roughly the shape of a letter B turned away from the town. It was a satisfying shape, wild and natural and yet cultivated. There weren't many people in the park that afternoon. I could hear the faint hum of traffic from Market Street; apart from that, I might have been deep in the countryside. It was even more secluded on the other side of the river; there were places in the forest scarcely five minutes' walk away where you couldn't see as much as a house chimney. But I didn't know this till much later.

I didn't bother to read my paper; and I stopped myself at the point of lighting a cigarette. There wasn't any need to fill the moment with trivialities – it was already filled to capacity. It was sufficient to sit there, to breathe, to look at the river and the trees, simply to exist.

I'd been sitting there for at least an hour when the wind turned cold and I began to shiver. I left the park and crossed into the Market Square for a cup of tea. I'd been sitting too long in the same position; as I put my hand to the door of Sylvia's Café I had a mild attack of pins-and-needles and one leg gave way under me. I swayed forward and put my other hand against the wall to steady myself. It was the most minor of mishaps and I recovered within a second; but the incident seemed, for the duration of that second, to jar my perceptions into a different focus. It was as if some barrier had been removed: everything seemed intensely real, as if I were watching myself take part in a documentary film – a really well-produced one, accurate, sharp, with none of the more obvious camera tricks. The black cobbles splashed green and yellow and red with squashed fruit and vegetables, the purple satin quilt held up in a bull-fighter's sweep by a fat man in his shirt-sleeves, a giggle of schoolgirls round a pile of brightly-coloured rayon underwear, the bells of the parish church striking the hour sad as Sunday, a small girl wearing an apron dress with one strap fastened by a

murderously big safety-pin – everything was immensely significant, yet neither more nor less than itself. There were no tricks
with the lens or the microphone, the buildings steadily obeyed the
laws of perspective, the colours registered without smudging, the
sounds were neither a symphony nor a discordance. Not one inch,
one shade, one decibel was false; I felt as if I were using all my
senses for the first time and then, turning into the café, I returned
to normality as smoothly as a ski-jumper landing.

I took a seat by the window and ordered a pot of tea. It was a
long curved window extending along the front of the café like a
ship's bridge. My table was placed at the centre of the window, and
I was able to see all the streets which led into the square. Market
Street was the broadest, forming one side of the square; three
other streets, narrow and cobbled, ran off it, one at each of the
top corners, another, scarcely wide enough to take two walking
abreast, halfway up the lefthand side. The two houses facing each
other at the end of this street were half-timbered; I recognised
them as genuinely Elizabethan, the beams an integral part of the
structure instead of laths nailed on plaster. There was a bridge of
wrought iron and glass connecting the next two houses; it seemed
to be the only thing which prevented them from sagging into
each other. The name of the street was Hangman's Lane; probably, I thought, a hangman had actually lived there, an interesting
bloody-handed Elizabethan hangman, not a seedy little bore in a
bowler hat.

Then at the moment the waitress brought the tea something
happened which changed my whole life. Perhaps that isn't entirely
true; I suppose that my instincts would have led me to where I am
now even if I hadn't been sitting at the window of Sylvia's Café
that afternoon. Perhaps I wasn't directed in the Ministry of Labour
sense, but I was certainly shown the way to a destination quite different from the one I had in mind for myself at that time.

Parked by a solicitor's office opposite the café was a green
Aston-Martin tourer, low-slung, with cycle-type mudguards. It had
the tough, functional smartness of the good British sports car; it's
a quality which is difficult to convey without using the terms of
the advertising copywriter – made by craftsmen, thoroughbred,

and so on – I can only say that it was a beautiful piece of engineering and leave it at that. Pre-war it would have cost as much as three baby saloons; it wasn't the sort of vehicle for business or for family outings but quite simply a rich man's toy.

As I was admiring it a young man and a girl came out of the solicitor's office. The young man was turning the ignition key when the girl said something to him and after a moment's argument he put up the windscreen. The girl smoothed his hair for him; I found the gesture disturbing in an odd way – it was again as if a barrier had been removed, but this time by an act of reason.

The ownership of the Aston-Martin automatically placed the young man in a social class far above mine; but that ownership was simply a question of money. The girl, with her even suntan and her fair hair cut short in a style too simple to be anything else but expensive, was as far beyond my reach as the car. But her ownership, too, was simply a question of money, of the price of the diamond ring on her left hand. This seems all too obvious; but it was the kind of truth which until that moment I'd only grasped theoretically.

The Aston-Martin started with a deep, healthy roar. As it passed the café in the direction of St. Clair Road I noticed the young man's olive linen shirt and bright silk neckerchief. The collar of the shirt was tucked inside the jacket; he wore the rather theatrical ensemble with a matter-of-fact nonchalance. Everything about him was easy and loose but not tired or sloppy. He had an undistinguished face with a narrow forehead and mousy hair cut short with no oil on it. It was a rich man's face, smooth with assurance and good living.

He hadn't ever had to work for anything he wanted; it had all been given him. The salary which I'd been so pleased about, an increase from Grade Ten to Grade Nine, would seem a pittance to him. The suit in which I fancied myself so much – my best suit – would seem cheap and nasty to him. He wouldn't have a *best* suit; all his clothes would be the best.

For a moment I hated him. I saw myself, compared with him, as the Town Hall clerk, the subordinate pen-pusher, halfway to being a zombie, and I tasted the sourness of envy. Then I rejected it. Not on moral grounds; but because I felt then, and still do, that envy's a small and squalid vice – the convict sulking because a fellow-prisoner's been given a bigger helping of skilly. This didn't abate the fierceness of my longing. I wanted an Aston-Martin, I wanted a three-guinea linen shirt, I wanted a girl with a Riviera suntan – these were my rights, I felt, a signed and sealed legacy.

As I watched the tail-end of the Aston-Martin with its shiny new G.B. plate go out of sight I remembered the secondhand Austin Seven which the Efficient Zombie, Dufton's Chief Treasurer, had just treated himself to. That was the most the local government had to offer me; it wasn't enough. I made my choice then and there: I was going to enjoy all the luxuries which that young man enjoyed. I was going to collect that legacy. It was as clear and compelling as the sense of vocation which doctors and missionaries are supposed to experience, though in my instance of course the call ordered me to do good to myself not others.

If Charles had been with me things would have been different. We had evolved a special mode of conversation to dispel envy and its opposite, forelock-tugging admiration. "The capitalist beast," Charles would have said. "Give the girl her clothes back, Lufford," I would have said, "she's turning blue." "Those big pop eyes of yours are glinting with lust," Charles would have said. "Is it the girl or the car?"

We would have continued in this vein for some time, becoming more and more outrageous, until we'd dissolve into laughter. It was an incantation, a ritual; the frank admission of envy somehow cleansed us of it. And very healthy-minded it all was; but I think that it fulfilled its purpose too thoroughly and obscured the fact that the material objects of our envy were attainable.

How to attain them I didn't know. I was like an officer fresh from training-school, unable for the moment to translate the untidiness of fear and cordite and corpses into the obvious and irresistible method of attack. I was going to take the position, though, I was sure of that. I was moving into the attack, and no one had better try to stop me. General Joe Lampton, you might say, had opened hostilities.

Four

B ob and Eva Storr came to tea the next day. I was to be very
friendly with them later; that afternoon I found them rather
intimidating. At first I thought that they were brother and sister,
they were so much alike – small, dark, with snub noses and big
mouths. They talked a lot, mostly about the Theatre, with special
reference to the Warley Thespians.

They'd seen all the latest plays and ballets and knew all about
the private lives of the famous. "And at the dress-rehearsal *fleets* of
taxis came," Bob would say, "disgorging *hordes* of pansies. The
theatre smelt like a brothel. And that, my dears, is the British
housewife's dream lover; they swoon over him in droves, the silly
sluts."

Then Eva would jump in with her piece of scandal. "He isn't
so bad, darling, I mean, he doesn't *corrupt* anyone, his boy friends
are corrupt already. What about poor Roger? He was so *delighted*
when he was given that part. And the things he was expected to
do . . ." She named an actor-manager whom I knew, from his publicity at any rate, as the apotheosis of wholesome masculinity.
"Roger was invited to dinner every Sunday. He used to try to make
him drunk, and when that wouldn't work he offered him more
salary . . . Of course Roger left the company. If I have to do *that*
to get anywhere in the Theatre, he said – you remember, Bobby
darling? – then I've finished with the Theatre. Poor lamb, he was
almost in tears."

I did for a moment examine the possibility of Roger not having
been very good at his job and inventing the story as an excuse
for having been sacked but I kept my mouth shut. By the time
they'd finished it appeared that there wasn't a normal person in the
whole theatrical profession; at the very best they were eunuchs or
nymphomaniacs.

They both talked as if they were in constant contact with the professional theatre. In actuality they knew only a handful of professionals, mostly young people like Roger not long out of the theatre school. And the Thespians occasionally had actors and playwrights visit them as lecturers, mostly down-at-heel non-entities but each with his or her stock of scandal in return for free drinks and, with luck, a substantial supper and bed for the night.

I wasn't aware of these facts till much later, of course; I thought Bob and Eva immensely sophisticated. They gave me the sensation of being in the know, of being close to a wicked, exciting, above all, wealthy world. Beside Cedric and Mrs. Thompson they seemed very young, not much older than myself, though he was thirty-seven and she was thirty-three and they had two sons.

Bob, it transpired, was in textiles but precisely what he did in textiles I couldn't discover. He'd lived in London and hadn't enjoyed it. "Got damned tired of it," he said. "Don't like being a little fish in a big pond. Glad to come home again, weren't we, Evie?"

I noticed that, when he remembered to, he clipped his words; he's learned that from Ronald Colman, I thought, and felt a little less impressed – it put him on the same level as the millhand with the Alan Ladd deadpan and the millgirl with the Veronica Lake hair style.

"Do you act?" he asked me.

"I have done," I said. "There's never been much time for it, though."

"You've a nice profile," Eva said, "and a deep brown voice. It's time we had a new man. This diminutive wreck plays practically all the juvenile leads. I joined the Thespians with the vision of being constantly embraced by handsome young men. And the only man who ever makes love to me is my own husband. I could do that at home."

"That's right," said Bob and gave her a facetious leer. Suddenly I had a mental picture of them in bed together. Eva gave me a cool, appraising look; I wondered if she knew what I was thinking.

"We'll introduce him to Ronnie, and arrange an audition," Mrs. Thompson said briskly.

"Don't introduce him to Alice," Eva said. "She's hunting for fresh meat. She's never really recovered from *Young Woodley*."

"Shush," said Mrs. Thompson, "you're giving Joe the wrong impression."

"Are you spoken for, Joe?" Eva asked.

"No-one will have me," I said.

"I'll see that you meet some really nice girls."

"Darling," Bob said, "what an awful combination of debauchery and respectability in that phrase. It always strikes me—"

Mrs. Thompson cut in. "No more of that *Design for Living* humour, Bob Storr." The smile which accompanied it took the sting from the reproof; but I was aware that she was in control of the conversation, that Bob had been steered away from some dangerous corner.

"They'd no business to do that play," Cedric said. "It should be *banned* to amateurs. Yes, *banned*. They only put it on to show off their evening dresses, anyway."

"I had a most glamorous evening dress," Eva said.

"Yes," said Bob, "and God only knows how it kept up."

Eva stuck her tongue out at him. Then she stretched her arms above her head and yawned, her eyes on me again.

I hadn't fallen in love with her. And I wasn't sex-obsessed – though there are worse things to be obsessed by. It was simply that I was an unmarried man of twenty-five with normal appetites. If you're hungry and someone's preparing a good meal, you'll naturally angle for an invitation.

The meal was on the table, so to speak, and it was a long time since I'd eaten. After a dance at the Dufton Locarno, to be exact; I couldn't even remember her name. It had been quick and sordid and I hadn't enjoyed it very much. I was beginning to dislike that sort of thing: it was typically Dufton, something I had to outgrow.

Suddenly I had an intuition that I could sleep with Eva. It was a genuine intuition, not simply a rationalisation of my desires. I've always found that intuitions are rarely wrong. Mine work very well because I'm not very fond of abstract thinking and I never expect anyone to be morally superior to myself.

After tea we went to the Thespians in Bob's car. It was a new Austin Eight; it was very difficult to get new cars – particularly small ones – at that time, and it occurred to me that whatever he did in textiles must be outstandingly profitable.

"You go in front with Bob," Eva said to Cedric. "Then you can stretch your legs. And you go in the back, Joan. And you too, Joe darling. Then I can sit on your knee."

"You'd better ask Bob's permission," I said, feeling foolishly pleased.

"Bobby dear, you don't mind if I sit on Joe's knee, do you? You're not going to be jealous and possessive and Victorian, are you?"

"I don't mind if he doesn't. He'll be sorry before the journey's over, I may add. She only *appears* light and fragile, Joe. I never let her sit on *my* knee."

"Pay no attention," Eva said. "Joe's strong enough to bear my weight. You like it, don't you, Joe darling?"

I tightened my hands round her waist. "Drive as far as you like, Bob," I said. I could feel the warmth and softness of her distinctly.

The quarter of Warley where the theatre was situated was, as Mrs. Thompson had said, a positive maze of little streets. They reminded me of Dufton for a moment; but they had a warmth and cheerfulness which Dufton never had.

Perhaps the presence of the theatre helped. Even the tattiest theatre radiates a certain gaiety, it's always as it were announcing the existence of a wider world, of things outside the drabness of washing-day and rate-demand. And of course Warley had never suffered very deeply from the Slump; its eggs were in too many baskets. Three-quarters of the working population of Dufton was unemployed in 1930; I remember the streets full of men with faces pasty from bread and margarine and sleeping till noon and their children who wore plimsolls in the depth of winter. And that river thick and yellow as pus – the final insult, worse even than Stag Woods, the last bit of unspoiled countryside in Dufton, which the Council cut down and surrounded with barbed wire fences, putting the dank orderliness of a pine plantation in its place. The slump didn't only make Dufton miserable and broken-spirited whilst it lasted, though; even when full employment came there was still an atmosphere of poverty and insecurity, a horde of nasty snivelling fears left in the town like bastards in the wake of an invading army.

I wasn't, I may add, bothered about all this from a political point of view. Though if I'd been in a job where I was allowed to take part in politics I might have tried to clear up the mess – eventually, I suppose, from a place like Hampstead, which, believe it or not, is where Dufton's Labour M.P. lives. (I voted for him in 1945, incidentally, partly because Mother and Father would have liked me to, and partly because the Tory candidate was a relative of the Torvers, who owned the biggest firm in Dufton, and I wasn't going to help *them* in any way – it would have amounted to licking their already well-licked boots.)

Mrs. Thompson's voice broke in upon my thoughts. "When I was a little girl, I always used to imagine the Sieur de Maladroit's door was somewhere around here. I loved to wander around, looking for adventures."

The little car smelled of leather and tobacco and scent; my thighs began to register Eva's body again. I was in Warley riding in a car to the theatre; Dufton was far away, Dufton was dead, dead, dead.

"Did you find any adventures?" I asked Mrs. Thompson. My face was against Eva's hair.

"Once a little boy kissed me," she said. "An awful little tough with red hair. He just grabbed me and kissed me. Then he hit me and ran away. I've been attached to the neighbourhood ever since."

"That man," said Bob gravely, "is today the richest in Warley. He has never looked at another woman since that fateful encounter. Everyone thinks him hard and unapproachable, caring only for money and power. But sometimes, sitting alone in his Georgian mansion right at T'Top, he remembers that winsome little girl, half-angel and half-bird, and tears soften his flinty eyes ... It's rather touching, really, like Dante and Beatrice."

He drew the car to a stop outside the theatre. "Dante had a wife and a large family," Cedric said mildly.

"You win," said Bob, getting out of the car. "It's a beautiful story nevertheless."

Mrs. Thompson said nothing, but smiled at Bob.

The theatre had a façade of glaring white concrete and a big illuminated sign over the entrance. Its lower-case lettering made the theatre look like a night club, which I assume was the impression that had been aimed at. The auditorium smelled of sawdust and paint and chalk. It was decorated in cream and grey with the usual picture-frame stage; the atmosphere was somehow educational; though I can't be sure whether this wasn't due to its schoolroom smell. There was nothing out of the ordinary about the audience; I'd half-expected the theatre to be full of people like Bob and Eva, being determinedly witty and theatrical at the top of their voices.

There was nothing out of the ordinary about the play either. It had run for three years during the war; I'd missed it, being in Stalag 1000 at the time it was produced. It dealt with a very charming upper-middle class family the members of which nearly committed adultery, nearly made a fortune, nearly made an unwise marriage, nearly missed their true vocation and so on, everything being made right in the end by the wise old grandmother who, rather daringly for this kind of play, spoke the prologue and epilogue swaying to and fro on her rocking-chair and fiddling about with a piece of knitting to break up her speeches.

I enjoyed it for the same reason that people enjoy *Mrs. Dale's Diary* – the characters belonged to the income-group which I wanted to belong to, it was like being an invisible spectator of life in one of the big houses on Eagle Road. It was all very soothing, right down to the comic servants with hearts of gold. (Nanny offered Master her life's savings when it seemed that he was going bankrupt and I distinctly heard a woman behind me sniffing back her tears.)

It was halfway through Act I that I saw Susan for the first time. She was the youngest daughter, the gay, innocent girl who nearly breaks her heart over an older man – at least, that's how the *Warley Clarion* put it. I remember her first line. "Oh hell and death, I'm late! Morning, Mummy pet." The swear words of course had been picked up from the Older Man, a debonair, greying composer; he used them when his new symphony wouldn't come right, this being a sure sign of his extreme sophistication and wickedness.

She had a young fresh voice and the accent of a good finishing school. She was supposed to be sixteen in that play, but she

had none of the puppy-fat and slight clumsiness of that age and
I judged her to be about nineteen. She couldn't act very well but
for me she brought the whole silly play to life. Not that the part
needed to be acted; it was tailored to fit any pretty young girl with
a proper mastery of the broad a and narrow u. What appealed to
me most about her was that she was conventionally pretty. Black
shoulder-length hair, large round hazel eyes, neat nose and mouth,
dimples – she was like the girl in the American advertisements
who is always being given a Hamilton watch or Cannon Percale
(whatever that is) Sheets or Nash Airflyte Eight. She might have
been the sister of the girl I'd seen outside Sylvia's Café.

Charles and I once worked out a grading scheme for women,
having noticed that the more money a man had the better looking
was his wife. We even typed out a schedule, the Lampton-Lufford
Report on Love. There was an appendix with Sex Summaries. I
remember that a Grade One woman gave one such a marvellous
time in bed that it was just as well that all Grade One husbands
had inherited fortunes because they couldn't possibly have had any
strength to spare for earning money. And Grade Four men were
awarded a little extra with each promotion (Oh dahling I'm so glad
the Directors are appreciating you at last, she said with her eyes
misty) and Grade Nine of course only indulged on Saturday night
and Sunday afternoon.

The grades corresponded, naturally, with the income of husband
or fiancé, running from One, for millionaires and film stars and
dictators – anyone with an income over £20,000 in fact – to Twelve
for those under £350 and not likely to get any more. Charles and I
belonged to Grade Seven, which was for the £600 and over deputy
and assistant head group; we really belonged to the grade below,
but the point of the whole scheme was that husbands were chosen
as much on eventual as actual salary, a certain level of intelligence
being taken for granted in women above Grade Ten standard. Our
schedule didn't work out perfectly, of course: sometimes men in
Grade Seven would have Grade Three wives, women capable of
acquiring £5,000-a-year men, and self-made Grade Three men
would have Grade Ten wives whom they'd been hooked by before
they'd made their pile. But the Grade Seven men generally lost

their wives to lovers who really understood and appreciated them
or, worse still, had to endure them grumbling about money for the
rest of their lives; and the Grade Three men generally got Grade
Three mistresses. This no doubt all seems very cynical but the fact
is that Charles and I could eventually work out husbands' incomes
to the nearest fifty pounds. There was a time when the accuracy of
our system profoundly depressed me. (That was when my horizon
was bounded by Dufton and the NALGO National Charter.) I
knew that I was equally as lovable and a damned sight more handsome than the Glittering Zombie, a young man with sleek black
hair, a shiny red face and a gold Rolex Oyster, gold signet ring, gold
cigarette-lighter and a gold cigarette-case; but, not having a father
who was a bookmaker, I could hope for a Grade Six wife at the best
and *he* would automatically attract a Grade Three.

Susan was Grade Two – if not One – whether or not she had
any money; but I had a shrewd idea that she'd qualify for the grade
financially as well as sexually. To be quite fair to myself, this wasn't
the only reason that I was excited by her, that the genteel com-
monplaces of the play seemed profoundly poetic, that it seemed at
any moment there'd be an annunciation which would transform
existence into what it ought to be, hold, as it were, to its bargain
the happiness which Warley had promised me. And I should have
felt exactly the same if I'd been an honest simple type to whom the
whole idea of grading women was beastly cynicism. She was so
young and innocent that it nearly broke my heart; in a queer but
pleasurable way it actually hurt me to look at her. If flesh had a
taste, hers, I imagine, would be like new milk. I fell in love with her
at first sight. I use the conventional phrase like a grammalogue in
shorthand, to express in a small space all the emotions she evoked
in me.

When we were putting on our coats in the foyer afterwards
Cedric said: "I assume you need some alcoholic refreshment after
that bourgeois gallimaufry, Joe." I heard the words but did not
connect them into a message.

"Susan Brown's very beautiful," I said. Then I realised what a
moon-struck calf I must appear and to my disgust found myself
reddening. Eva laughed.

"I'm *livid* with jealousy." She gave me a blow on my chest with more force than playfulness behind it. "As soon as I meet a handsome young man he falls for that flibbertigibbet."

"She always seems a bit *insipid* to me," Bob said, "strictly the bread-and-butter Miss."

"Oh no," said Eva quickly. "It's very nice of you, darling, to say she is not attractive, but it just isn't true. Joe has good taste. She's beautiful, yes, really beautiful, fresh as a rose on the day of battle or whatever that poem is, and a truly sweet-natured child."

"Who wouldn't be, with a rich and adoring papa?" Bob said.

"I think Joe had better meet her," said Mrs. Thompson.

"No more of this prattle of beauty and sweetness," said Cedric impatiently. "I lust for strong drink. We'll see you at the Clarence if you're going backstage, Bob."

He went out into the street, his scarf tucked into a pocket of his raincoat and trailing almost on the floor. He was talking at the top of his voice. "No life, no vigour, no poetry!" I heard him say as he went out of sight, Mrs. Thompson walking sedately beside him with her head cocked slightly to one side, an attentive but slightly amused expression on her face.

"You really *are* smitten, aren't you, Joe?" Eva said as we walked down the passage behind the foyer.

"I suppose she's already attached to someone," I said gloomily.

"She's not engaged," Bob said. "But watch out for Jack Wales. Bags of money, about seven foot tall and a beautiful RAF moustache."

I laughed. "I eat those types for breakfast," I said. "Besides, my admiration is purely artistic." Even to me it didn't sound very convincing, but I felt myself being pushed into the position of the poor man at the gate, the humble admirer from afar.

The dressing-room was already crowded when we reached it. It was a narrow room with a concrete floor and a long table with lighted mirrors above it. It smelled agreeably of makeup and tobacco and well-fed, well-washed bodies.

Susan had just taken off her makeup and was wiping the remaining cream from her face. I noticed with a shock of pleasure how white and delicate her skin was.

"This is Joe Lampton," Eva said. "He's come all the way from Dufton. He liked the show very much."

"Particularly you," I said. Her hand was childishly warm and soft and I would have liked to have held it far longer, but ineffectual contacts like that were Zombie habits – trying to make a dinner out of hors-d'œuvres – so I didn't extend the handshake for more than a second.

"I'm not awfully good really," she said. I was close to her but I had to strain to catch the words. Susan always lowered her voice when she felt shy.

"If I'd known, I'd have brought you some flowers," I said. Her dark lashes came down over her eyes and she looked away from me for a moment. It was the kind of gesture which only a virgin could have got away with; because it was so natural and unstudied it moved me almost to tears.

"If you'd known what?"

"If I'd known you'd be so beautiful."

Her blouse had a button too many unfastened. She saw me looking at her but made no effort to fasten the button. The revelation of some kind of promise, though it hadn't, I was sure, been deliberate.

"Coming over for a drink, honey?" Eva asked her.

"I'd love to, but Jack and I are promised home for supper."

"Bring Jack too," Bob said. "I want to explain the function of the cyclorama. His dawn came up like thunder, which is splendid for Burma but not the Home Counties."

"You're horrid," Susan said. "It was a perfectly *sweet* dawn." She spoke as if the dawn were a small cuddly animal.

They began to argue about it and then Jack came in. I knew it was him straightaway. The big RAF moustache was worn with the right degree of nonchalance; he'd been an officer, it was an officer's adornment. I never grew one myself for precisely that reason: if you wear one and haven't been commissioned people look upon you as if you were wearing a uniform or decorations you weren't entitled to. What annoyed me the most about him was that he stood four inches above me and was broader across the shoulders. He had an amiable, rugged face, the Bulldog Drummond type, and no doubt, I thought viciously, well aware of it.

"Hello there, Sue," he said. He looked at his watch. "One nine three oh precisely. Operation Supper to begin." He laughed, well-pleased with his own facetiousness. "Lord, what a pong," he said. "Don't know how you stand it, Sue."

He looked at me sharply. "This is Joe Lampton," Bob said. "Jack Wales, Joe Lampton. You should have something in common. You were both intrepid birdmen, weren't you?"

Jack laughed and put out a ham-like hand. He tried to out-grip me but he couldn't manage it.

"Speaking for myself," he said. "I'm glad its over. Flying's fun, but being shot at is most disconcerting."

"Too true," I said. "Not that the fun of flying didn't pall upon me eventually."

"What blasé young men you are," Eva said. "Can we ask you to have a drink, Jack?"

"Terribly sorry," he said, "but you know what a stickler for punctuality Papa Brown is. Some other time, we'd be delighted. Or rather, I'd be delighted—" he winked heavily at Eva – "we'll leave the others behind. Just you and me, eh?"

We were all listening to him as if he were Royalty explaining graciously that it was impossible, owing to other engagements, to open the bazaar but perhaps some other time . . . When he and Susan left there'd be an emptiness in the room, they'd be travelling into warmth and luxury and gaiety and we, somehow, would be left to a cold Monday drabness.

I didn't add my pleadings to Eva's; though I had an intuition that Susan would have liked to have gone with us.

"Tha doesn't have to coax *me* to sup some ale, lass," I said to Eva, deliberately dropping into broad Yorkshire to counterattack Wales' genuine officer's accent, as carelessly correct as his tweed suit. "Coom on." I turned to Susan, giving her my best smile, which I've had to practise a great deal because my teeth, though passable, only remain so by reason of a yearly agony at the dentist's. I would have liked to have had teeth as white as my rival's (for so I had already thought of him) but a smile with the mouth closed and the eyes wrinkled a little at the corners can be just as

effective with women as the showing of the teeth; or at least so
I thought at that moment, seeing her blush. "I'll remember the
flowers next time," I said.

"Thank you," she said. Her eyes were shining; I know that this
is due to excess moisture, possibly in her case to the irritation from
too generously applied mascara, but it made her look like a child at
Christmas. I wondered if she got many compliments from the big
lummox standing possessively beside her.

When we were outside in the street Eva gave me another mock-
playful blow in the chest.

"You're a very *direct* sort of a person, aren't you?"

"I always go straight for what I want."

Bob grinned maliciously. "Jack didn't like your promise of
flowers. I detected signs of jealousy."

"He's not engaged to her."

"Ah, but he's known her all his life. Childhood sweethearts and
all that."

"How pretty," I said.

Five

Two months after I was in the Public Library trying to explain
elementary book-keeping to the Chief Assistant, a dapper
little man whom I'd met at the Thespians. He'd made a dread-
ful mess of his Cash and Deposits book; such a mess that for a
moment I suspected him of teeming and lading. Then I discovered that he'd overpaid by ten shillings out of his own pocket. Like
a great many people who are very bright in other directions he
lost all his wits when confronted with a column of figures; it had
apparently never occurred to him that the deficit might be due to
a simple error of entry.

"I'm no good at this sort of thing," he said querulously when
I'd finally straightened the matter. "I'm spending an hour a day on
these damned books. Seems a bit of a waste. Not to mention your
time."

"That old boy's going to explode soon," I said, watching a

whitehaired man trying to explain what he wanted to one of the junior assistants, a thin youth, who'd already acquired the librarian's stoop. "Look, Reggie, I'll see Hoylake about the C. and D. There must be some easier way."

Either we could cut down the numbers of different receipts, I thought, or else take over the whole business ourselves, collecting the money and entering it up each morning. Whatever my suggestions were, Hoylake would listen to them. He was a great improvement over the Efficient Zombie. Even now, I don't like to remember the Efficient Zombie. He had a large head with short oiled hair and an absolutely immobile face. It wasn't dignified or even stony, it was dead; he seemed to take all the oxygen out of the air around him. I managed to flannel him into the belief that I approved of his particular brand of efficiency, and he liked me as much as he could like anyone. But working under him was always a strain.

He was one of those local government officers who have a guilty feeling about security of employment and the thirty-eight hour week; he was continually reminding us of the toughness of the world outside. And he was always worrying about what the Council thought of us. He needn't have done; the majority of the members of the Council wouldn't have noticed if the entire Town Hall staff had gone to work naked. But there were some who, for the sake of publicity in the local rag, appointed themselves as scourgers of the pampered bureaucracy. Whenever there was a headline in the *Dufton Observer* (Councillor Hits Out At Conference, Let Town Hall Punch Time-Clock, Salary Increase Fantastic) the Efficient Zombie would be stirred to increased activity and there would follow a spate of typewritten notices beginning, It has been brought to my attention, and ending THIS MUST STOP. Worse still, there were what he called Pep Talks which were made specially gruesome by the fact that, since he seemed to be able to speak and scarcely open his lips, his clear metallic voice seemed to come from nowhere.

We were expected to work all the time, which appears reasonable enough. The drawback was that we were always beginning jobs and then being forced to break them off which in the long

run wastes more time than the odd ten minutes spent smoking or
flirting with the typist. And we worked overtime at least one evening a week; this pleased him very much, especially if a member
of the Council heard about it, but had his staff been allowed to
establish their own rhythm of working it wouldn't have been necessary.

Hoylake was everything that the Efficient Zombie wasn't. He
was short and tubby and amiable with an odd little toothbrush
moustache and black library spectacles; he always reminded me of
Robertson Hare except that he had a slight Yorkshire accent. He
left us to our own devices; he didn't give a damn how the work was
done as long as it was finished when we'd promised, and he refused
to be bothered with details. His department in consequence was
much more efficient than the Efficient Zombie's: we were a team
of professionals, not a collection of adding-machines.

That was, so to speak, another gift from Warley: I was for the
first time completely happy in my work. And I'd joined the Thespians and was beginning to mix with people of a kind I'd never
mixed with before. The Thespians was like a club – one which,
particularly if you were a young man, was very easy to join. It
was exclusive too; though there was nothing to stop working-class
people joining it they somehow never did. Apart from that the
Thespians gave me something which I'd never enjoyed before: the
sense of belonging, of being part of a community. Perhaps that
sounds portentous, but let it stand. All in all, I was happy and contented; too much so perhaps. I'd already forgotten the resolution I
made that afternoon at Sylvia's Café.

We were going over the C. and D. in the small room by the
Lending Library counter which the Chief Assistant liked to call
his office, though in actuality it was only a workroom. I saw Eva
through the glass partition. The Chief Assistant beckoned her
inside.

"Come and testify to my character, darling," he said. "Joe's practically accused me of cooking the books."

"My favourite man is never wrong."

"I thought *I* was your favourite man," the Chief Assistant said.

She patted him on the hand. "Until Joe came along, Reggie dear."

She looked at the rows of new books. "Have you anything really shocking, Reggie? I adore mucky books, and you never have any in stock."

She was wearing a scent like burnt roses; it seemed to fill the room, overlaying the smell of books and Pollywog paste.

"Do you know any good ones, Joe?" she asked me.

"I like my pornography in real life," I said.

"Well, what are we waiting for?"

Reggie was watching us with a curious intentness; the Library was the clearing-house for all the town's gossip. I decided to change the subject.

"Did you know I'm playing Joshua?" I flexed my biceps and threw out my chest. "The strength of a giant and the heart of a child. Led away by a wicked woman—"

"Damn the Casting Committee," she said, "*I* wanted to lead you astray, why didn't they give me the part?"

"The housekeeper's much nicer," Reggie said. "Needs real acting. Anyone can play Leda."

"Maybe," Eva said gloomily, "but I'm fed up with being wholesome. I *long* to be seductive and tempting. What's Alice got that I haven't got?"

"Who's Alice?" I asked.

"You've met her, you dope. Tall and slim and blonde. Used to act in Rep. You might have noticed her if you hadn't been making eyes at Susan."

"Is she married?"

"I hope so, she's been living with him nearly ten years. George Aisgill; you've met him too, he came to the last Social Evening. Lots of money. They seem happy enough—" She stopped, as if she were on the verge of indiscretion.

"I remember her now," I said. "She seemed a bit offhand. In fact, definitely cold."

"You mean that she didn't succumb immediately to your charms," Reggie said. His tone was light, I couldn't take offence but I resolved to be more careful in front of him in future.

"You should never look at one woman when you're talking to another," Eva said. "No wonder the poor darling was offhand.

Alice is a very sweet person indeed and I won't hear a word against her, so there."

"She a damned good actress," Reggie said. "God, she was wonderful in *The Playground*. Absolutely *exuded* sex. Two old dears walked out in the middle of Act Two."

"Well, not quite as wonderful as all that," Eva said. "I saw it in London, and she'd pinched a lot of La Thomas's business – you remember the way she took off her shoes? But she'll manage the part. She'll teach Joe a lot."

"Tall and slim and blonde. Goodgoodgood, I'm willing to learn."

"You'll have to keep an eye on him," Reggie said. His dark little face seemed rather wistful.

"Ee, lad, doan't tak on soa," Eva said, quoting from the play, "T'world's not ended 'cos tha's made a gurt fooil of thisen. We'll mak summat of thee yet."

Reggie put away the C. and D. "I'd better make sure that my staff isn't making a gurt fooil of itsen," he said, as he went out of the room to where the whitehaired man was still trying to explain what he wanted to the junior assistant.

"Come and help me pick my books, Joe," Eva said, taking my arm. "Our Mr. Scurrah's quite agreeable, isn't he? A trifle flabby though. It's no job for a man."

"They're not all the same," I said.

Eva felt my biceps with hard little fingers. "You're a strong brute."

"I used to box."

"Don't you any more?"

"I didn't see the point of getting bashed up for nothing and I wasn't good enough to be a professional."

"You be a professional," she said, "and I'll run away with you. I couldn't resist a big, brutal, sweaty boxer."

I glanced quickly round the Library. We'd gone over to the Drama section, an alcove on the far side of the Lending Library. No one could see us, even if they'd been looking that way.

"I thought you were going to run away with me," I said. "Just for a weekend."

"I don't know what you mean." Her voice had lost its flirtatiousness.

"You said on Sunday—"

"So that's it. Merely because I let you give me a beery kiss in the Props Room, you think the balloon's going up . . . No, dear, but no definitely."

"What did you promise for?"

She shrugged her shoulders. "You seemed to expect it. Besides, I'm not sure that I did promise you anything."

I felt a spasm of lust and anger. When I had kissed her on Sunday it had seemed that everything was going my way. At last, I thought, feeling her body against me, soft and scented, clean all over, above all, *expensive*, I was going to have a woman who would neither weep with shame afterwards nor eat fish and chips whilst she was doing it. I would have done better for myself at the Dufton Locarno.

"You're a genuine flirt, aren't you, honey?" I said to her. "Hasn't anyone got really annoyed with you?"

"I only mix with civilised people," she said coldly.

I took a deep breath. Being angry wouldn't help. "Don't worry. I won't bother you." I forced a smile. "You're too attractive, that's the trouble."

There was a pause. When she spoke again her voice had softened. "Joe, you're very inexperienced. You can't get everything you want all at once. Will you remember that?"

"I'll remember," I said, not knowing then what she really meant.

Six

It was the first reading of *Meadowes Farm* that evening. When I arrived at the Thespians the producer, Ronnie Smith, was already there. He worked in a bank, though you wouldn't have believed it at first sight. He was wearing green suède shoes, a very old pair of flannels, a yellow crewneck sweater and a golf jacket; with his seamed face and brilliantined hair thinning at the temples he looked like a middle-aged actor, which I suppose was exactly what he wanted.

"Hello there, Joshua," he said or rather shouted, that being part of the theatrical pose. "God, you've got a lovely part. Out of this world." He repeated the phrase with relish. "Yes, out of this world. You'll have to work though, God, you'll have to work!"

"You're scaring him," said Eva, who'd just entered with Alice. "T'lad's cum to enjoy hisen, 'aven't you, luv?"

"Hello, Eva," I said. "Hello, Alice. You look most seductive, I must say."

"That's very kind of you," she said. "Actually I feel terrible." Her voice wasn't very friendly; she certainly wasn't succumbing instantly to my charm.

At the side of Eva, who had a rosy complexion and a bouncing vitality, she did in fact look pale and haggard. She had honey coloured hair which at that time she wore in a bun, and thin features. She had an angular fashion plate figure, to which her big breasts didn't seem to belong; in the white sweater she was wearing they seemed to sag with their own weight. In a way this appealed to me more than firmness; it was a guarantee of reality. I could imagine myself touching them.

I repressed the thought. It wasn't any use. I remembered Eva rubbing herself against me: You're wonderful, we must do something about this, we'll go away – a lot of good it had done me. I remembered Susan at the last Social Evening: Jack had never let her out of his sight and had whisked her straight home in a shiny new M.G. Alice wasn't for me; I might as well abandon that idea before it took too firm a hold.

I looked at the rest of the cast. Herbert Downs owned a small weaving mill, Johnnie Rogers' father owned a coal business, Anne Barlby's father owned three groceries; Jimmie Matthews, the youngest was attending classes at the Leddersford Technical College; Jimmie was going to help his daddy in the family firm, as no doubt Johnnie was. Anne's big brother was learning the grocery business of course, right from the bottom just like anyone else: Anne was going to the Leddersford School of Art which would keep her out of mischief till she got married, possibly to Johnnie, whose father's business was expanding rapidly under the wicked Labour government. They all had more money than me, but it wasn't big money. It was all too easy to reach their grade, so consequently I didn't respect them very much. I looked at them gesturing freely but jaggedly as they talked in their best accents about *The Lady's Not for Burning*, and jeered at them mentally, one of the landed gentry watching the tradespeople ape their betters. But my feeling of superiority was short-lived; the first reading went very badly. Perhaps because I was still irritated about Eva and Susan, I made a thorough hash of my lines, mispronouncing the simplest words and emphasising almost every sentence incorrectly. We had to stop for a moment when I referred to a roadman's brassière; I joined in the laughter but it was a considerable effort.

"D'Eon Rides Again," said Alice. "What a thought – erotic vices among the working-classes." She spoke directly to me. "I am working-class," I said sulkily. "And you needn't explain your little quip. I know all about the Chevalier. I read a book once."

She flushed. "You shouldn't—" she began, then stopped. "I'll tell you afterwards." She smiled at me and then turned back to her script.

I kept glancing at her throughout the rest of the play. Sometimes when she wasn't reading her part she looked plain, in fact downright ugly: her chin had a heavy shapelessness and the lines on her forehead and neck were as if scored with a knife. When she was acting her face came to life: it wasn't so much that you forgot its blemishes as that they became endearing and exciting. She made the other women look dowdy and careless; Eva, too, I realised with astonishment.

When we'd finished, Ronnie sat staring at us for a moment, puffing his pipe noisily and fiddling with a sheaf of notes and a gold Eversharp pencil. "We'll have to work very hard, people. The play's a great deal more subtle than it appears." He took his pipe out of his mouth and then pointed the stem at me. "Joe, remember that you're an honest simple farmer. And for Heaven's sake be careful about – er – articles of ladies' underwear." Everyone except me giggled. "In fact, you'd better cut that bit."

"Watch out, Joe," Eva said. "Ronnie loves cutting. You'll have no part left if you're not careful."

Ronnie beamed at her. "All plays should be cut by half," he said.

"Me and Orson Welles," Alice murmured into my ear.

"All right, people," Ronnie said. "That's it for tonight. Herbert and I will now try to make sense of the author's lighting plot."

"Would you like some coffee?" I asked Alice as she rose.

"No, thank you."

To hell with you, I thought, and turned on my heel.

"You can buy me a beer though."

"The Clarence?"

"Too many Thespians there. Too clean and well-lighted. They'll be installing neons soon. The St. Clair's much nicer. Dark and smells of beef and tapers."

Her car, a green Fiat 500, was parked outside. She unlocked the righthand door then hesitated. "Can you drive?"

"Oddly enough, yes," I said.

"Don't be so bloody thin-skinned."

"I wasn't—"

"You damn well were. I just thought you might like to drive. Most men hate being a woman's passenger. I'm an awful driver anyway."

I didn't say anything but sat in the driver's seat and opened the other door for her.

It was pleasant to be driving a car again; not that I'd ever had one of my own. I'd learned to drive in the RAF: I'd shared an Austin Chummy with three of the aircrew. As I engaged first gear I was again riding through the flat desolation of Lincolnshire with a crate of beer in the back and Tommy Jenks leading the chorus of *Cats on the Roof-tops* or *In Mobile* or *Three Old Ladies*; I felt a nostalgia for those days, when I could afford to spend four pounds a week on beer and cigarettes and the silver half-wing was a passport to free drinks and high-grade women. The Austin wasn't up to much – and no wonder, after seventeen years' misuse – but a quarter of it belonged to me. Tommy smashed it up on the North Finchley Road, together with himself, a WAAF corporal, and the G.I. who drove the jeep he crashed into.

"You're scowling," Alice said. "You look like a gangster in that hat, did you know? Turn to the right here, will you?"

"Where are we?"

"Nearly in St. Clair Road. It's on my way home actually."

"You live right at T'Top, of course?" There must have been a sneer in my voice; I saw her wince, and wondered what devil had got inside me.

"I live in Linnet Road," she said. "I didn't choose the house. Though I think it's a very pleasant one. You live in Eagle Road, don't you?"

"I lodge there," I said.

We were driving down Poplar Avenue. From a big house to our left came a blaze of light and music. There was a gate half-open in the high wall; I caught a glimpse of water and a white platform. "My God," I said, "a swimming-pool."

"That's where Sue Brown lives," Alice said. "It's her birthday party tonight."

"How nice for them," I said. "I expect Jack's a guest. If I may refer to him with such familiarity."

Alice didn't seem to have heard me. "Turn down to the left here," she said. We went down a narrow road and into a little square. The houses were smaller in this quarter: the big house at the top of the road was the last outpost of the world of private swimming-pools and poplars and the new M.G.'s. The working-class area by the station extended further than I'd thought, coming between Poplar Avenue and the smoke of the valley like a shield. A narrow flight of stone steps led up from the square into a ruler-straight street of millstone grit. The St. Clair was down an alley at the end nearest to the square.

As Alice had said it was dark and smelled of beef and tapers. The little room behind the bar was empty except for two old men huddled round the fire. There were two old prints of Warley hanging on the walls, and a photograph of a house with its roof blown off by the whirlwind of 1888. The space left uncovered was occupied by glittering horse brasses and warming-pans. The seats which ran round the walls were leather upholstered and well padded.

Alice looked round her with satisfaction. "This is what I *call* a snug," she said. "So damned cosy it's almost sinister."

The landlord, a thin grey-haired man, shuffled in, "Good-evening, Mrs. Aisgill. Good-evening, sir. What can I get you?"

"Try the Old," Alice said. "It's *real* beer, isn't it, Bert?"

"A lovely drink, Mrs. Aisgill," he said in his deep lugubrious voice. "A beautiful beer."

It was in fact very good beer, dark and sweet and smooth. It was warm and restful in the Snug and I liked being with Alice; I didn't feel any necessity to make love to her, and consequently had no fear of rejection. I gave her a cigarette. When I'm on edge I somehow forget to smoke; it was my first cigarette that evening and the tobacco tasted pleasantly strong, a hair's-breadth from being acrid, which is how I like it best.

"Look, Joe," Alice said, "we're going to be working together, so we ought to get everything straight between us. For God's sake take that chip off your shoulder. I didn't like telling you when the others were around – but you were bloody offensive to me. Have you got an inferiority complex, or what?"

"No," I muttered.

"What is it?"

"I thought you were coming the Lady of the Mansion over me, that's all. My father didn't own an engineering works or a mill but that doesn't mean that I've never read anything or that I can't drive a car." I was aware that this wasn't an adequate explanation; for I wasn't really angry with Alice at all.

"But Joe dear," she said, "who cares about these things? I don't. The Thompsons don't. Eva doesn't—" She frowned. "It's Eva, isn't it? She leads young men on and then she turns prim and proper on them. She's a born teaser, she'll never change. You know, it wouldn't at all surprise me if – no, I'd better not say it."

I ordered more beer. "Now you've begun, you'd better finish."

"It wouldn't surprise me if she didn't tell Bob about her young men's antics. They're cold fishes, both of them. You didn't take her seriously, did you?"

"It depends on what you mean by seriously."

"The same thing as you mean, honey."

"My God, no. Not for one moment." I laughed. "What a big fool I must have seemed." Then I remembered my main grievance. "Jack Wales," I said. "Patronising me, talking about the Officers' Mess, forgetting my name when I speak to him . . ."

"He'll be back at the University soon," she said. "Besides that's not why you're angry with him. He's staked out a claim to Susan. That's why, isn't it?"

I didn't answer. I was wondering just how we'd reached this stage. I was talking with her as freely as I would with Charles; the realisation was rather disconcerting.

"Isn't that why?" she repeated.

"All right. That's why. Plain jealousy. It's as if people like him take everything worth having by a sort of divine right. I've seen it too often."

"I could hit you," she said. "She's not engaged to him, is she? You're not married yourself, are you? Or are you frightened of him? Why don't you 'phone the girl and ask her to go out with you?"

"I never thought of that," I said weakly.

"You'd rather feel sorry for yourself," she said. "Instead of doing something about it, you're just lying down. Perhaps you feel Jack's superior to you?"

"No," I said. "It wouldn't matter anyway – whether or not he were superior I mean – if she wanted him. I have a feeling that she doesn't. She's got used to having him around, that's all . . . I *know* she could be interested in me. That's what's so damned annoying. I suppose you think I'm conceited."

"No," she said. "Young and terribly inexperienced. If that's what you truly feel about her, straightaway and instinctively, then you must be right."

The belief in intuition isn't exclusively my property but to hear her expressing it made me feel that I could hide nothing from her.

I looked at my empty glass. "I can't drink in halves," I said, and fished in my pocket for money.

"Let me get it, will you?" Alice said.

"I can afford it—"

She held up her hand to silence me. "No. I won't argue. I always pay for my own. I learned that in Rep a long time ago."

"But I'm not in Rep."

"Oh shut up. I don't care if you're the Borough Treasurer, I don't care if you own the bloody pub. *I'm* independent, I can afford to pay for my own. See?"

I took the money and ordered the drinks. I was glad of it, to tell the truth, because the Old cost two shillings a pint and at the rate we were drinking it would have meant at least nine bob's worth before the evening was out. I had eight hundred in the bank, this mostly being my parents' insurance and my accumulated pay from Stalag 1000. But I never touched it; I wasn't likely to acquire so much money so quickly again. I lived on my salary; and it didn't allow for casual expenditures of nearly ten bob.

I looked at Alice with affection. "Would you like some potato crisps, love?"

"Yes, please. They've Smith's on Mondays. Ask him for some salt, will you? I can never find those beastly little blue packets."

"I like salty things with beer," I said. "Pickled onions and fat pork are best, though."

She grinned at me. It was a companionable grin with no sex behind it. "Me too. I've low tastes. What's more, I can drink as much beer as you."

"I'll take you up on that."

"I'll hold you to it. I was brought up on beer but all the men I seem to meet drink whisky and gin. They think I'm joking when I say I like beer and I get gassy bottled stuff and lager."

The Old was stronger than I'd thought; halfway through my third pint a warm rush of affection came over me.

"I'll tell you something, Alice. I like you. I don't mean sex, I mean I like *you*. I can talk with you like a man. I can tell you things —Oh Lord, what a lot of I's . . ." I took another swig of beer and then crunched a mouthful of the crisps.

"I like you too," she said. "You look about eighteen at times, do you know that?"

We stayed till closing time and then she drove me home. It wasn't until I was in bed that I realised that I'd never told any woman as much about myself – not only that but I hadn't any fears of having said too much, of having made a fool of myself. The pillow smelled faintly of lavender; it reminded me of something. It was her scent, cool as clean linen, friendly as beer; I went off to sleep without knowing it, into a dream in which I was riding in the Fiat with her, the car skidding wildly round fantastic bends in a country a mixture of Lincolnshire and Prussia; then she was Susan, her eyes shining, her face distorted with pleasure, and suddenly I was lost in the wild open country, sand and pines and heather, calling out not Susan's name but Alice's, and then I was awake in my room at Oak Crescent looking at the Medici reproduction of Olympe, smooth and white and lovely, and well aware of it: the picture grew in size until it covered the whole wall and I put my hands over my eyes and tried to scream and found myself awake in Warley to the alarm clock ringing and the sound of bacon frying in the kitchen.

Seven

The Library shared the same building as the Town Hall, I called there at ten the following morning and found out that Jack would be returning to the University in a couple of days.

I stood in the little alcove they called the Reference Department, feeling absurdly exultant and at the same time envious. Cambridge: I had a mental picture of port wine, boating, leisurely discussions over long tables gleaming with silver and cut glass. And over it all the atmosphere of power, power speaking impeccable Standard English, power which was power because it was born of the right family, always knew the right people: if you were going to run the country you couldn't do without a University education.

Jack's father, among other things, manufactured cars. Business was booming; though even if it hadn't been, it wouldn't greatly have mattered, since he'd built up a cosy little vertical trust. Whenever he spent more than a certain amount on any component, he bought the firm which made it; he owned a plastics factory, a tannery, a bodywork builders and even a laundry and a printing firm. Beside Ford or Lyons or Unilever it was a small combine; but I'll be very surprised if the old man cuts up for less than a million.

Cedric had explained to me the reason for Jack's taking a science degree. "Whoever runs the combine can't specialise," he said. "He must be able to think *generally*. If he knows too much detail he won't be able to grasp the whole. So Jack's going to Cambridge to learn how to think." Cedric had given me a conspiratorial smile.

"Not that it makes much difference. The accountants and the engineers run the show no matter who's in charge. All that's necessary is that Jack meets the right people and learns how to get on with them. Blinding with science – isn't that the phrase?"

All right, I muttered to myself childishly, I'll pinch your woman, Wales, and all your money won't stop me . . .

I went out to the 'phone kiosk opposite the Town Hall and called Susan. Waiting for the operator to put me through I was half inclined to abandon the whole attempt. If she hadn't answered the 'phone it's doubtful whether I would have tried again.

"Susan Brown speaking," she said.

"Joe Lampton speaking. How official we sound." There was a pane missing in the kiosk and a cold wind blew in. My hands were shaking with excitement. "I've got two tickets for the ballet on Saturday night, I wondered if you'd care to see it."

"Saturday night?"

"I mean evening," I said, cursing myself.

"I'd love to see it. Just a minute, Joe, I'm all tangled up, I've just had a bath."

I imagined her nakedness, young and firm and fragrant. Then I put the idea out of my head. It was something I didn't want to think about. It wasn't that I didn't desire her physically; but to strip her mentally was adolescent and pimply, it didn't express my true feelings. This I can honestly say: my intentions towards Susan were always those described as honourable. Any other response to her beauty would have seemed shabby. Even apart from her money, she was worth marrying. She was the princess in the fairy stories, the girl in old songs, the heroine of musical comedies. She naturally belonged to it because she possessed the necessary face and figure and the right income group. And that's how it is in all the fairy stories: the princess is always beautiful, and lives in a golden palace, and wears fine clothes and rich jewels and eats chicken and strawberries and cakes made from honey and even if she has bad luck and has to go to work in the kitchen the prince always spots her because she's left an expensive ring in the cake she's baked for him; and the shock almost kills him when she's brought to him in her donkey skin with her face and hands dirty from menial labours because he thinks he's fallen in love with a common working-girl, Grade Ten in fact. But she takes off the donkey skin and he sees her fine clothes and she washes her face and hands and he sees her white delicate skin. So it's all right: she's Grade One and they can marry and live happily ever after. The qualifications for a princess are made brutally clear.

Susan was a princess and I was the equivalent of a swineherd. I was, you might say, acting out a fairy story. The trouble was that there were more difficult obstacles than dragons and enchanters to overcome, and I could see no sign of a fairy godmother. And that morning I couldn't tell how the story would end. When she left the 'phone she seemed to be away for a long time; I thought for a moment that she'd hung up on me but somewhere in the background I could hear a vacuum-cleaner and women's voices.

"I'm sorry for keeping you waiting," she said, "I couldn't find my engagement-book. Saturday evening will be all right, Joe."

The first dragon was killed, even if it was only a small one. I tried not to sound too exultant. "Grand. I'll call for you at a quarter-past six, shall I?"

"No, no," she said quickly, "I'll meet you at the theatre."

"A quarter to seven then."

"Golly, here's Mummy. I must rush. Goodbye."

"Goodbye," I said, feeling a little puzzled. Some of the gilt had already been taken off the gingerbread. Why should she panic when her mother came into the room? It was as if she hadn't wanted it to be known that she was going out with me. Wasn't she supposed to go out with anyone except Jack? And was I, unlike him, not good enough to call at her house?

When I returned to the Treasurer's Teddy Soames was drinking tea and flirting with June Oakes, the Health Department typist. June was just twenty with red hair and clear skin and, I was fairly sure, a silly but loving disposition; but I knew better than to become mixed up with her. Office affairs are easy to begin and difficult to finish, particularly in a small town.

However, I joined in the flirtation. It was reassuring to my ego to be with a woman who was within my reach, who wouldn't, I thought, looking at her full moist lips, egg me on unless she meant business, and who would be absolutely delighted to have me call at her home.

"Hello, queen of my heart," I said, taking a cup of tea. "It's always nice to see you. Every day you look more beautiful. I'm glad you don't work at the Treasurer's though."

"Wouldn't you like me to?"

"I'd be too busy looking at you," I said. "I'd never get any work done."

She giggled. "I hear that you're *looking* at someone else."

"Only because you won't marry me."

"You haven't asked me."

I went down on one knee and put my hand on my heart. "Dear – or may I say dearest? – Miss Oakes, I offer you my hand and my heart—"

"Don't listen, June," Teddy said. "He goes boozing with married women."

I straightened myself up. "I don't know what you mean."

June giggled again. "Her name might begin with A. She's *much* too old for you." She had a voice which was very light in timbre, almost a squeak; it combined oddly with her magnificent bust.

"Oh *that*," I said lightly. "She was giving me a lift home. We were discussing the play. Teddy wouldn't understand. Our relationship is strictly platonic."

"Yes, I understand," Teddy said, putting his arm round June's waist. "I'm trying to take June on a platonic weekend. Of course, it'll be too bad if she has a platonic baby." He gave one of his loud artificial laughs and nuzzled June's cheek.

"Oh, you are awful," she said. "No, Teddy. No, you mustn't. What if Mr. Hoylake comes in?"

"He'll order me to leave you alone and let *him* have a cuddle," Teddy said.

"I won't speak to you again *ever*," she said. "You've got an awful mind." She smiled at me. "But Joe's a gentleman."

"Don't depend on it," I said.

She came closer to me; she had a strange smell, not perfume, not soap, not sweat, almost rank, but clean. I was strongly tempted to caress her, or at least make a date with her; but the one would have been unsatisfying and the other dangerous. So I smiled back at her. "You're lovely," I said.

"You've gorgeous eyes," she said. As she went out she laid her hand on mine for a second. "What's wrong with we young spinsters?" she asked. It was as if Teddy weren't there.

"Don't mind me," he said. "You're quite a boy for the women, aren't you?"

"They queue up just to speak to me."

"You can have June," he said. "She's only a kid. But Mrs. A. – now *her* I really envy you."

"There's nothing to envy me for."

"She's lovely," he said. His thin tough face was wistful.

"She's all right. Never thought of it."

"By God, *I'd* think of it. She's—" he searched for the word and then used it rather shamefacedly – "she's a lady. She's a woman too. Every time I see her I sweat and shake – you know."

"You lewd young man," I said. "You know what the Good Book says about committing adultery in your heart."

"Her husband's committing it elsewhere."

"That's no excuse. What's he like, by the way?"

"Wealthy woolman. Sleek and pale, talks well-off."

"Who's the other party?"

"A girl from his office. Young and plump and dumb. It's been going on for a year."

"They're worse than animals," I said indignantly. "Why can't he be content with Alice?"

"She's thirty-four and they've been married nearly ten years and they haven't had any children." He grinned. "I'd help him out. Willingly."

I shrugged my shoulders. "She doesn't attract me in that way." I was thinking about Susan; it gave me a queer little thrill in the pit of my stomach when I remembered. I badly wanted to tell someone, to boast about it discreetly. I rather hoped that Teddy would introduce her name into the conversation and then I could drop a casual statement about our date. He didn't mention her, however, but continued to drool over Alice.

That evening I went to the second rehearsal of *Meadowes Farm*. Ronnie was in great form, puffing violently at his pipe, running his hands through his hair to indicate nervous tension, and scribbling frantically in his interleaved script. "This evening, people," he said, "you're just *bodies*. And very fine bodies too, if I may say so. I want you to clarify these moves, and then we can get on with some acting..."

Alice and I had three torrid love scenes. I expected to find them embarrassing, but she was so impersonal in her attitude, so free of embarrassment herself, that our embraces were like slow dances. We worked so well together that Ronnie didn't have to correct me more than twice each move, which is pretty good at that stage of production. I took my lead from her; which of course was quite correct because I was supposed to be seduced by her.

Ronnie was moved to praise afterwards. "Your love-scenes are beginning to shape well already, Joe. I can foresee trouble elsewhere" – he twinkled at me over his spectacles – "you know, the dull necessary business of entrance and exit and sitting down and standing up. You sit down as if – well, I won't be vulgar. And you rise as if you'd sat on a tin-tack. And you're *most* awkward with Anne and Johnnie. But with Alice you really come to life."

"Alice would bring a dead man to life," I said. I smiled at her; to my surprise she coloured a little.

When Ronnie had finished speaking to the cast I followed her off the stage into the auditorium. She took up her coat from where she'd left it in the stalls; I helped her put it on. The second before I took my hands off her shoulders she relaxed against me; it was as impersonal as our stage embraces.

I put on my own coat and sat down beside her. "I followed your suggestions."

"Which suggestions?"

"I 'phoned Susan. We're going to the ballet." Somewhere in the flies I heard the voices of Ronnie and Herbert: a blue light illumined the stage with its litter of cigarette ends, the trestle tables and Windsor chairs and the horsehair sofa on which I'd been making love to her. It was only a small theatre but suddenly it seemed big and echoing and desolate.

"Susan?" she said. "Yes, I remember." The light turned to a warm pink. "You can't go wrong if you're advised by me. Auntie Alice is always right."

"You're not an aunt," I said. "They're forty and smell of camphor."

She grimaced. I noticed that her chin sagged a little underneath. "Well at least I don't smell of camphor. I'm behaving like a *Woman's Chats* auntie, though. Or Juliet's nurse." Her tone seemed bitter.

"But no," I said. "I saw *Romeo and Juliet* once. She was an evil old bitch. You're nice and exciting. And rather—" I stopped. I was going into dangerous territory.

"Rather what?"

"Don't be angry with me. Promise."

"All right," she said impatiently, "I won't be angry even if it's indecent. I promise."

I floundered. "It seems so silly. I can't—"

"This is just like *At Mrs. Bean's*," she said. "You *are* irritating, Joe. Go on, for God's sake."

"You're rather – no – not pathetic. But lost, like a little girl. As if you were looking for something. Oh God, I sound like a cheap film. Forget I said it, will you?"

She was silent for a moment. Then her eyes moistened. "What a strange thing for you to say. No, I'm not angry, darling." She fished in her handbag. When I gave her a light I was surprised to find my hand trembling.

At that moment George Aisgill came in. He was wearing an enormously thick overcoat, which he wasn't tall or broad enough to carry. He had small well-shaped hands, the nails shining from a recent manicure and he wore not only a signet ring on his third finger but a diamond ring on his little finger. His features were neat and smooth and his moustache looked as if it had been painted on. Despite the manicure and the diamond ring he didn't look effeminate; though he didn't look masculine either. It was as if he'd deliberately chosen masculinity because it was more comfortable and profitable. I disliked him at sight but in a different way from Jack Wales; there was no real harm in Jack, but George Aisgill had a watchful coldness about him which almost frightened me: he looked utterly incapable of making a fool of himself.

"I've come to take my wife away from you rogues and vaga-bonds," he said. "My wife having messed up the Fiat."

"This is Joe Lampton," Alice said to him. "My lover."

"Dear me," he said, "I'm sorry. Have I spoiled it all?"

"We've met before," I said.

He gave me a quick exhaustive glance. "I remember," he said. He nodded towards the stage. "How's it going?"

Something in his manner suggested that we were all indulging in a scruffy kind of charade.

"I can't tell you," I said. "You'll have to ask Alice."

"Oh, it's not more than usually bloody," she said in a flat voice. "We continue to amuse ourselves."

Her whole manner had changed with his coming. She wasn't subdued or frightened or over-bright; it was very difficult to put one's finger on the difference, but I noticed it at once. She became the sort of person that up to the evening before I'd thought she was – cool, blasé, superior, only half-alive.

"You're a Town Hall wallah, aren't you?" he asked me.

The outdated temporary gentleman phrase set my teeth on edge. "Treasurer's."

"Must be a bit dull."

"You'd be surprised," I said lightly. "There's always some busi-ness man trying to fiddle. My God, how those boys hate paying rates!"

"Not guilty, old man," he said. "My mill's not in Warley."

"We don't like that either. You're depriving your home town of money."

"When the Council encourages business I'll build a mill at Warley."

"When we find a business man who thinks our smoke abate-ment policy isn't merely words, we'll welcome him."

He smiled showing sharp white little teeth. "Where there's muck—"

I was just going to retort that he took damned good care to live outside the muck when Alice broke in.

"No shop," she said. "Don't you ever get tired of it?"

He threw up his hands in a gesture of mock resignation, the diamond on his little finger glittering coldly. "You'll never understand that we men live for our work. As soon as we talk about anything interesting, you complain we're talking shop."

Against my will I felt pleased that he should have considered my remarks interesting, though I knew that it was Dale Carnegie stuff, a small, apparently casual compliment. The others imperceptibly gathered round him, in much the same way, I thought, as they'd gathered round Jack Wales. He represented the power of money as Jack did: he was another king. As I watched them all paying court to him, I wondered how on earth he came to marry Alice, how the thin lips under the neat moustache brought themselves to frame – as they surely must have done – the words *I love you*. I just couldn't imagine them in bed together, either. They weren't the same kind of person; they hadn't, as all the happily married do, acquired any likeness to one another.

I rose and said to Alice that I was going.

"You're coming our way, aren't you?" she asked.

"There won't be room," I said.

"Nonsense," George said. "You haven't an engagement, have you?"

"There's plenty of room," Alice said. "Do come, Joe."

I looked at her sharply. It was as if she were asking me for protection.

George's car was a Daimler 2½ litre. I settled down in the back with Johnnie Rogers and Anne Barlby. I'd never ridden in a privately owned Daimler before. George switched on the roof-light for a moment: the soft light enclosed us in a private world, warm and cosy, tough and adventurous too, arrogant with speed and distance.

Johnnie passed round cigarettes and I leaned back against the deep cushions, letting myself be absorbed in the private world, letting the atmosphere of luxury rub against me like a cat. Johnnie talked cars with George; he was, of course, going to buy one soon. We used RAF slang, which personally always makes me want to vomit: unless exceptionally well-done it stinks of newspapers and films. "I wish you could see this Bug," Johnnie was saying. "It's wizard, sir. Bang-on . . ." But he was harmless, only just twenty, with a snub nose and curly hair and an air of morning baths and early to bed and plenty of exercise.

Anne Barlby was his cousin. She was talking to Alice or rather, trying to make her feel thoroughly uncomfortable by references to her good fortune in possessing a Daimler and to the good looks of her lover – "The spit-and-image of Jean Marais, darling." I was Alice's lover of course; the joke was wearing thin.

Anne wasn't like Johnnie in temperament, but looked very like him, with the same fresh look and curly hair. Unfortunately, she had a nose which would have better suited a man, big and shapeless, nearly bulbous. It didn't look bad from some angles and was passable on the stage; but she was unduly sensitive about it. She needn't have worried: she had a trim figure, was bright and intelligent and, though not exactly an heiress, had money behind her. In the meantime she was inclined to be bitchy. She especially disliked me and never lost an opportunity to be unpleasant. Looking back, I know the reason for her dislike: I didn't take sufficient pains to disguise the fact that I found her physically unattractive. A little gentle flirtation, even a discreet sort of pass, would have changed her attitude entirely. She behaved as if she wouldn't welcome sex from me in any shape or form; and I took her at her face value. Which is the last thing that any woman wants.

The Daimler took St. Clair Road with no effort. It was like being in a mobile drawing-room; except that it was a great deal more comfortable than many drawing-rooms. George drove with a chauffeur's neat efficiency; I couldn't help comparing his technique with Alice's slapdash recklessness.

"We'll leave you here," Anne said halfway up St. Clair Road. "It's a lovely car, Mr. Aisgill. Much nicer than the Fiat. You can only squeeze two into the Fiat, can't you, Joe?"

"My God," Alice said, when George had started the car again, "what a poisonous little cat *she* is. Dripping nasty insinuations in that chorus-girl accent! She'll wait a damned long time before I ride in the same car with her again. Shall I confess all, George? Shall I throw myself upon your mercy? I gave Joe a lift home last night and we called at the St. Clair. There now, our guilty secret's out. Of all the scandalmongering, gossiping, evil-minded places—"

"All small towns are like that," George said indifferently. "Anyway, why bother with the St. Clair? Take Joe home if you don't like people gossiping. There's plenty to drink in the house, isn't there?"

He overshot Eagle Road and I didn't notice myself until we were half-a-mile past, nearly at the top of St. Clair Road.

"I'll walk down," I said to him.

"You might as well come and have some supper," he said. "You can 'phone the Thompsons."

"Do come," Alice said.

"The rations—"

She laughed. "Don't worry about that, honey. It won't be a banquet anyway, just bits and pieces."

We'd reached the top of St. Clair Road. From Eagle Road it was open country – pasture land bordered by trees, with a few big houses set well back from the road. On the left, half-hidden by pines, there was the biggest house I'd seen in Warley. It was a mansion, in fact, a genuine Victorian mansion with turrets and battlements and a drive at least a quarter-of-a-mile long and a lodge at the gate as big as the average semi-detached.

"Who lives there?" I asked.

"Jack Wales," George said. "Or rather the Wales family. They bought it from a bankrupt woolman. Colossal, isn't it? Mind you, they don't use half of it."

My spirits sank. For the first time I realised Jack's colossal advantages. I thought that I was big and strong; but there was a lot more of that house than there was of me. It was a physical extension of Jack, at least fifty thousand pounds' worth of brick and mortar stating his superiority over me as a suitor.

The Aisgills' house stood at the end of a narrow dirt road just off St. Clair Park. It was 1930 functional in white concrete, with a flat roof. There were no other houses near it and it stood on the top of a shelf of ground with the moors behind it and the park in front of it. It looked expensive, built-to-order, but out of place, like a Piccadilly tart walking the moors in high heels and nylons.

Inside it was decorated in white and off-white with steel and rubber chairs which were more comfortable than they appeared. There were three brightly coloured paintings on the walls: two of them were what seemed to me no more than a mix-up of lines and blobs and circles but the other was a recognisable portrait of Alice. She was wearing a low-cut evening dress in a glittering silver cloth. Her breasts were smaller and firmer and there were no lines on her face. The artist hadn't prettified her; I could see the faint heaviness of her chin and the beginnings of lines.

"Don't look at it too closely, Joe," she said, coming up behind me. "I was ten years younger then."

"I wish I were ten years older," I said.

'Why, Joe, that's very sweet of you." She squeezed my hand but didn't release it straightaway. "You like the room?"

"Very much," I said. But I wasn't quite sure that I did. It was a strange room, very clean, very bright, in good taste, but somehow without comfort. The low white-painted shelves across the wall opposite the fireplace were full of books, mostly brand-new, with their jackets still on; they should have humanised the room but they didn't; it seemed impossible that they should be read; they were so much a part of the room's decorative scheme that you wouldn't have dared to have taken one.

"Drink?" George asked, going to the cocktail cabinet. "Gin, whisky, brandy, rum, sherry, and various loathsome liqueurs which I can't really recommend."

"Whisky, please."

He gave me a malicious look. "It's not Scotch, alas. An American customer gave me a crate. Tastes like hair-oil. I warn you."

"I drank a lot of it in Berlin," I said. "No soda, thanks."

It left a warm glow inside my stomach after it had for a split second dried my mouth and sent a little rush of air up my throat.

"Alice says you're from Dufton." He filled up his glass with soda-water and sipped it like a medicine.

"I was born there."

"Been there on business once or twice. My God, it's depressing!"

"You get used to it."

"You'll know the Torvers, I suppose."

I did know them in the same way that I knew the Lord Lieutenant of the county. They were Dufton's oldest mill-owning family; in fact, the only mill-owning family left after the Depression, the other mills having gone either into the hands of the Receiver or London syndicates.

"My father worked at their mill," I said. "He was an overlooker. So we never met socially, as you might say."

George laughed. "My dear Joe, no-one ever meets the Torvers socially. No-one would want to. The Old Man hasn't had one decent emotion since he was weaned, and Dicky Torver spends what little time he has left over from the mill-girls in drinking himself to death."

"We used to call Dicky the Sexy Zombie," I said.

"Damned good. I say, damned good!" He refilled my glass as if he were giving me a little reward for amusing him. "That's *just* how he is with that awful pasty face and that slouch and that *fishy* gleam that comes into his eyes whenever he sees a bedworthy woman. Mind you, he's a good business man. You'd have to get up very early to catch Dicky Torver."

"He's a horror," said Alice, entering with a tray of sandwiches. She poured herself a whisky. "I met him at the Con ball at Leddersford. He made a pass within the first five minutes and invited me to a dirty weekend within another five. Why doesn't someone beat him up?"

"Some women might find him attractive," George said. He nibbled a cheese biscuit.

"You mean that their husbands might want to do business with him?" I said.

He laughed again. It was a low, pleasant laugh; he could evidently call it up at will. "Not that way, Joe. It's like bribing an executioner; if you're reprieved, he says it's due to his efforts and if you're hanged you can't talk. If someone's wife is – well, *kind* to Dicky, and the husband lands the contract or whatever it is, then Dicky's kept his side of the bargain. If the husband doesn't land the contract he can hardly make a public complaint. No, business isn't as simple as all that."

"It happens," said Alice.

"Occasionally." His manner indicated the subject was closed and I'd been put in my place.

"Joe," Alice said, "do have a sandwich. They're there to be eaten."

The sandwiches were the thinnest possible slices of bread over thick slices of cold roast beef. The plate was piled high with them. "You've cut up all your ration," I said.

"Oh no," she said. "Don't worry about that. We've lots more. Truly."

"The farmers have meat," George said, "I have cloth. See?"

It was perfectly clear; and I enjoyed the meat all the more. It was like driving Alice's car; for a moment I was living on the level I wanted to occupy permanently. I was the hero of one of those comedies with a title like *King for a Day*. Except that I couldn't have deceived myself as long as a day, and I could, in that room, tasting the undeniable reality of home-killed beef and feeling the whisky warm in my belly, put myself into George's shoes.

Alice was sitting a little away from the table, facing me. She was wearing a black pleated skirt and a bright red blouse of very fine poplin. She had very elegant legs, only an ounce away from scragginess; her likeness to a *Vogue* drawing struck me again. I looked at her steadily. We were the same sort of person, I thought fuzzily, fair and Nordic.

George poured me another Bourbon. I swallowed it and bit into a second sandwich. Alice gave me a light little smile. It was no more than a quick grimace, but I found my cheeks burning as I realised that I'd like to be in George's shoes in more ways than one.

Eight

Waiting for Susan on Saturday evening I was as excited as if it had been the first time I'd taken a girl out. I was standing in the foyer of the Leddersford Grand; it was the usual sort of theatre foyer with red carpets, white pillars, photos of stars with white teeth and glossy hair and sparkling eyes, and over it all a faint smell of cigars and perfumed disinfectant, but at that moment it seemed to possess a sort of innocent splendour. I experienced so many different emotions that I was like a child with one of those selection boxes the chocolate manufacturers used to bring out before the war. I was undecided as to which to taste first; the plain dark chocolate of going out with a pretty girl, the Turkish Delight of vanity, the sweet smooth milk of love, the flavour of power, of being one up on Jack Wales, perhaps the most attractive of all, strong as rum.

If she'd come then I would, so as to speak, have eaten the whole selection box. But at three minutes to seven there was no sign of her, and the whole evening began to turn sour on me. I heard again the panic in her voice. 'Golly, here's Mummy.' Why should she be so frightened of her mother knowing about me? Why shouldn't I call at the house? And why should I? I saw myself as Mummy would see me, uncouth and vulgar and working-class – with all the faults of the *nouveau riche*, in fact, but none of those solid merits, such as a hundred thousand in gilt-edged securities, for the sake of which so much can be forgiven. "That awful Lampton boy with the funny teeth," I heard Susan say. "He's pursuing me. Yes, really! I don't know why, but I said I'd go to the ballet with him. Yes, I know, it was silly of me, but I wasn't *thinking* . . . Well, my dear, I *forgot*! It went *right out of my head*! For all I know, he's still waiting. Aren't I *awful*?"

I was elaborating this dialogue with a drearily masochistic relish when I felt a tap on my shoulder.

"I've been watching you," she said. "You look awfully bad-tempered. Are you very angry with me?"

"Not now you've come."

"I'm very sorry for being late. Herbert gave me a lift and something went wrong with the magglet."

I laughed. "That's very serious. Are you sure it was the magglet?"

"I don't know about cars," she said. "Should I?"

"There's no law that enforces you to. Magglet's very good anyway. All cars should have a magglet." I took her arm. "We'll have to hurry. Two minutes to zero."

She was wearing a furtopped Cossack cap and big fur gloves and a full-skirted cashmere topcoat. Her eyes were sparkling and her cheeks flushed a little and there was about her that clean smell – like baby-powder mixed with new-mown hay – which I had noticed the first time I'd met her.

When I handed the tickets to the usher she caught sight of their price. "Four and six," she said. "Golly. Isn't that frightfully expensive?"

I looked at her sharply; did she expect a box? But I saw that she was quite serious and I was astounded and delighted at her naïvety; the clothes she was wearing must have cost a good fifty pounds.

We settled down to watch *The Haunted Ballroom*. I passed her a block of milk chocolate; my hand brushed hers and hovered over it for a second but it had no responsiveness; if a girl wants her hand to be held it tightens over yours the moment it's touched.

Somehow it seemed tremendously important that I should hold her hand. Contact with her, I felt, would be as different from contact with ordinary women as singing is to speaking. It seemed tremendously important; and yet I didn't want to touch her at all. Brought out, perhaps, by the music and the dancers blown across the stage by it like pieces of coloured paper, a deeply buried instinct asserted itself: I wanted simply to admire what is, after all, a rare human type: a beautiful and unspoiled virgin. Even when I let my eyes rest on the outline of her firm small breasts beneath her sweater it was without a trace of lasciviousness; I was visited, in fact, by the emotion of our first meeting. This time it was more real, there wasn't the annoyance of other people's presence and Susan was herself, speaking her own words, not a fictitious character seeable for half-a-crown.

I took her to the bar at the interval.

"Mummy would be awfully cross if she knew I was here," she said, looking doubtfully round her at the rows of coloured bottles and the gilt mirrors and the framed playbills and cartoons and the usual beefy men and plump women, smelling of bay-rum and violets, whom one never sees in any number except in theatre bars and who always seem to be comfortably installed before one's arrived.

"Is she teetotal?" I asked.

"She thinks pubs are low. But this isn't a pub really, is it?"

"Not really," I said. "What would you like to drink?"

"You won't laugh if I have a grapefruit, will you?"

"There's no law against it." I smiled at her. "Have whatever you like, honey."

When I'd got the drinks I offered her a cigarette.

"No, thank you," she said. "I don't smoke."

"You're the sort of girl I like to take out."

She gave me a look which was coquettish in a naïve sort of way. "Why am I the sort of girl you like to take out?"

"You've no expensive vices."

"Are your usual girls very expensive?"

"I haven't any girls," I said. "There's never been any. Only you."

"Now you're telling fibs. *Wicked!*"

She had an intonation for the word which was altogether charming and innocent but at the same time faintly provocative.

I put my hand on my heart. "There's no-one but you."

"You haven't known me very long. How can you tell?" She looked a little frightened; I'm going too fast I thought.

"You're not a dear kipper," I said, as if I hadn't heard her question.

The phrase instantly distracted her, as I'd calculated it would. "A dear kipper?"

"My mother used to call me that when I wanted something that cost more than she could afford."

She clapped her hands. It was a gesture which I'd read about but never seen, so childish and outmoded that only Susan, I think, could have got away with it. "A dear kipper. A dear kipper. Oh, how *lovely*. You know, I'd rather like to be a dear kipper."

I sipped my gin-and-lime. I'd chosen it because it wouldn't make my breath smell, but quite apart from the fact that the price is sheer robbery, I don't care for the stuff. For a moment I had a fierce longing to be drinking Old at the St. Clair with Alice.

"Are you enjoying the show?" I asked Susan.

"It's *gorgeous*. I adore ballet. And the music – it makes me feel all *squashy* inside – I feel, oh, ever so excited and squiffy." She put her elbow on the table and cupped her chin in her hand. "It's ever so difficult to explain . . . it's like being inside a house all painted with beautiful colours and when you listen it's like touching the paint, the colours all run over your mind – does that sound silly?"

"No. Not one little bit. I've always felt like that myself, only I can't put it as well as you." I was lying, of course; as far as I'm concerned ballet is something with which to occupy the eyes whilst listening to music. But I wouldn't have dreamed of saying so; it was essential that I should appear to share Susan's interests – or rather, that they should appear to coincide. I'd discover something unimportant to disagree with her about so that she'd think me an intelligent type with a mind of my own.

"I'd like to take you to Sadler's Wells," I said.

"Have you seen Fonteyn?"

"All of them." I talked about ballet till the bell rang, managing – rather skilfully, I thought – to conceal the fact that I'd only been to Sadler's Wells once and that Fonteyn was the only prima ballerina I'd ever seen.

After the show had ended to the usual tumultuous and idiotic applause I asked her if she'd like some coffee. I was helping her on with her coat; I remember noticing with approval that she took the courtesy for granted.

"Coffee? Oh, that's sweet of you. I'd love some."

"You can have some cakes too," I said, "I know a café where they're eatable."

"I'm awfully hungry. I didn't have any dinner, I was in such a rush."

"You should have told me. It's silly to miss meals in winter."

"I'll be all right. I eat a *terrific* lot, really I do. But I'm *starving*. I could eat lots and lots – oh dear!" She put her hand to her mouth. "You'll think I'm a dear kipper," she said dolefully.

I laughed. "Don't worry about that." It was charming when she put her hand to her mouth; entirely natural, but stylised and graceful. She made all the other girls I'd been out with seem dingy and clumsy and old before their time: the thought came to me tinged with apprehension – I wasn't playing for matches any more.

The café was just outside the theatre. It was the sort of place I didn't normally go to then – oak panelling, deep carpets, a four-piece band, and an atmosphere of exclusiveness. I don't mean that I personally was overawed by all the splendid people there – they were mostly fat old woolmen anyway. But I always had the fear of doing the wrong thing, of making a fool of myself in front of the higher grades. Saying the wrong thing to the waiter or picking up the wrong fork or not being able to find the cloakroom immediately wouldn't have mattered in an ordinary café. In fact, there wouldn't have been any possibility of me making any faux pas. In front of those with no more money than me there would be no necessity to be careful, people in one's own income group can't be enemies. The rich were my enemies, I felt: they were watching me for the first false move.

It's queer when I remember it – I have even bought meals at cafeterias when for a couple of shillings extra I could have had an eatable meal at a good restaurant. That evening with Susan, though, I walked into the café quite happily: she was my passport, it was her sort of place.

"Isn't it nice here?" she said. "All Dickensy. And look at that little waiter there with the funny quiff. He's utterly *squoo*. Don't you think so, Joe?"

The waiter came over to us with the flat-footed glide of the professional servant. We'd hardly taken our seats before he came over; I wondered for a moment if he'd have come so quickly if I'd not been with Susan. When he'd gone off with the order Susan looked at me and giggled. "Do you think he heard me? I don't care, he *was* squoo. Awfully sad and yet perky like a little monkey. I wonder if he likes his job? I wonder what he thinks of his customers?"

"He'll think you're the most beautiful girl he's ever seen," I said, "and he'll think me extremely fortunate to be in your company. He's sad because he's married and has twenty children and you're forever unattainable and he's perky because no man could help being happy when you're around. See?"

"You're making me blush." She kept on looking round the place with a frank and lively interest. There was a middle-aged woman at the far side of the room with black dyed hair and a sort of deliquescent distinction; she was talking in a hoarse but still attractive voice to her companion, a mousy little woman with a pink openwork jumper revealing at my estimate eight shoulder-straps. The middle-aged woman's face was set in an attitude of ashamed disillusion as if she'd lost her vitality as suddenly and ludicrously as underwear when the elastic snaps in the street. When she saw Susan looking at her she smiled. For a moment she looked her real age and her real age didn't matter. I don't know why I should remember this, nor why it should hurt me when I remember. Susan returned the old woman's smile and continued to look round the place, examining every person there with the frank and lively interest of a child.

I laughed. "You're as bad as my mother." I kept my tone light and bantering because, though a dead mother is useful in boosting the emotional atmosphere, to have used a sepulchral tone would have spoiled the particular line I was trying to use. "She used to know everything that went on in Dufton. She was *interested* in people, like you. She said that there was something wrong with you if you didn't take any notice of what your fellow-humans did."

"She sounds nice. I'd like to meet her."

"She's dead."

"I'm sorry. Poor Joe—" She put her hand on mine very quickly, then withdrew it.

"Don't be sorry. I like talking about her. I don't mean that I don't miss her – and my father – but I don't live in the graveyard." I was, I realised, quoting Mrs. Thompson. That was all right; I meant what I said. Why should I feel guilty about it?

"How did it happen?"

"A bomb. Dufton's one and only bomb. I don't even think it was meant to hit anything."

"It must have been awful for you."

"It's a long time ago."

The waiter set down the coffee and cakes and left us as silently as he came. He smiled at Susan; it was his real smile too, a warm flicker, constrained a little, not a waiter's grin. The coffee was very strong and the cakes were fresh and of the kind which young girls like – meringues, éclairs, chocolate cup-cakes, marzipan rolls.

"He really does like you," I said. "Everyone else has been given Madeira cakes and rock buns."

"You're horrid. He's a *delectable* little man and I like him very much." She bit into an éclair. "We didn't see much of the war in Warley. Daddy used to work awfully hard at the factory, though. Sometimes he used to stay up all night."

What fun he would have had too, I thought. The rich always had the most fun during the war. They had the double pleasure of influencing the course of events and making themselves still richer. I elaborated the thought with no real satisfaction. Suddenly I felt sad and lonely.

"Don't you miss your father and mother terribly sometimes?" she asked.

"Often. But generally when I think of them it makes me happy in a queer sort of way. Not happy because they're dead, but because they were good people."

It was perfectly true. But, as I looked at Susan's rosy young face – so young that the full neck and firm little breasts seemed at moments not to belong to her but to have been borrowed for the occasion like an older sister's stockings and lipstick – I felt guilty. I was manœuvring for position all the time, noting the effect of each word; and it seemed to devalue everything I said.

Nine

I was depressed for some time afterwards. It wasn't a tangible sort of depression: it was rather like that washing-day sadness which came to one on waking to the realisation that the £75,000 cheque, so convincing even to the twopenny stamp, was, after all, only a dream.

I began to shake it off a little when I went to the Thespians the following Monday. There's an atmosphere about a theatre at rehearsals that's as comforting as cloves for toothache. It's dusty, it's dry, it's chilly, and at times it seems to be a huge reservoir of silence into which all one's words take belly-flops. But at the same time it's as warm and cosy and private as a nursery and every activity, even just waiting for one's cue, is important and exciting, every moment is handed to one like a hot buttered muffin.

When Alice came to sit beside me the sense of pleasure increased. I felt reassured, too, protected like a child. I could tell her everything and be sure that she'd understand. It was like the way I'd feel when, the Efficient Zombie having been even more bloody-minded than usual, I'd see Charles and know that I'd be able to talk away all my accumulated anger and humiliation. Except that I'd never had the least desire to undress Charles and, I realised with a shock, I wanted to undress Alice. I was angry with myself for the thought; I felt as guilty as if it had been Mrs. Thompson I was lusting after. I honestly didn't want to spoil the relationship that was building up between us; I could get sex at any pub or dance-hall but not the friendship which Alice had given me from that first evening at the St. Clair. It had come to us quickly and smoothly but without hurry; we could not only talk about every subject under the sun but we could sit together in silence and be happy and contented.

"It's good to see you," I said. This was the standard Thespian greeting; but I meant it.

"It's good to see you too, Joe." When she smiled I could see that there was a speck of decay on one of her upper incisors and another seemed to be more filling than tooth. They weren't bad; but they were no better than mine and this fact gave me a kind of shabby kinship, as if we'd both had the same illness. It was a kinship which I could never share with Susan: I loved looking at her teeth, white and small and regular, but they always induced an uncomfortable inferiority.

"I know my lines now," I said. "And I can say the Song of Solomon bit backwards. It's *lush*."

"Don't let Ronnie see that you're enjoying yourself or he'll cut it."

"We'll knock 'em in the aisles," I said.

When my cue came a moment later I didn't walk on to the stage, I made an entrance. I was supposed to stand glancing at Herbert and Eva for a moment before I spoke; until that evening I'd always made a mess of it, either holding the silence too long or not long enough. That evening I timed it perfectly: I knew instinctively that a fraction of a second less would have seemed pointless and a fraction more would have seemed as if I needed a prompt. And I knew that the reason for my glowering was that I wanted my mistress badly and was as frustrated as a tethered bull in spring. Everything clicked into place, I found it impossible to go wrong; and when Alice entered something happened which is rare with amateurs; we achieved exactly the right tempo. I found myself thinking, or rather sensing, that at some places I must go slowly and at others more quickly and that the slowness and the quickness hadn't, as it were, to be dumped in heaps but to be spread smoothly. And for the first time in my life I became aware of my own body and voice without conceit, as instruments. Alice and I were a team; she was no more to me and no less, than the Theatre Sister to the surgeon; she wasn't Alice Aisgill whom I'd just wanted to undress, she was Sybil whom I'd already undressed in the other world bounded now by stacked-up flats, tangles of wires and ropes, and the smell of new paint.

"You were pretty good tonight," Alice said in the Fiat afterwards.

"Not so good as you," I said. I turned the ignition key, her praise brandy to my self-esteem. The engine started immediately, though I always had trouble with it normally. I wish often that I could have fixed my life at that moment – the car rolling smoothly down the narrow street with the gas lamps washing the cobbles with orange light, the smells of East Warley tugging at me for attention like children on their father's birthday – malt, burning millband, frying fish, that wonderful bread-and-butter smell coming from the open spaces nearby – and inside the car, the masculinity of steel and oil and warm leather and, best of all, Alice, her smell of lavender and her own personal smell as musky as furs and as fresh as apples.

We left the quarter all too quickly. It was the part of Warley I came to like best; that evening it was as if there were an invisible street party: each house was my home and the blackened millstone grit looked soft as kindness. I remember that the curtains of one house weren't fully drawn and I caught a glimpse of a young man in overalls tickling the waist of a red-haired girl. I knew somehow that they weren't long married and I watched them with tenderness, in a queer bless-you-my-children way without the least trace of, as Charles used to put it, the bog-eyed hogger.

Even the long drabness of Sebastopol Street, with no building along it but Tebbut's Mills, seemed part of my happiness. The sound of the looms filled the air, a loud clicking that didn't seem like a naturally loud noise but a small one deliberately amplified to annoy the passer-by; and the fluorescent lighting inside, the daylight, if it is daylight, of hangovers and executions, made the workers at their looms look like the inhabitants of a vast aquarium; but I could translate them both, the noise and the light, into prosperity, into marriage and meat and dancing.

And when we came to Poplar Avenue I was able to laugh at Susan's home without anger or frustration. I imagined her sitting at a dressing-table of polished walnut with a litter of silver brushes and bottles of expensive scent in front of her. The white carpet would be ankle-deep and the sheets of her bed would be silk. There would be a lot of photographs; but they wouldn't be the cheap kind that seem deliberately to have caught their subjects in positions so unnatural that to hold them for one moment longer would cause actual physical pain. They would be the very best, not one under a guinea, the work of professionals who could make the pretty beautiful, the passable pretty, and the ugly interesting. Surrounded by these glossy pieces of well-being, Susan would be brushing her hair, that was as smooth and shining as a blackbird's wing, not thinking, not wanting, not making plans, but quite simply *being*.

Again I felt that I was part of a fairy story. There was a melancholy pleasure in the thought of her inaccessibility. I could hardly believe that I myself had thought of marrying her: it seemed like the crazy prophecy of some old witch. I was grateful that she should exist, just as I was grateful that Warley should exist. The road was rustling with dead leaves, the air was smoky and mellow as if the whole earth were being burned for its fragrance like a cigar; I felt suddenly that something wonderful was going to happen. The feeling was sufficient in itself; I didn't expect anything material to result from it. I was honoured by the gesture; life doesn't often bother to be charming once childhood has passed.

"You're smiling," Alice said.

"I'm happy."

"My God, I wish I were."

"What's the matter, love?"

"Never mind," she said. "It's too damned sordid and boring to explain."

"You need a drink."

"Do you mind if we didn't?" She laughed. "Don't look so woebegone, honey."

"You want to go home?"

"Not particularly." She switched on the car radio. A brass band was playing *The Entry of the Gladiators*; the huge bombast of the piece seemed to blow the little car along.

"I'd like to go to Sparrow Hill," she said.

"It's cold up there."

"That's what I want," she said violently. "Somewhere cold and clean. No people, no dirty people . . ."

I turned the Fiat into Sparrow Hill Road, narrow, twisting, steep, with the fields and weeds on either side stretching out into the black and endless distance. Alice switched off the radio as abruptly as she'd switched it on and there was no sound but the Fiat's self-satisfied little hum and the moan of the wind in the telephone wires.

"Far away, far away, Are the lands where the Jumblies live. Their hands are green and their feet are blue, And they went to sea in a sieve . . ." Her voice was dreamy and there was something about its tone which for a second made the hairs on the nape of my neck bristle. In the half-light I could see her profile with the straight nose and the chin a shade too heavy and beginning to sag underneath; I could smell her again, too, but this time the smell wasn't part of the evening but the whole evening.

The fields and woods clinging to the hillside gave way to the plateau of Warley Moors; a little ahead I saw the old brickworks and hard by them Sparrow Hill rising abruptly from the surrounding flatness.

There was a dirt road by the brickworks; I stopped the car by the little corrugated-iron office which stood at the top. The door was boarded up and the windows broken; as I looked at it and the big mouldering kiln towering above it like a red igloo I felt a not unpleasant melancholy, though I generally dislike dead places and would rather look at a prosperous mill than the most beautiful ruin. Here on the moors it was different: it was as if someone had been playing a game with those bricks and corrugated iron, leaving them there in that lonely spot to assert the fact of human existence.

"We're too visible here," said Alice. "Turn to the left behind the hill." Sparrow Hill is set back some two hundred yards from the road; the side facing the road is bare except for short, sheep-nibbled grass but the far side is covered with bushes and bracken and there's a big grove of beeches at the foot of the hill.

"Follow the road," she said. "You can see the concrete verges – it ends just beyond that farmhouse on the right. They were going to have all sorts of things at Sparrow Hill once, but it all came to nothing."

I stopped in the shelter of the trees. My heart was beating hard and when I gave Alice a cigarette my hand was trembling. *We're too visible here*: I knew exactly what the words implied. And somehow I didn't want them to imply anything. I wanted to postpone what was going to happen within the next few minutes: I was on the verge of a new territory and it frightened me. Alice was much more than a pair of willing thighs and she would ask for much more than quick comfort. I didn't at the time put it to myself as clearly as this; but I definitely remember thinking that I felt exactly as I did when I had my first woman – a plump WAAF whose name I've forgotten – at the age of eighteen.

So I talked to her. I talked without stopping, and I don't remember what I talked about. It was as if I were putting in a filibuster: a kind of bill was to be passed which would alter my whole life and I wasn't sure that I wanted my whole life to be altered. Then I stopped talking; or, rather, my voice trailed off into silence independently of me. I looked at her. She was smiling with that tight, almost painful expression which I'd noticed when we'd had supper at her house. Her hands were clasped over her knees, her skirt drawn back above them.

I leaned over towards her. "I've been thinking about you all week. I've been dreaming about you, do you know that?"

She put out her hand and touched the nape of my neck. I
kissed her. Her lips tasted of tobacco and toothpaste; they were
held moistly and laxly against mine in a way that was entirely new
to me, utterly different from her dry and light stage kisses. Her
breasts felt astoundingly heavy and full against me; she seemed
to be much younger, much more feminine and soft than ever I'd
imagined her to be.

"I'm all twisted," she said. "This is a terribly moral kind of car."

"We'll go outside," I said hoarsely. She kissed my hands.
"They're beautiful," she said. "Big and red and brutal . . . Will you
keep me warm?"

I remember those words especially. They were empty and
tawdry, they didn't match what took place in the beech grove soon
afterwards; but they were Alice's own words and I preserve them
like saints' relics. And yet there was no great physical pleasure for
either of us that night: it was too cold, I was too nervous, there
was too much messing about with buttons and zips and straps. It
was best when we'd finished; it was like having a cup of really good
coffee and a Havana after an indifferently cooked but urgently
needed meal. It was a clear starlit night: through a gap in the tree
I could see the distant hills. I kissed Alice on the little wing of hair
just above the temple. The hair at that point always seems to me
to smell differently from the hair on the rest of the head; it's vulnerable and soft and somehow babyish. She pressed herself more
closely against me.

"You're all warm," she said. "My dear overcoat. I'd like to sleep
with you, Joe. Truly sleep, I mean, in a big bed with a feather mattress and brass rails and a china chamberpot underneath it."

"I wouldn't let you sleep," I said, not then understanding.

She laughed. "We will sleep together, pet, I promise you."

"It's never been like this before," I said.

"Nor me."

"Did you know this was going to happen?"

She didn't answer. After a moment she said: "Please don't fall in
love with me, Joe. We will be friends, won't we? Loving friends?"

"Loving friends," I said.

When I was starting the car going back she didn't speak at all.

But she was smiling to herself all the way; perhaps it was only a trick of the light but her hair seemed as if it were glowing from within. I drove fast along the narrow switchback of Sparrow Hill Road, taking the corners as if on rails. I couldn't go wrong; the car felt as if it had two litres under its bonnet instead of just over a half. I was the devil of a fellow, I was the lover of a married woman, I was taking out the daughter of one of the richest men in Warley, there wasn't a damn thing I couldn't do. Say what you like of me when I was younger; but I certainly wasn't blasé.

Ten

I spent Christmas at my Aunt Emily's. It snowed in Warley the night I left, just a light powdering, a present from Raphael's and Tuck's and Sharpe's to make the girls' eyes sparkle and the waits sing in tune and to turn the houses taller and crookeder and all's-well-in-the-end adventurous; the town was crammed with people, all of them none the less absolute tenants of happiness because they'd been shepherded into it by the shopkeepers and the newspapers and the BBC: you could sense that happiness, innocent and formal as a children's story, with each snowflake and each note of the Town Hall carillon.

It was hard to leave Warley then; I felt as if I were being sent home from a party before the presents had been taken off the tree. In fact, I'd felt out of things all December: I'd gone to the Thespians' Christmas party, and been the back end of a horse in the children's play, and kissed all the girls at the Town Hall after the traditional lunchtime boozeup, but I knew that I wasn't part of Warley's festival, because I was leaving before the preparations began to make sense, before that short turkey and spice-cake and wine and whisky period when every door in the town would be wide open and the grades wouldn't matter. Not that I really believed such a thing could happen; but in Warley it at least was possible to dream about it.

No dreams were possible in Dufton, where the snow seemed to turn black almost before it hit the ground; Christmas there always seemed a bit ashamed of itself, as if it knew that it was a wicked waste of good money; Dufton and gaiety just weren't on speaking terms. And the house at Oak Crescent was small and dark and smelly and cluttered-up; it wasn't that I didn't care for Aunt Emily and her family, but I was too much of T'Top now and, half-hating myself for it, I found myself seeing them as foreigners. They were kind and good and generous; but they weren't my sort of person any longer.

I told Charles something of this on Boxing Day at the Siege Gun just outside the town. The Siege Gun was our local; it stood on the top of a little hill overlooking a wilderness of allotments and hen-runs. It was about half-an-hour's walk from Oak Crescent; for some reason it was the only respectable pub in Dufton. The others weren't exactly low, but even in their Best Rooms you were likely to see the overalled and sweaty. The landlord at the Siege Gun, a sour old ex-Regular, discouraged anyone entering the Best Room without a collar and tie. Consequently his pub was the only place in Dufton where you'd find any of the town's upper crust, such as it was. I'd had some good nights at the Siege Gun but, looking around me that lunchtime, I knew that there wouldn't be any more. It was too small, too dingy, too working-class; four months in Warley had given me a fixed taste for either the roadhouse or the authentic country pub.

"I couldn't bear Dufton sober," I said to Charles.

"Too true," he said. "I'll be damned glad when I get to London."

I'd known for a month that he'd landed a job there, but when he spoke so lightly about going away I felt lonely and lost; I wanted him to stay permanently in Dufton, I suppose, so that I'd at least be able to depend upon my hometown providing me with company. Dufton's only virtue was that it never changed; Charles to me was part of Dufton. Now that he was leaving the town, the lever had been pulled that would complete its journey into death.

"You slant-eyed Mongolian pig," I said. "What do you want to go away for? Who'll I have to talk to now when I come home at weekends?"

Charles took out a grubby handkerchief and pretended to wipe his eyes. "Your beautifully phrased appeal to my friendship moves me inexpressibly. But I can't stay in Dufton even to please you. Do you know, when I come into this pub, I don't even have to order? They *automatically* issue a pint of wallop. And if I come in with someone else I point at them and nod twice if it's bitter. I'm growing too fond of the stuff anyway . . . it's the only quick way out of this stinking town." He looked at his pint with an expression of comic gluttony on his plump, strangely cherubic face. "Lovely lovely ale," he said. "The mainstay of the industrial North, the bulwark of the British Constitution. If the Dufton pubs closed for just one day, there wouldn't be a virgin or an unbroken window left by ten o'clock."

"There's not many left of either as it is," I said.

"I do my best," he said. "How's *your* sex-life, by the way?"

"Satisfactory. I see Alice every week."

"Weather's a bit cold for it," he said.

"She borrows a friend's flat in Leddersford."

"You be careful, chum."

"She's not possessive. It's not that sort of an affaire—" What sort exactly was it, though? I remembered once, through half-closed eyes, watching her take up my shirt from beside the bed and kiss it. When she saw me looking at her she blushed and turned away. I felt myself blushing too.

"It's perfect," I said firmly. "She's wonderful in bed, and she wants nothing else from me."

"She will."

"Not Alice."

"Keep right on believing that, and it won't be long before I see your name in the Sunday papers."

"Phooey," I said. "It's a simple straightforward transaction. Just for the sake of our health, that's all. Besides, it helps me keep myself pure for Susan."

"You've not said much about her lately. The Lampton charm not working?"

"I've been out with her about half-a-dozen times now. The theatre and the cinema and a five-bob hop. All most genteel. Costs me the hell of a lot of money – flowers, chocolates, and all the rest of it – and I get nothing in return."

"You mean old swine."

"Mind you, she thinks I'm wonderful. Like an elder brother. I keep paying her compliments and I treat her with great respect et cetera et cetera. It's not entirely without effect – I suppose that Wales takes her for granted, the big slob."

"Their daddies will have arranged it all," Charles said. "I don't see why he should put himself out. Damned if *I* would. You haven't a cat in hell's chance, frankly. Unless you thoroughly misbehave, if you see what I mean."

"I see what you mean. But it's easier said than done. She doesn't want me to make love to her – I can always tell."

"Perhaps you're trying too hard. Why not leave her alone for two months or so? Don't quarrel with her, don't attempt to discover how you stand. Simply stop seeing her. If she's at all interested in you, she'll be a bit huffed. Or she'll wonder what's wrong with her. Remember, she's got into the habit of seeing you, poor bitch. But don't" – he wagged his finger at me – "say a word to anyone else. If you do run across her, behave as if nothing had happened." His face looked very red above his stiff white collar; there was a chess-player's intentness in his pale blue eyes. "It should be *very* interesting. Report back with full details, Sergeant, if you survive."

"She mayn't give a curse whether I see her or not," I said. "She probably won't even notice that I've gone."

"In that case, you'll have lost nothing. And you'll have saved your pride."

"I'd be scared of losing her," I said. "I'm in love with her."

He snorted. "In love with her! Drivel! In lust with her. And Daddy's bank balance. I know you, you scoundrel. Do what Uncle Charles advises, and all will be gas and gaiters."

"I might try it," I said. "Another beer?"

"Wait," Charles whispered as a young man in a Crombie overcoat came through the door. "The Glittering Zombie's being democratic. After all, we went to school with him."

He waved at the newcomer. "Come over here, Cyril." He winked at me. "By Jove, old man, it's nice to see you. What are you having?" He was using his Captain's accent, I observed with amusement. It was a wartime acquisition; he'd learned it in ten days flat after he'd seen a young Cockney sub-lieutenant driven to suicide by the jeers of the Standard English types. He did it rather well; the Glittering Zombie, a simple soul whose father had been a Corporation dustman before the war, was, as always, impressed and flattered.

"Let *me*, Charlie," he said quickly. "Something short, eh?"

I returned to Aunt Emily slightly oiled.

"Hello, love," she said when I came in. "Been with Charles?"

"Talking over old times," I said. "We're going out tonight. I'll have supper at his place."

"Where are you going?"

"I don't really know yet."

"Not far from a bottle, if I know Charles."

She was sitting by the fire with her hands folded. It was quite dark in the Front Room; the fire burned with a kind of restrained brightness, reflecting itself gently from the unscratched furniture. A faint smell of cigars and wine and chocolate still hung over the room. Aunt Emily looked very much like my mother; her face had the same thin elegance and the same air of restrained energy. Aided by the beer and the whisky and the faint sadness of the Front Room, the tears came to my eyes.

"What's up, lad?"

"You made me think of Mother."

She sighed. "Ee, I remember her well as a young lass. She used to run the house after Father died. She wor proper determined, wor your mother. Your grandma had all t'heart knocked out of her when your grandpa wor killed at t'mill. During t'first war, that was, and them coining money then, but not a penny-piece of compensation did your grandma get. T'same people went bankrupt in 1930. T'owd meister shot himself."

"Good," I said.

"It wasn't good for those that wor thrown out of work." She looked at me sternly. "Think on how lucky you are, Joe. T'Town Hall can't go bankrupt. Tha'll never go hungry. Or have to scrat and scrape saving for thi old age."

"It's not so bad in the mills now," I said. "No-one's out of work. Dammit, some of the millhands are better off than me."

"Aye," she said, "they can get ten and twelve pounds if they work fifty and sixty and seventy hours a week in t'heat and t'din and t'muck. But how long will it last?"

She rose. "Ah'll make some tea," she said. "Your uncle's having a lay-down and t'boys are out playing." She winked. "So there's only thee and me in t'house, and we'll have a right cup of tea. Ah've been putting a bit aside for you coming home."

Moved by an impulse of affection, I kissed her on the cheek. "Make it so t'spoon'll stand up in it, love," I said. "And I want a pint-pot." I kissed her on the other cheek. "You're very good to me, Auntie," I said.

"It's t'beer that's making thee so sloppy," she said, but I could see that she was pleased by the springiness of her step as she went out.

When she came back with the tea I offered her a cigarette. To my surprise, she accepted it. "I am a devil, aren't I?" she said, puffing away inexpertly.

The tea was both astringent and sweet, and she'd put some rum in it. "That's t'first right cup of tea Ah've had sin' Ah left home," I said.

"Time you had a home of your own."

"I'm too young yet," I said weakly.

"You're old enough. Old enough to be running after all t'lasses in sight, Ah do know."

"No-one'll have me, Auntie. I'm not rich enough."

"Fiddlesticks. You're not bad-looking and you have a good steady job. And you're not shy, you're brass-faced, in fact. Don't try to tell *me* you can't get a lass, Joe Lampton, because Ah'll noan credit it. Haven't you met anyone at this theatre you keep writing about?"

It was no use; I never could withstand her questioning for very long. (I think that perhaps I was unconsciously making up to Mother through her for all the times I'd answered perfectly reasonable questions with boorish grunts or studied vagueness.)

"There's a girl named Susan Brown," I said. "I've taken her out a few times. She's rather attractive."

"Who is she?"

"Her father owns a factory near Leddersford. He's on the Warley Council."

She looked at me with a curious pity. "Money marries money, lad. Be careful she doesn't break your heart. Is she really a nice lass, though?"

"She's lovely," I said. "Not just lovely to look at – she's sweet and innocent and good."

"I bet she doesn't work for a living either, or else does a job for pin money. What good's a girl like that to you? Get one of your own class, lad, go to your own people."

I poured myself another cup of tea. I didn't like its taste any longer; it was too strong, stuffy and pungent like old sacking. "If I want her, I'll have her."

"I wonder how fond you really are of her," Aunt Emily said sadly.

"I love her. I'm going to marry her." But I felt shamefaced as I spoke the words.

On my way to the Siege Gun that evening I went past my old home. Christmas Eve's snow had already melted, and it was cold with a damp enclosing coldness; it was like being locked in a disused cellar. I paused by the gap where our house had stood; I had no desire to receive old memories but instantly, unbidden, the events of that morning in 1941 – the Bad Morning, the Death Morning – unreeled themselves like a film.

It was the smell which had upset me most. There was nothing there now but a faint mustiness; but on the Bad Morning it had been chokingly strong – the blitz smell, damp plaster and bone-meal. I'd accepted it as part of the atmosphere in London and the Home Counties, but here in Dufton it was as incongruous as a tiger.

There was no rubble now, no broken glass, no fluttering shreds of wallpaper. The pavement had been roped off that morning: among the debris was the bathroom mirror, which somehow had survived the explosion and seemed to wink derisively in the August sun, as if it had survived at my parents' expense. For a moment I'd pretended that the bomb had fallen on some other house, and that very soon I'd be talking the whole thing over with

Mother. The houses were so much alike with their oak-grained doors, lace curtains, yellowstoned doorsteps, and fronts of stained Accrington brick (good for a thousand years) that it was easy to see how the Town Hall had made the mistake. Come to that, the front of the house had been so neatly sheared off that it was possible to imagine some macabre practical joke having been played – hadn't Charles and I often agreed that Zombies have a queer sense of humour?

There'd been the usual group of spectators with the usual expression of futile excitement, voyeurs of disaster; I didn't speak to any of them because I hated them so much that I couldn't speak. I shut them out of my mind because if I'd lost control of myself I should simply have been providing them with an extra pleasure, an unexpected titillation.

I'd ducked under the ropes and entered through the front porch, which was still standing, the door ajar. I could have entered with equal ease at any point where the wall had stood; but it would have been disrespectful, like dropping ash on a corpse.

"Clear out," the man in overalls had said. He was standing at the far corner of the living-room with a small red notebook in his hand. His ARP helmet had been pushed back to show a mop of thick white hair; he was wearing heavy horn rim spectacles and a bushy white moustache. He was small and square-shouldered and stood with his feet wide apart as if the floor were swaying. "Clear out," he repeated. "That wall's coming down soon. Christ, haven't you ever seen a blitzed house before?"

"I used to live here."

"I'm sorry." He'd taken off his spectacles and started to clean them with a little square of cloth, his face becoming weak and plump and civilian. "It was a terrible thing to happen. Terrible." He'd looked at the half-wing on my tunic. "You'll get your revenge," he said. He'd replaced his spectacles, his face regaining its purposefulness. "Yes," he said, "give the bastards hell."

Had he really said that, or had I imagined it? But he *had* used those exact words; I remembered how he'd stuck out his chin and frowned, trying to look like a MOI poster. The background was ideal – the wringing-machine blown through the kitchen window, the stone sink cracked in two, a heavy grey sock, darned at the heel, lying half under a lump of plaster, and all the crockery, except one thick half pint mug, mixed up in fragments with butter and sugar and jam and bread and sausages and golden syrup.

Father and Mother had gone to bed when the bomb dropped. The syren had sounded but it was unlikely that they'd taken any notice. Dufton simply wasn't worth the trouble of raiding. They'd died instantly – at least, that was the phrase which Zombie Number One (looking uncommonly prosperous in a new suit and a Macclesfield silk tie) had used, standing with the Town Clerk and the Efficient Zombie in a group of official condolence. There'd even been whisky, offered with an air of ceremonial furtiveness. And I'd wanted to laugh when drinking the whisky because I was suddenly reminded of the picture Charles used to paint of the Council cache of liquor – a huge cellar crammed with rare liqueurs and vintage wines, guarded by huge eunuchs with drawn scimitars. I'd had an insane impulse to ask if they still stocked the Zombie specialities like blood-and-Benedictine.

I stepped forward into the bareness which had been the living-room. Quite calmly now – more calmly than I had done that August morning – I reconstructed it in my memory. I was sure about the cream valance, the red velvet curtains, the big photograph of myself as a child which had hung over the mantelshelf; but I couldn't be quite certain about the location of the oak dining-table. I closed my eyes for a moment and it came into focus by the far wall with three Windsor chairs round it. And there was the sofa with the blue cloth cover; it was most important to remember that. When its springs began to perish, my father brought a leather car-seat from a junk-dealer's. The sofa-cover was loose, and when my parents both went out I used sometimes to take it off and, sitting on the righthand side, drive Birkin's Bentley or the Saint's Hirondel for hours at a stretch.

The walls had been decorated half in fawn and orange paper and half in imitation oak panelling. The paper was reduced to a few shreds now, the imitation oak panelling was pulped with dust and smoke and weather. There had been a pattern of raised beads; I struck a match and held it close to the wall and I could still see some of the little marks where as a child I'd picked the beads off with my fingernails. I felt a sharp guilt at the memory; the house should have been inviolate from minor indignities.

The fireplace had survived the bomb untouched; the two loose bricks on its lefthand side had still been projecting like buck teeth. For as long as I could remember they'd annoyed me; but on the Death Morning they seemed unbearably pathetic. And the draught control handle over the fireplace – a chromium hand clutching a rod – which had frightened me in my dreams, seemed frightening no longer, but lost and in pain, a sick child's.

Everyone had been very kind and there'd been a constant stream of callers at Aunt Emily's. A shower of gifts had been pressed upon me by every organisation in the town and there was even talk of some kind of fund being opened for me. The truth was that the whole elaborate machinery for the relief of blitz victims had been unemployed until Father and Mother were killed, so it had set enthusiastically to work on me, like an elephant picking up a peanut. In a way, though, I'd rather enjoyed being the centre of attention, warm between the cosy breasts of sympathy.

A sluggish wind crept down from the Pennines, cold and damp and spiteful, trying to find a gap in my defences. It retired, defeated by alcohol and meat and the thick wool of my overcoat and the soft cashmere of my scarf; it had no power over me now, it was a killer only of the poor and the weak. I looked at the small space which had once been my home; I'd come a long way since 1941.

Too far perhaps; I thought of my father. He was a good workman; too good a workman to be sacked and too outspoken about his Labour convictions to be promoted. He told me this entirely without bitterness; in fact, I'd detected a note of pride in his deep, slow voice. "If Ah'd joined t'Con Club, lad, Ah'd be riding to work in mi own car . . ."

I didn't, at the age of fifteen, share my father's pride, because the hypothetical car which he'd so highmindedly rejected was all too real to me. So instead of the look of approval which he expected he received merely a sullen glare.

My mother knew what was in my mind. "You've never gone short, Joseph," she said. She always called me by my full name when she wanted to read the Riot Act. "Your father would starve before he'd sell himself for a handful of silver" – this was one of her favourite quotations and her use of it, I don't know why, always embarrassed me intensely – "but he'd never see his own in want. I knew that when I married him. I could have had a common, fat man with a motor-car, but I wanted something better than that."

She smiled at Father; intercepting that smile, I felt shut-out, bewildered, childish. My father was sitting in the armchair to the left of the fireplace, smoking his pipe and listening to, of all things, Noel Coward's *The Stately Homes of England*. He was as completely relaxed as the grey tomcat asleep by the fire with its head on my feet. That, I might say, was as far as the image extended; there was nothing even remotely feline about my father. He had a face like the statue of some Victorian industrialist, heavy and firm and deeply lined, giving an impression of stern willingness. He was, in fact, a very handsome man; his features were regular, his hair thick and bright, and his teeth – this was rare in Dufton – were white and even. It was an obsolete handsomeness, a Charles Hawtrey, bay-rum, Sweet Adeline kind, solid and male and wholesome. Mother had a thin lively face which only just missed horsiness. She was never still and rarely silent. She had a fresh, rosy complexion and clear blue eyes; at thirty-eight, her hair was already greying but the effect, paradoxically, was to make her look younger, as if she were only pretending to be old.

Father rose. He rose very quickly and smoothly. He was a big man (six foot and over fourteen stone) but he hadn't the ponderous clumsiness of most big men. He moved rather as a young bull moves, but without its blind menace.

"Ah'm bahn for a gill, lass," he said. He ruffled my hair as he passed. "Mind what Ah say, Joe. There's some things that can be bought too dear."

Then I remembered the bomb, and the whole scene dissolved. It was as if my mind were in watertight compartments. Behind the doors of this particular compartment, even six years after, were things I couldn't face. It was bad enough when these things hap-pened to strangers; I remembered the WAAF messroom at my first station after a direct hit. I'd stood that better than I'd expected, thinking of it simply as a mess to be cleared up, even after I'd seen that fair-haired girl from Doncaster with both eyes running down her cheeks. But what made me really sick was treading on a piece of flesh which squirmed from under my foot like a mouse. The invasion of the abattoir, the raw physical horror suddenly becoming undisputed master – I couldn't connect it with Father and Mother, I refused to accept it.

I turned away from the house and walked quickly away. It had been a mistake to go there. The watertight compartments were out of order; images of pain and distress, more memories of things I'd seen during the war and would rather have forgotten, rose to the surface of my mind. As long as I kept on walking they'd remain mixed and chaotic, like imperfectly recollected books and films; once I stopped they'd become unbearably organised; if I walked quickly I could cram my mind with the speed of my own movement, with the grocer's shop and its frosted window and the Christmas tree, with the men's outfitters and the awful American ties, with the Board School and its murderous asphalt playground – and then I stopped trying. It was futile; here on the left stood the huge bulk of Torver's Mills where Father had worked for twenty years; here was the Wellington, his local, and here was the greengrocer's where he bought muscatel raisins for our Sunday walks – wherever I looked there was a memory, an italicising of death.

Why hadn't I noticed it before? Because Warley had shown me a new way of living; for the first time I'd lived in a place without memories. And for the first time *lived* in a place; in the three months I'd been there I was already more a part of the town, more involved in its life, than ever I had been in my birthplace. And even for three days only, I couldn't endure the chilly bedroom with its hideous wallpaper and view of mill-chimneys and middens, the bath with its peeling enamel, the scratchy blankets – my aunt and uncle were unselfish and generous and gentle, they spoke only the language of giving, but no virtue was substitute for the cool smoothness of linen, the glittering cleanliness of a real bathroom, the view of Warley Moor at dawn, and the saunter along St. Clair Road past the expensive houses.

"Dead Dufton," I muttered to myself. "Dirty Dufton, Dreary Dufton, Despicable Dufton—" then stopped. It was too quiet. There were lights in the windows but they seemed as if put there to deceive – follow them and you were over the precipice, crashing into the witch's cave to labour in the mills for ever. There were cigarette ends and orange peel and sweet wrappers in the gutter but no-one living had smoked those cigarettes or eaten those sweets; the town reminded me of those detective stories in dossier form which used to be sold complete with clues – cigarette-ends, poisoned lozenges, hairpins . . . I walked over the suspension bridge at the top of the town; the river was running faster than usual, swollen with melted snow and harried by the north-east wind; the bridge was swaying and creaking beneath my feet, and I suddenly was afraid that it might deliberately throw me into the water like a vicious horse; I forced myself to walk slowly, but the sweat was dripping off my brow.

Eleven

Alice took hold of me by my hair. "You've a nice body, do you know that? Hairy but not too hairy. I never could bear animated hearthrugs."

I felt as if I were choking. "God, you're lovely. You – I don't know what to say, you're so beautiful."

"What, an old woman like me?"

"You're not old."

"Oh yes I am, honey. Much older than you."

"I wish you wouldn't talk as if I were a minor," I said with some irritation. "I'm twenty-five and I've had a lot of experience."

"I'm sure you have." Her dark blue eyes were tender and amused. She pulled my head down to her breasts. "There now, my sweet baby, there now. You're very old and very mature and you're going to be a great man."

I could see nothing but her body, breathe nothing but that

peppery odour of lavender and the indescribable, infinitely good smell of woman's flesh. I pressed my face tighter; the thin hands on my head tightened convulsively.

"Oh God," she said, "you're so good. You're so good to me. You're so kind. There was never anyone so good to me before. I'm alive now, all of me's alive. I'm feeling things I'd forgotten, the nerve's regenerating. It hurts sometimes . . . I don't care." She covered my face with kisses.

The kisses did more to me than the longest kiss on the mouth could have done. They weren't preliminaries; they were complete in themselves. She kissed me as moistly as a little girl; and I was glad of this; I was discovering that I never had really made love to a woman before or truly enjoyed a woman's body. The sort of sex I was used to was sex as it would be if human beings were like screen characters – hygienic, perfumed, with no normal odours or tastes – as if flesh were silk stretched over rubber, as if lips were the only sensitive part, as if the natural secretions were shameful.

Alice was no more greedy of actual sex than the others; but she was shameless in love, with no repugnances, no inhibitions. In her arms I was learning quickly; so that now I actually found myself drinking the moisture from her lips. I didn't want to wash it off, I wanted it to stay, for her to become a part of me.

"You beautiful brute," she said, and drew the bedclothes aside. "You beautiful uncomplicated brute."

"No," I said. "As they say in the films, I'm just a crazy mixed-up kid."

She ran her hand delicately over my chest. "You should have been a navvy. I hate to think of you ever wearing clothes."

"Navvies don't go about naked. If anything they wear far more than accountants."

"I wish you were one just the same. I'd let you beat me every Saturday night . . . Joe, will you tell me something?"

"What, darling?"

She pulled a hair from my chest. "There, I'll keep that as a souvenir." She put her face against my chest and lay silent.

"That wasn't what you wanted to ask me about," I said. "Besides, you took it without asking."

"It's a funny question. All ifs. Look, supposing you'd met me before I married, supposing I were ten years younger – how would you have felt about me?"

"That's simple. Like now."

"That's not what I meant. Would you have taken me seriously?" Her voice was muffled against my chest.

"Yes. You know that I would. But what's the use?"

"Don't be practical, Joe. Please don't be sensible. Just imagine me as I was ten years ago. And you as you are now."

I looked into her eyes. I could see my face in her pupils, flushed, with my hair tousled. "You're looking babies," she said, almost coyly. "If you look long enough, you'll see a baby."

I had the same sensation that I had when as a child of ten I'd seen my Aunt Emily with her son at her breast. And it was, too, like the sensation I'd had when I'd intercepted looks and actions of my parents – the secret, bold look before bedtime, the hand on the knee – it was as if I'd stumbled upon something bigger than myself. Something which was uncompromisingly real, something which I couldn't avoid but which, I felt ashamedly, I was trying to avoid. There was happiness at its centre but it was a frightening kind of happiness.

"There were no lines then," she said. "And I was firm here—" she put my hands on her breasts. "Everything was ahead of me. I couldn't sleep sometimes, wondering what would happen to me – I knew that it would be wonderful, whatever it was . . . No, that would be when I was nineteen. Yes, imagine me nineteen. That's the best age. I used to feel happy, terribly happy, all of a sudden, and there'd be no reason for it. And I'd cry easily but I'd enjoy it and it never made my eyes red. Would you have taken me seriously?"

"You probably wouldn't have taken *me* seriously."

"I'd have been silly enough for that . . . I had a *career* then. I'd just graduated from the drama school – a broken-down place with a broken-down old ham in charge of it – the best Mummy could afford. It was a cheap finishing school, you see. Mummy hoped that I'd learn to speak and move properly there and acquire a sort of polish and a little glamour – and then hook a rich young man and retrieve the family fortunes."

"That I couldn't have done at any time. What about Alice at twenty-five?"

"Oh, I was awfully smooth. Worn smooth, I think. I'd been in London three years. It's a hellish place when you're poor – I had to keep up appearances too. I took some awful jobs when I was resting. Cinema usherette, snack-bar attendant – everything but a life of shame. But I was still young. I'd lots and lots of bounce left in me."

"You have now."

"Yes, but I have to live to a regime to possess it. I just had it then, whatever I did. Would you have liked me then, would you have been romantic about me?"

"You might still have broken my heart. How could I have helped an ambitious young actress? I'll take you as you are now."

She got out of bed. "I'll make some coffee."

"Tea would be nicer."

"Poor Elspeth," she said. "She lends us her flat and we pinch all her precious tea."

"I'll get her some more."

She wrinkled her nose and put her hands palm upwards; as I watched her, her face seemed to grow male and vulpine and her nose to lengthen. "Vat, are you in the racket too?" She started to dress.

"I hate you to put any clothes on," I said.

"That's sweet of you, but I'm too old to walk about in the nude." She wriggled into her girdle.

"I like watching you dress, though." She came over in her slip and kissed me. I stroked her back; she was already a different person in the blue silk garment, smaller but already less vulnerable, more controlled. It was a little hard to imagine her as being the same person who, scarcely half-an-hour since, had been moaning in my arms in the last extremity of a pleasure almost indistinguishable from pain.

She moved gently out of my embrace and picked up her dress. She went into the kitchen; I heard the flare of a match and the hiss of a gas-ring. I dressed quickly; by myself I felt an obscure uneasiness at being naked. I lit a cigarette, the first for two hours, and inhaled deeply.

It wasn't a big flat; the block was one of the mansions in which the wool lords of Leddersford had once lived; this room had probably belonged to one of the servants. It was furnished in a middle-class, *démodé*, vaguely theatrical kind of way. The big bed was covered with a mauve quilt; there were pouffes, a satin-walnut table, and a great many photographs of actors and actresses. The white carpet was very thick, and the chairs gilt and spindly-legged. There was a profusion of dolls on the dressing-table; it was a boudoir, faintly naughty, rather too feminine. I felt not quite in place there, as if I'd got into the wrong room by mistake.

I went into the tiny box of a kitchen. Alice was watching the kettle and tapping her foot impatiently. "It won't ever boil if you do that," I said, and took hold of her waist. She leaned back in my arms; I put my face against hers, breathing in her scent. It was as if we shared the same lungs. We were breathing deeply and slowly; I was utterly secure and warm. The kettle whistled; at that moment it had the effect of a mill-hooter at six in the morning. I let her go reluctantly.

"Note," she said. "Teapot to kettle, water mustn't be left to boil. Teapot is warm but dry. Now leave for three minutes. Synchronise your watches, men. 2020. Roger?"

"Roger," I said.

Her watch was a thin gold wafer with jewels for numerals. "At least, I think it's 2020," she said. "This is very pretty but difficult to tell the time by."

"I'd like to buy you something like that." I would have liked to stamp on it. Then I reflected that, through taking Alice, I had in a sense, taken away the value of the watch; but even that thought didn't console me very much. She didn't seem to have heard what I said. "Honey, take this stuff in the kitchen. You're hungry, aren't you?"

"I'll eat anything. Iron Guts they used to call me."

"That's lovely, I'll always call you Iron Guts. Take these sandwiches in there too, Iron Guts. And the pickles. We'll have a proper do." She giggled like a schoolgirl, her face suddenly losing its harsh lines.

The bread was fresh and well-buttered and the sandwiches were fried chicken, crisp and golden-brown. We sat beside each other in comfortable silence; now and again she'd smile at me. When we'd finished eating she went into the kitchen to cut some more bread. I sat with my eyes half-closed, sipping the strong tea. Suddenly I heard her call my name. She was standing at the breadboard with her right fore-finger dripping blood.

"It's nothing," she said, but her face was white. I took her to the sink and washed her finger with hot water. I noticed the first-aid cabinet over the sink and after a little rummaging (Elspeth seemed to have been using the cabinet as a make-up box) found some T.C.P. and a bandage. I poured out a cup of tea and held it to her lips.

"I want a cigarette," she said.

"Drink that first."

She drank it obediently. The colour returned to her cheeks. I lit a cigarette for her and she leaned back against my shoulder.

"Silly of me to carry on like that. It was the shock, I think. I hate blood . . . You're very competent, aren't you, Joe?"

"I've bound up worse than that."

"Joe, have you seen a lot of horrid things? In the RAF, I mean."

"Just the average amount. You soon forget."

"You look so young. Except for your mouth. Are you sure you've forgotten?"

"Sometimes something happens to bring them out. They poke out their heads and growl and then you shove them back in the cage. Why are you asking? Afraid I'm neurotic?"

She kissed me on the cheek. "You're the least neurotic person I know. It's just something I've been curious about for a long time but I haven't really known anyone whom I could ask. George wasn't in any of the Services. He has a perforated eardrum and they wouldn't look at him." She looked at me a little angrily. "It wasn't his fault."

"I haven't said a word."

"It's all so safe and civilised and cosy," she went on, half-dreamily. "All these men, so well-mannered and mild and agreeable – but what's behind it all? Violence and death. They've seen things which you think would drive anyone mad. And yet there's no trace.

There's blood on everyone's hands, that's what it amounts to . . . everything so damned insecure—" I felt her shiver.

"Don't think about it, love," I said. "The world's full of violence. But it always has been. There's probably someone being killed not ten miles away from here at this very moment—"

"Don't remind me," she said.

"It's different in wartime, too. You didn't have time to be sickened. There was too much to do. Anyway, you can't help anyone by being sensitive."

"I know, I know," she said impatiently. "Oh God, everything's going so fast. There's no way to stop the merrygoround. You never feel safe. When I was young I used to feel safe. Even if Father and Mother quarrelled they were kind to me. The house was solid too. That bloody concrete barracks I live in now – it's so clean and streamlined that I wouldn't be at all surprised if it took to flight."

"You talk too much," I said, and drew her upon my knees. "Quiet now, not another word." I stroked the smooth skin of her forearm; she closed her eyes and went limp in my arms.

"You can do that all night," she said. "I won't stop you." She sighed. "You make a lovely seat. I could purr like a cat."

The smoothness of her arm, the warm weight of her upon my lap; I too could have done it all night. And I could have taken her again; but the act of love was becoming not distasteful, not unnecessary, but only one of a series of pleasures; of pleasures which were solely dependent upon her.

The doorbell rang; three shorts, one long, three shorts. "Elspeth," I said. I was going to rise, but Alice pulled me back.

"Don't be so bourgeois," she said. I put my arms more tightly round her.

Elspeth's head came round the door with a roguish smile on it which would have suited her better in the days when she was touring in *A Little Bit of Fluff.* She danced rather than walked into the room, her skirt flaring up round her. A heavy smell of Phul-Nana came in with her. "Hello, dears," she said in her husky fruity voice. "Do hope I haven't disturbed you. I try to be discreet, but I *had* to come in. It's cold outside."

"I'll make you some tea," Alice said, and went into the kitchen.

Elspeth threw herself down into an armchair. "Me oh my, what an evening I've had. You not only produce, you teach 'em how to act. Honestly, ducks, they can't understand the simplest thing. I don't know why I went in for the stage, I don't really." She pirouetted to the piano and started to sing *Don't put your daughter on the stage, Mrs. Worthington*, her husky voice still clear and full.

She whirled the piano stool round when she'd finished and sat facing me, her hands held outwards. "Not that it's anything else but cabaret stuff," she said. "No body in it somehow . . ."

"If you're going to give us a concert, you'd better have some food," Alice said from the kitchen.

"Lovely, dear," Elspeth said. She lowered her voice. "You're a very lucky young man, Joe. Alice is an angel, a real angel. A heart of gold." Her black button eyes were looking at me intently. In the old painted face they were shockingly youthful. She was sitting with her legs slightly apart and her skirt had ridden up above her knee; I turned my eyes away, feeling a little disgusted. Her legs too were the legs of a much younger woman: cut off from the waist, sheer pornography. However full her skirt, Elspeth always gave the impression that it was inadequate.

She pulled it down over her knees. "I always forget," she said. She smiled at me, her head a little on one side. "If you'd seen that much of me once, you wouldn't have stayed in that chair for very long."

"I'm sure I wouldn't."

She blew me a kiss. "Ah, I don't blame Alice. You're the sort of man I like, big and beefy. There's too many pansies about these days. I knew a lot of big men once; they're all dead now and a little skinny thing like me lives on . . ." Her picture-postcard face with the dyed red bubble-curls and the Lily Langtry nose and chin was sad as a sick monkey's. "It's as if the bigger and stronger they are the more the illnesses have to feed upon. I remember the night Laird died. I can't breathe, he said, and he started tearing at his collar. Then he just fell, straight forward. My God, the dressing-room shook. We picked him up and he was dead. Thirty-five, with his whole life before him. It makes you wonder, don't it?" She lit one of her Turkish cigarettes; the sweet, pungently archaic odour

– *The Bing Boys* and Romano's and Drury Lane – filled the room like incense. "He was made for me to go away with him," she said. "Sometimes I wish I had. My husband wasn't much good even then. I was too independent and he wanted to own me. He was a devil when he was drunk. A big strong man too – I never could resist big strong men . . . Do you love Alice?"

"Yes," I said without thinking; the question was so abruptly put that it caught me off balance.

"I thought you did," she said calmly. "I saw the way she was sitting with you. She doesn't know it yet—" she put her hand on mine – "Don't hurt her. Don't hurt her."

I had a sensation of black water closing over my head; the room seemed airless, too heavily scented, somehow decadent; the raddled intent face before me was an old witch's. I'd suddenly awaken and find myself turned into an old man and see her laughing at me, a girl again, rosy and plump with my stolen youth.

She started talking about the old days at Daly's Theatre; I hardly listened because suddenly I wanted to be out of the room, to walk over the moors, to have the wind and the rain in my face.

When Alice came in with the supper tray I saw her for a moment as the same kind of person as Elspeth, an inhabitant of a shut-in musty world, tatty as running greasepaint, and the tenderness I had felt evaporated; it seemed impossible that I'd embraced her naked body, that the whole evening hadn't been a rehearsal for some naughty bedroom farce, a bored routine the colour of a provincial theatre's faded gilt and plush.

Twelve

The Bar Parlour of the Western Hotel, just opposite the Town Hall, is a remarkable one in its way. It's the best-furnished in the place, with cushioned benches and a thick grey carpet and glass-topped tables and basket-chairs and photos of local cricket and football teams and a wallpaper in a soft, subdued orange and grey which is, if you care for that sort of thing, a pleasure to look at. It's for men only; the other rooms, even the Lounge, are rather scruffy, with iron-legged tables and hard benches and Windsor chairs. Consequently the pub is much used by solid business men and Town Hall officials, who like to drink without women but who have no taste for the sawdust and spittoons of the tap-room. The Western has always been the venue for the Warley NALGO Men's Evening, the Town Hall's annual stag-party. The routine is to meet in the Bar Parlour for a couple of pints, have dinner upstairs and a couple more pints, then return to the Bar Parlour for some serious drinking. One unwritten rule of the Men's Evening is to mix with other departments; that evening, I remember, I talked mostly with Reggie from the Library.

I'd taken Charles' advice and hadn't tried to see Susan since Christmas. I hadn't much hope of his plan working; in fact, I'd almost decided to write her off. But that evening – probably as a result of the four pints inside me and the odd feelings I'd had about Alice in Elspeth's flat the day before – I started to daydream. I did the job thoroughly too. There was a letter from Susan inviting me to a party and asking plaintively if she'd done anything to offend me. Or, better still, the doorbell would ring one wild wet evening and she'd be standing there, her face rosy with the wind; perhaps she'd come ostensibly to see the Thompsons on Thespian business or perhaps she might simply say "I *had* to come, Joe. You'll think I'm shameless but—" And I'd kiss her and there'd be no need to speak; we'd stand there listening to the rain walling us up into happiness together and then we'd go out to Sparrow Hill – "I love walking in the rain with you," she'd say – and we'd walk on and on, the good clean air fresh in our lungs, walking on for ever, the fairy story come true . . .

But it wasn't quite like that. I was sitting in the Bar Parlour with Reggie after dinner, feeling agreeably full of food and beer but not so full that there wasn't room for a few more pints. I'd just finished telling Reggie a dirty story, the sort that one can only tell at stag parties.

"That's the muckiest I've ever heard," he said admiringly. "Where the devil do you get 'em from, Joe? That reminds me. Ran across Susan the other day."

"Susan Brown?" I kept my voice flat deliberately.

"We had quite a cosy little chat. I bought her a coffee at Riley's. After all, if *you* won't look after the girl, someone's got to. We talked about you most of the time."

"You couldn't choose a better subject."

"I don't think so, old man. I kept trying to point out my own merits in a discreet sort of way but it was all Joe Lampton. Isn't Joe handsome, isn't Joe clever, wasn't Joe wonderful in *The Farm* – I got sick of it."

"You're joking."

"Wish I were. You haven't seen her for a bit, have you?"

I drained off my pint. "Another?" I tried to keep the triumphant smile off my face.

"I haven't your monumental capacity," he said. "Just a half, please."

I beckoned the waiter over. Hoylake came in at that moment, twinkling and dapper. He saw the empty seat beside us and came over. "I'm not intruding, boys?"

"Not at all," I said. "Won't you have a drink, Mr. Hoylake?"

"You have one with me, Joe. And you too, Reggie. I only dropped in for five minutes. Must encourage NALGO activities. Though I like mixed events best. All-male social functions have rarely appealed to me. I hope you weren't talking shop. I hate talking shop."

A little hush had come over the room; but it didn't last long. He wasn't the sort of chief who paralysed conversation; not that I was entirely taken in by his chumminess. It was all very nice of him to call us Joe and Reggie but, I reflected, he wouldn't have been pleased if we'd called him Fred.

"We were talking about a young lady," Reggie said.

"Good, good," Hoylake said. He looked over the top of his glasses with mock severity. "You weren't taking her name lightly, I hope?"

"We were taking her very seriously," Reggie said. "We're deadly rivals for her affections. We contemplate a duel in Snow Park."

"What crowded lives my colleagues lead," said Hoylake. He lifted his whisky. "All the best, boys."

"I shall lose both ways," Reggie said. "If I win, she won't have me; I shall have hurt her precious Joe. If I were her I wouldn't look at him. What do you think of a young man who takes a sweet young girl out for months, then drops her flat, Mr. Hoylake?"

I found myself blushing. "Don't believe a word he says. She couldn't care less."

"Couldn't care less indeed!" Reggie laughed. There was a look of faint malice on his face. "She lights up when she hears his name. And he just doesn't bother. The best-looking girl in Warley too."

"They all fall for Joe," Hoylake said. "When he collects the rates at Gilden all the women come in droves. They pay twice over to have five minutes longer with him." He sighed. "Mind you, when I was younger I'd have given him a run for his money."

I was thinking about what Reggie had said with increasing jubilation. I shut my mind against entire acceptance of his words; it was possible that her only feeling was one of hurt – at least slightly damaged – pride. If I asked her to go out with me again that would retrieve her pride; if she used some transparently contrived excuse to put me off, she'd be completely revenged. But I knew, almost as soon as these thoughts passed through my head, that they were all nonsense; Susan simply wasn't the vendetta type.

"The prettiest girl in Warley," Hoylake said ruminatively. "Now, who could that be? Unmarried, I trust. Joe would meet her at the Thespians, I should imagine. Let me see – her name would begin with an S? Surname with a B? Dark hair and not entirely unconnected with the Chairman of the Finance Committee?"

"You're a first-rate detective," Reggie said.

"I'm an old busybody," Hoylake said. "We all are in Warley. Mind you, there's a lot to be said for it even when, though don't quote me—" he snickered as if deprecating his slight touch of self-importance – "it takes the form of scandal-mongering. It indicates interest in one's fellow-humans, which surely is an admirable thing. I'm glad that Joe here is beginning to take some part in the community life of Warley, and isn't living outside the town. I thoroughly dislike commuting – people should live and work in the same place. But here I am, on the verge of talking shop . . . I see your chief, Reggie. I must have a word with him. See you later."

He went over to the Librarian; I noticed that he took his drink with him, barely touched. He was paid twice as much as the Librarian, and didn't wish to force him into buying expensive drinks.

"He's a clever little devil," Reggie said. "Not much he misses. Every move taped out."

"As long as I get on with him he can be as clever as he likes," I said. "Look, Reggie, are you really serious about Susan? I mean, did she really say all those things?"

"Why on earth should I joke about it?" He seemed a little indignant. "It's absolutely true. I mentioned *The Farm* – and then I talked about your performance. Among others, of course. I wasn't terribly impressed with you – she absolutely leapt to your defence. From then on, the conversation never left you. She lit up from inside when she talked about you. It's quite unmistakable, that look – a sort of dopy joyfulness. You're wearing it at present, incidentally."

"You want another drink," I said hastily.

"It's my turn. Don't try to sidetrack me."

"I drink two to your one, so it's fair enough."

"That's ridiculous," he said weakly, but I could tell that he was relieved. He looked round the room. "Small-town officials. My God, what a crew! You know something, Joe? I'd give a year's salary to get out of this town."

"I don't agree with you. I'm all for small towns. If they're the right kind."

"It's all very well for you, chum. You're a bright, efficient type. You stand out in a crowd. You're bound to get ahead in a place like Warley. And, of course, it's a novelty to you. If you'd lived here all your life you'd feel differently."

"I hate my own hometown," I said. "But that's different. Look, Dufton's awful. It stinks. Literally. It's dead as mutton. Warley's alive. I felt that from the first moment I set foot in the place. And there's so much of it, too, in five minutes you can be right away from everything. It's even got a history, you can find out something fresh about it every day . . ." My voice trailed off; I was giving too much of myself away.

Reggie smiled. "Anyone'd think you were talking about a woman and not a perfectly ordinary market town with a few mills. You're a funny chap, Joe."

Teddy Soames came over to our table at that moment. "We're all funny here," he said. He belched loudly. "Excuse me, I'm a trifle intoxicated. Not that I should be. When I was in the RAF the amount that I've forced down me tonight wouldn't have made me turn one of my Brylcreemed hairs." He sat down heavily. "Roll on the next war."

"Speak for yourself," Reggie said. "I never was so miserable in my whole life."

"It was monotonous at times, I grant you that," Teddy said. "But you had no worries and plenty of money. Plenty of beer and plenty of cigarettes and plenty of women. Shall we give them an old RAF song, Joe?" He started to sing softly. "Cats on the roof-tops, cats on the tiles—"

"Whoa," I said. "It's too early for filthy ballads."

"I'd forgotten I was respectable," Teddy said. "I've sung that at all the best hotels in Lincolnshire. With Wingcos and Group Captains joining in. Happy happy days!"

"It may have been like that for you," Reggie said. "As far as I was concerned, war was hell. All I did at first was drill under a blazing sun in itchy woollen underwear. Then I peeled potatoes. Later on I became the British Army's most inefficient clerk. For a while I was quite happy. At least I didn't have to handle loaded weapons and such-like dangerous objects. Then some inhuman planner at the War Office started cutting down administrative staff. So I became the British Army's most frightened infantryman. The day I put on my demob suit was the happiest day of my life. Granted, I came home to discover that the bloody Library Association had made their exams ten times as difficult, thus giving a flying start to the women and the conchies—"

"No shop," Teddy said. "The Library Association's shop. Definitely." He looked at me then put out his hand to feel the texture of my suit. "Highgrade worsted," he said. "And look at that shirt and tie! My goodness, Mr. Lampton, however do you manage on your coupons?"

"He has connections," Reggie said.

Reggie gave the clenched-fist salute. "Joe for King! Vote Labour!"

"You idiot," I said. "You know what Hoylake's like about politics."

"That's not politics," Teddy said. "Just a saying. Reggie used to chalk it on his tank before he went into battle."

"I never saw the inside of a tank," Reggie said. "I once saw a Jerry open the turret of a Sherman and throw in a hand-grenade. The feeling of security they gave you at first sight was entirely ill-ill-illusory. Frankly, I've always believed in the old-fashioned war of attrition, when you stayed in a cosy concrete dugout and let the artillery do the fighting. I never could get HQ to agree with me, though. I always seemed to be advancing regardless. All over Africa, all over Italy."

"I thought I recognised you in Desert Victory," Teddy said. "A gallant figure with a bloodstained scarf round your head waving your men onwards."

"I wish it had been me you saw," Reggie said. "I was one of the poor devils who got waved onwards."

I heard the Librarian laughing. He had a high-pitched, rather effeminate laugh.

"That's his dirty joke laugh," Reggie said. "He has a special one for every occasion. A respectful laugh, a refined laugh, a derisive laugh when I say something he doesn't agree with . . . If he'd been my sergeant I could always have found a chance to shoot the bastard. I should have stayed in the Army."

"You intellectual types," Teddy said. "Never content."

The Librarian joined us. He was a small man with eyes so deep-set that they gave the effect of being mounted horizontally. He was about thirty-five, and didn't look as if he'd ever been any younger.

"Enjoying yourselves?" he asked.

"We're just fighting the war over again, sir," Reggie said. He winked at us. "We decided that we should have let the Russians polish off the Germans and then gone in and polished off the Russians with the atom bomb." He winked again at us.

"Just what I've always said." The Librarian fizzed with enthusiasm. "The Allies have paid dearly for their mistake. When I was in Germany I saw what the Russians were really like. I don't mind admitting that I was a bit of a Communist before the war, but I soon changed my tune . . . What are you lads drinking?"

"We've ordered, thanks," I said. "Won't you have one with me?"

"Do you know, I think I will. They're all plutocrats at the Treasurer's, Reggie. That's always how it is: we torch-bearers of culture are paid starvation wages, and the hard materialists, the men of facts and figures, are the lords of creation. I'll have a half of bitter, Joe."

"Pints here," I said. "Nothing but pints."

"We *are* making a night of it, aren't we?" He laughed, but I couldn't classify the laugh this time. "Mr. Hoylake has just imparted a rather clever story. Two old colonels were sitting in their club one day—"

I didn't listen; I was remembering the way I'd checked Teddy and Reggie, I was remembering the way Hoylake had, in effect, refused a drink from me and then from the Librarian. He'd bought the drinks, not out of kindness but because of a protocol that wasn't, when one weighed it up, very much less rigid than diplomatic protocol. But the prizes were so small; Hoylake was the richest man in the room with a salary of a thousand. George Aisgill, I was certain, would spend that amount on food and drink and petrol alone. Even Bob Storr wouldn't get much less than a thousand. In business, I ruminated, I'd have to soft-soap people whom I despised, I'd have to steer the conversation towards their favourite subjects, I'd have to stand them meals and drinks. But the game was worth the candle; if I sold my independence, at least I'd get a decent price for it.

"—And the second old colonel said: '*Female* camel, of course. There's nothing queer about old Carruthers.'" The Librarian threw back his head and laughed shrilly.

The beer was beginning to take hold of me; I realised that I'd had seven pints without noticing it. I worked out a little sum in my head: five one-and-fours plus one one-and-four minus one one-and-four from Hoylake—

"I meant to tell you, Joe," the Librarian said, "how much I enjoyed your performance in *The Farm*."

"Hell," Teddy said, "so did he. I bet he rehearsed those love-scenes! Admit it, you young ram."

"Tut tut," I said. "My relations with Mrs. Aisgill are pure as the driven snow."

"Funny old driven snow," Reggie said.

The Librarian giggled. "You really shouldn't cast aspersions. Though to tell you the truth I shouldn't personally object to a pure friendship with the lady to whom you refer." He wiped the sweat from his brow and took a long pull from his pint-pot. Like most inexperienced drinkers, he felt obliged to keep up with the rest of the party; with an heroic effort, he drained off the rest of the pint, then hiccuped painfully. "Excuse me, gentlemen, I must go to change the goldfish's water, as the French say." He went out hastily, looking pale.

When he'd left, we burst out laughing. "Wine is a mocker, strong drink is raging," Reggie said. "The poor devil's not used to it, is he?"

"It's the thought of Alice," Teddy said, "unchaste thoughts are running riot."

"Tell the truth, Joe," Reggie said. "Aren't you doing a bit for her?"

"You mustn't ask me such questions. If I say yes, I'm a cad, and if I say no, I'm a liar." I grinned maliciously. "Would you like her yourself, Reggie?"

"My God, would I not! She's terrific. A trifle long in the tooth, mark you, but she has style, real style."

"What about June?" Teddy said. "Say a kind word for June. She has the merit of being a virgin too."

"She's only a child," Reggie said. "I'd feel the hot breath of the Sunday press on my neck if I made a pass at her. There's no comparison."

I felt a deep exultation. Whatever desires they had been tormented by, I'd fulfilled, and in six days would fulfil again. I was given for the asking what they'd never get in a thousand years; and I'd be given Susan too; and, if I wanted her, there was no reason why I shouldn't be given June.

Then I thought of Sparrow Hill and Warley Moor again. I knew that there was a cold wind outside and a light covering of snow. It would be quiet there and untouched and clean. The beer went dead inside me; I felt choked with my own selfishness as nasty as catarrh; there was nothing in my heart to match the lovely sweep of the moor and the sense of infinite space behind it and a million extra stars above. Then I shook the depression off me.

"Let's have a song," I said. "Clean but not too clean. Music, Teddy, please. *The Foggy Foggy Dew.*"

Teddy struck the first keys on the cottage piano in the corner and I started to sing. Soon everyone was singing. "*I loved her in the winter and in the summer too and the only thing I ever did wrong was to shield her from the foggy foggy dew . . .*" Out of the corner of my eye I saw Hoylake humming the tune to himself, an expression of benign approval on his face.

Thirteen

"Y ou're quiet, darling," Alice said.
      "I was admiring your figure," I said. "My God, you are beautiful. I'd like a picture of you like this. I'd keep it locked away, and look at it whenever I felt depressed . . ."

Looking back, I can see exactly how it happened. It need never have happened; those were the key words, spoken idly in Elspeth's flat one Friday evening. If, out of any of the countless million at my disposal, I'd used any other words, then my whole life, and hers, would have taken different courses. But her next words, spoken as idly as mine, started the avalanche.

She laughed. "There *is* a picture of me in the nude," she said. She named a Home Counties town. "It's still at the municipal gallery, as far as I know. I was an artist's model once."

It was as if the soft hand gently caressing me had turned hard and big and hit me. I felt sick and betrayed and dirtied. I moved away from her in the bed. "You never told me. Why didn't you tell me?"

"I'd almost forgotten about it. It wasn't very important, anyway. I badly needed money, and I met this artist at a party and he wanted a model. I modelled for a photographer too. That was all. I didn't do it again."

"Didn't you?" I asked hoarsely. "Are you sure?"

"I don't tell lies," she said quietly. "You know that." Her eyes were cold. Then she smiled and stretched out her hand. "Darling, what a pother about nothing at all! I'd never have told you if I'd known you'd carry on like that. I didn't sleep with either of them, if that's what you're thinking, so you can set your mind at rest."

"Oh God," I said miserably, "what did you do it for? You didn't have to, there's millions of women have been as poor as you were and they'd rather have died than expose themselves like that for a few lousy shillings. Damn you to hell, I'd like to beat you black and blue."

"Damn *you*," she shouted, "what's it to do with you? It was years before I met you. Was I supposed to starve because some day I might meet a narrow-minded prude from Dufton who wouldn't like the idea of me showing the body God gave me?"

She got out of bed and began to dress hastily. "Since your beastly little provincial mind doesn't like nudity I'd better cover myself up, hadn't I?"

I started to dress too. If only either of us had laughed it would have been different; the sight of us both reversing our usual procedure and hurrying to put our clothes on, modestly averting each other's eyes, was actually very funny. But I was too angry and too sick; the idea of being naked for one moment longer turned my stomach.

She came over to my side of the bed to fasten up her stockings. "That's what you like, isn't it?" she said viciously. "Leg-show and lingerie—" She spat out the last word.

I took hold of her by her shoulders. "You stupid bitch, it isn't that at all. Can't you see that it's the idea of other people looking at your nakedness that I hate? It's not decent, don't you see?"

"Let me go," she said icily. I dropped my hands.

"My God," I said, "I understand now what makes men kill women like you."

"You're very brave," she said. "Highly moral too. It isn't decent of me to pose for an artist who sees me simply as an arrangement of colour and light, but it's perfectly OK for you to kiss me all over and to lie for an hour just looking at me. I suppose it gave you a thrill, a dirty little thrill, I suppose I'm your own private dirty post-card. You can't conceive that a man could look at a naked woman without wanting to make love to her, can you?"

"It's not that at all," I said wearily. I went across to the cupboard and poured myself a gin. I took it in one gulp and poured out another.

"Elspeth isn't rich, you know," Alice said waspishly. Her face was white and ugly and old. "You needn't take all her gin."

I took a pound-note from my wallet and tossed it to her. "Give that to her. Tell her I broke the bottle."

She let it fall to the floor. I was tempted to pick it up; I knew very well that she'd buy Elspeth some more gin. But there are times when a man's dignity is worth more than a pound. I filled my glass again and lit a cigarette. I couldn't trust myself to speak.

"To think that I let you even touch me," she said quietly. "Look at you now. The typical attitude – glass in hand, big red face glow-ering with outraged respectability. I thought you were different, but you're not. You're typical – the decent chap who likes a little bit of fun but who knows where to draw the line. I'm your little bit of fun, I'm the slice off the cut cake that'll never be missed . . . You smug hypocritical swine!"

I found myself crumpling up my freshly-lit cigarette. I threw it away and lit another with a shaking hand. She kept on talking, her voice low and controlled. "Get this clear. I own my body. I'm not ashamed of it. I'm not ashamed of anything I've ever done. If you'd ever mixed with intelligent people you'd not be looking at me now as if I'd committed a crime." She laughed. It was an ugly harsh laugh which made my hair prickle. "I can just see you in Dufton now, looking at the nudes in a magazine, drooling over them. Saying you wouldn't mind having a quick bash. But black-guarding the girls, calling them shameless——" The word came from her lips like a gobbet of phlegm. "Yes, look shocked. You've used the word often enough with your boozy friends, though, haven't you? I was damned near starvation when I transgressed your peculiar morality. You wouldn't understand that, would you? You make a great to-do about your humble beginnings, but you've never gone hungry." Her eyes narrowed. "I wonder. I wonder.

Probably someone else went short for our darling Joe, the fair-haired charmer."

I took another drink. It had a musty taste. "What do you think a POW gets to eat?" I asked bitterly.

She laughed again. "You didn't starve even then. You got extra because you looked so clean and Nordic, you told me so. Oh yes, you always fall on your feet. Why didn't you escape like Jack Wales?"

That was more than I could stand. "Don't mention that swine's name to me," I said furiously. "It was all right for him to escape. He had a rich daddy to look after him and to buy him an education. He could afford to waste his time. I couldn't. Those three years were the only chance I'd get to be qualified. Let those rich bastards who have all the fun be heroes. Let them pay for their privileges. If you want it straight from the shoulder I'll tell you: I was bloody well pleased when I was captured. I wasn't going to be killed trying to escape and I wasn't going to be killed flying again. I didn't like being a prisoner but it was a damned sight better than being dead. Come to that, what did you do in the Great War?"

"All right," she said in a tired voice. "You can stop defending yourself. I needn't have brought that up. It's useless trying to explain that what I did isn't important and that there's nothing wrong in it. We're different kinds of people, and there's nothing more to be said."

"Isn't there? It doesn't seem any use trying to explain to you either. I'm not a hypocrite and I'm not a moralist; I don't care if you did sleep with the artist. It's just the thing itself that hurts me – God, I never thought of it till now, why should I? I feel just as if I'd been kicked between the legs."

"I can't help that. You're making your own misery." The tears began to roll down her cheeks. "Oh, damn you, damn you, damn you!"

"You'd better have a drink." I gave her a glassful; she drank it, coughing a little. I wanted to take her in my arms and tell her that it didn't matter and that I was wrong and I was sorry; I couldn't bear to see her tears. She looked thin and bedraggled; not unlike the thin women one sees in pictures of mine disasters, disconso-

late and old and ugly against the pithead wheel. But, remembering
the way she'd repulsed me when I'd touched her, I didn't attempt
it.

"I'd better make some tea," she said. She turned at the doorway.
"It's all over," she said. I could scarcely hear the words. "It's all
over, Joe."

I went into the lounge and sat in the armchair by the fire,
feeling sick and cold. I'd never been in a quarrel like that before.
When Father and Mother had differences, they were no more than
tiffs; he was too easygoing and she recovered from her anger too
quickly. I couldn't even remember being shouted at. It was all over;
Alice was quite right. I felt as if I had lost all my strength; there was
no way of being comfortable, my body was a shameful encum-
brance, there was no sleep ahead of me. I thought of Susan, but it
didn't help; she was on the same side of the fence as Alice. Perhaps,
I thought, one was earmarked from birth, and only the scoundrels
and the geniuses ever rose out of the class into which they were
born.

Alice came in with the tea. "You don't want anything to eat?"

"I couldn't. For once I'm not Iron Guts." I achieved a weak
smile.

She poured out the tea. "We might as well be sensible. We did
agree, didn't we, that there'd be nothing permanent about it?"

I heard my own voice uttering words which I wasn't aware of
having chosen. "We'll call it a day."

"Yes, we'll call it a day." She put her hand on mine; it was dry
and hot. "I won't be possessed, Joe. I won't be dominated. I won't
be owned by anyone. Don't think badly of me."

"I won't. I'm very grateful to you." I was retreating, I wasn't
fighting; but from where was I retreating, and who was I fighting?
"It's been wonderful, Alice. I'm sorry about all this."

"Forget it," she said. She lifted the teacup to her mouth but her
hand was shaking so much that she spilt half of it. I looked at the
pound-note on the floor and suddenly discovered that I didn't give
a damn about it.

Fourteen

I left the flat before Alice, as I generally did. The flat was on the top floor and the lift was out of order; I remember that the stairs seemed never to end and I remember the deep silence of the place. The building had been decorated in the usual post-war manner and had the air of a big ship. There was a queer dry smell like hot toast and chlorine. The stairs were broad and the thick grey carpeting seemed to blot up all sound. It was all very clean and shining; very nice too, except that it gave me the impression that no human beings had ever lived there. I imagined nothing but emptiness behind those white doors with their chromium numbers and neat little name-cards.

Once all the rich people in Leddersford had lived in the district round the flats. As cars had become more dependable and the city had become more dirty, the rich people had moved out to towns like Warley. The houses which hadn't been converted into flats and private hotels now belonged to doctors and dentists and photographers. There were a lot of trees and the roads were broad; in a way it reminded me of Warley. But it had ceased to be a place a long time ago.

It was a clear evening with a warm wind. Spring was on the way; not that it made much difference there. The laurels and pines and firs would look exactly the same all the year round, dark and melancholy and alien. I wasn't due home until ten; it was only half-past eight. There was a vast useless stretch of time to fill; I occupied my mind with dreariness like a starving man eating earth. It's all over now, the sensible part of me said, you're well rid of the neurotic bitch. You're out of the danger of scandal, you're out of the danger of being possessed. But another side of me kept remembering the big tears rolling down her cheeks, remembered, with shocked tenderness, how they had washed away her attractiveness.

Then I thought of her lying naked beside me, and the pain

returned, as real as toothache. The strange thing was that I hoped she had lied to me, that she had slept with the artist. That would have made it bearable. What hurt me was the fact of her exposing herself unemotionally, as if her body were of no importance. An arrangement of colour and light – as if an arrangement of colour and light could cut its finger with the breadknife, get married, make love, receive my most secret confidences – it was the excuse, the palliative for my jealousy, that hurt me most. I called her the worst names I could think of, repeating them again and again under my breath, but it didn't relieve my feelings very much. (There are, after all, only about a dozen foul words in the English language and nine of them aren't, properly speaking, foul, but merely physiologically descriptive.)

I thought with bitter regret of the time when she had been a stranger to me and I wouldn't have cared if she'd walked the streets naked in broad daylight. She'd done *that* as if I hadn't existed – I bit my lip sharply, drawing blood. My head was throbbing and my mouth tasted of vomit and my throat was dry. I put my hand against the wall. It was as if I were being attacked by an invisible enemy. I crossed the road and kept on walking. It was a street of large terrace houses; I remember that one had its curtains drawn back and that inside there was a crowd of young people and a sound of music. As I passed they drew the blinds. I walked on; the houses became smaller and there were no more trees and the mills loomed up at me from the gathering darkness. I didn't want to think of what Alice had done and yet my imagination persisted in returning to London ten years ago: I saw her, innocent, firm, smelling of youth, going into the studio, undressing behind a screen then, quite naked, a little abashed perhaps, being reassured by the artist. He looked rather like Jack Wales, but he had a beard. I saw her sitting on the model's throne, her legs parted a little . . . That was as far as I got; savage, useless, sick anger took over again. I thought of Charles and me looking at the nudes in Leeds Art Gallery, and of the time we'd been to a London revue. "Of course," Charles had said, "they're no better than prostitutes. Wouldn't care to marry a woman who'd show all she'd got to dirty young men like thee and me."

I wondered if George knew. If he did, would he care? I frowned with concentration. If it would hurt him, then he was my kind of person, and some of the pain was, as it were, shared. But I knew very well that it wouldn't matter to him; if he thought of it at all, it would be with amusement. So that was an extra torment – illogical, but there, indisputably, the fact was.

I saw a large pub standing a little off the road. I went in; it being Thursday, it was nearly empty. Drinking my pint, I began to go over my last lesson in economics. The theory of surplus value states . . . I have normally a memory like a sponge; I used often to fill in spare moments by presenting pages of print before my mind's eye. But now I saw the lesson torn into scraps of paper, the facts were totally unrelated. On the page I was looking at I could only see Nude; I closed my eyes for a second and saw a red blur and then opened them to see the word again. I looked at the far corner of the room and saw the poster, THE NEATEST NAUGHTIEST NUDES IN SHOW BUSINESS – SANDRA CAROLE ELISE LIZBETH . . . And Alice. I wondered if she'd done that too, if that were another thing she hadn't bothered to tell me about, if she had stood in the pink spotlight in a spangled head-dress and a gold fig-leaf with a thousand eyes settling on her naked flesh like leeches. I couldn't be sure that it hadn't happened, that she, with her bright, quick mind and sharp tenderness, hadn't descended to this last tatty extreme; it was as if I'd seen her given over to torture in some shabby cellar. That was what hurt me. It wasn't the fact of modelling, but of Alice modelling. Some of my standards were still Dufton standards, and in Dufton artists' models were thought of as tarts, not quite professionals, but simply the kind who couldn't be bothered to say no. It was unbearable to think of Alice in that way; and I didn't know, or didn't want to know, why it should affect me at all. And I was jealous retrospectively – it was almost as if I were standing frustrated outside the studio, a pimply sixteen.

Looking back, I see myself as being near the verge of insanity. I couldn't feel like that now; there is, as it were, a transparent barrier between myself and strong emotion. I feel what is correct for me to feel; I go through the necessary motions. But I cannot delude myself that I care. I wouldn't say that I was dead; simply that I had begun to die. I have realised, you might say, that I have, at the most, only another sixty years to live. I'm not actively unhappy and I'm not afraid of death, but I'm not alive in the way that I was that evening I quarrelled with Alice. I look back at that raw young man sitting miserable in the pub with a feeling of genuine regret; I wouldn't, even if I could, change places with him, but he was indisputably a better person than the smooth character I am now, after ten years of getting almost everything that I ever wanted. I know the name he'd give me: the Successful Zombie.

I don't of course care whether that young man looking at the theatre bill was wiser or kinder or more innocent than the Successful Zombie. But he was of a higher quality; he could feel more, he could take more strain. Of a higher quality, that is, if one accepts that a human being is meant to have certain emotions, to be affected strongly by all that happens to him, to live *among* the people around him. I don't mean that one has to love people, but simply that one ought to care. I'm like a brand-new Cadillac in a poor industrial area, insulated by steel and glass and air-conditioning from the people outside, from the rain and the cold and the shivering ailing bodies. I don't wish to be like the people outside, I don't even wish that I had some weakness, some foolishness to immobilise me amongst the envious coolie faces, to let in the rain and the smell of defeat. But I sometimes wish that I wished it.

What has happened to me is exactly what I willed to happen. I am my own draughtsman. Destiny, force of events, fate, good or bad fortune – all that battered repertory company can be thrown right out of my story, left to starve without a moment's recognition. But somewhere along the line – somewhere along the assembly line, which is what the phrase means – I could have been a different person. What has happened to my emotions is as fantastic as what happens to steel in an American car; steel should be always true to its own nature, always have a certain angularity and heaviness and not be plastic and lacquered; and the basic feelings should be angular and heavy too. I suppose that I had my chance to be a real person. "You're always in contact," Alice said to me once. "You're *there* as a person, you're warm and human. It's as though everyone else were wearing rubber gloves." She couldn't say that now.

Fifteen

I looked at the invitation as I drank my final cup of tea at breakfast. It was a fine morning; the sun had melted all but the last traces of snow in the valley, and one could almost smell the green things growing. For the first time in a week I didn't think of Alice.

"Sally Carstairs has asked me to her birthday party," I said to Mrs. Thompson.

"She's a thoroughly nice girl. Weren't you in *The Farm* with her?"

"She helped with the props. Don't know her very well, though. What should I give her?" I tried to sound matter-of-fact but I was excited and delighted. The Carstairs had plenty of money – they ran a chain of cafés – and lived in a big house at Gilden, right on top of Warley Moors.

"You leave it to me. I know Sally's mother very well."

"How much should I spend?"

"Leave that to me too. I won't break you, I promise."

"It's in your hands," I said. I was leaving more and more in her hands, I thought, those thin long-fingered hands so much like Alice's – I shied away from the name like a horse from a corpse. I looked at my watch. "Time to get my nose to the grindstone." I said goodbye to Mrs. Thompson; when I passed her chair I wanted to kiss her. Not passionately, I may add, but as I would have kissed my mother on my way to work.

Walking down Eagle Road, I wondered dimly if I might achieve something with Sally. She was small and slim and bright as a budgerigar and was training at the Leddersford Art School; my mind shied away again, but this time it was more of an automatic side-stepping from what might disturb me than a violent and painful revulsion. As I walked down the hill I experienced the conqueror's sensation again. Warley was below in the valley waiting to be possessed, I'd just come from a beautiful room as near T"Top as made no difference, I was going to a rich house to meet rich people and who could say what would come of it? Perhaps Susan might be there; not that it mattered very much. It wasn't that I disbelieved Reggie; but at the moment I didn't feel prepared for that particular sector of the battlefield.

Gilden is a rather grim mill village north-east of Warley. It has the appearance of being ready for anything: the narrow windows of the millstone grit houses might suddenly sprout rifles, beyond the next corner of its twisting streets and alleys it's not fantastic to imagine the glint of bayonets, the two Crimean War guns in the Memorial Park are ready for action, the General Stores in the High Street has rations for a five years siege. The village ends abruptly at the Ebenezer Methodist chapel with its crammed graveyard; beyond it is nothing but the moors and a few sheep and curlews and a solitary farmhouse a mile west. That too has a military air; the moors are Gilden's maquis and behind its walls are planned the sudden raid into the valley, the ambush in the village, the last desperate stand with the enemy corpses piling up behind the drystone walls.

The Carstairs home stood apart from the village, an opulent neutral. It wasn't merely its ten rooms, its raw newness, its glaring red brick of the type which is supposed to mellow with wind and weather, that made its Gilden address simply a geographical term; it was sited where it was not to be near the business or the estate or other houses or the road, not for any practical reason at all, but simply because Carstairs père had fancied a house on the moors. That was why I liked it: it hadn't the remotest connection with any sort of economic necessity, it was a rich man's vulgar solid self-indulgence.

Reggie and I shared a taxi from Warley; the 'bus ran only hourly. As we turned into the Carstairs drive, we passed the 'bus; I saw an old man, a gang of children, a young couple holding hands. I recognised the middle-aged woman in front, her frowning face looking like a dull pudding under her off-white headscarf; she never paid her rates until the last moment, and the answer was, I fancied, in the village pub of which her husband was Gilden's most devoted mainstay. I felt a spasm of pity for her; as we passed it seemed that two worlds were meeting. The world of worry about rent and rates and groceries, of the smell of soda and blacklead and No Smoking and No Spitting and Please Have the Correct Change Ready and the world of the Rolls and the Black Market clothes and the Coty perfume and the career ahead of one running on well-oiled grooves to a knighthood; and the party in the big house at the end of the pine-lined drive at which, I felt in a sudden accession of pessimism, I would very quickly be shown that my place was in the world of the poor with its narrow present like a stony hen-run.

A grey Jaguar coupé drove away as we reached the house. The woman driving it gave Reggie a circumscribed wave and a quick cold smile. She had black hair and a fur jacket and sat bolt upright and disdainfully, as if giving the car its orders rather than driving it.

"Mama Brown," Reggie said. "That's her runabout. Hubby has a Bentley, and they keep a V8 shooting-brake as a spare."

"She seems well aware of it," I said.

"Not half, old man. The last of the St. Clairs and stinking with money. She's an old tough too; a place for everyone and everyone in their place. She practically ran a young man out of town for making a pass at Susan."

I paid the taximan. "I didn't know Susan was coming."

"There's a lot you don't know," Reggie said as the maid opened the door for us.

The hall was as impersonal as a hotel lounge. The walls were hung with trophies – buffalo horns, lions' heads, a Fokker airscrew – but they gave the impression of having all been bought at the same time, they were too clean, too neatly arranged, too new. Everything from the silver cigarette-boxes to the inlaid ash-trays was new and heavy and expensive. When the maid took my coat I took a quick look at myself; I had an uneasy feeling that my fly was open or my shoelace broken or that I'd put on odd socks.

There were about twenty people at the party, most of whom I hadn't met before. The girls were dressed to kill; I remember that Sally was wearing a blue dress which exposed a great deal of a very pleasant bosom and even Anne Barlby looked bedworthy in white and rose chiffon. The room we stood in was the largest I'd ever seen in a private house, and it had the first parquet floor I'd seen outside a library or museum. The furniture was of the kind that was to become fashionable ten years later, and each wall was in a different shade of green.

But as soon as I saw Susan I stopped noticing my surroundings. She was wearing a black taffeta skirt and a white broderie anglaise blouse; she made all the other girls look worn and shopsoiled. If anyone ever needed a justification of the capitalist system, I thought, here it was: a human being perfect of its kind, a phœnix amongst barnyard fowls.

"Hello," I said. "You look good enough to eat." My eyes were holding hers; mine were the first to drop. "I didn't know you were coming here."

She pouted. "Do you mean you wouldn't have come if you'd known I'd come?"

"On the contrary. I couldn't hope to enjoy myself without you. You're a festivity in yourself."

"You're making fun of me," she said in a low voice.

"I'm quite serious. Not that I've any right to be."

She didn't speak for a moment, but stood looking at me intently. I noticed for the first time that her eyes were flecked with gold, bright and alive and dancing. Looking into them and smelling her scent I felt my head swimming.

"I don't see why you haven't any right to be serious," she said. "It's not – not fair if you're joking."

I've never loved her more than I did then. I forgot the Jaguar and the Bentley and the Ford V8. She loved and she wanted to be loved, she was transparent with affection; I could no more deny that correct response in my heart than refuse a child a piece of bread. In the back of my mind a calculating machine rang up success and began to compose a triumphant letter to Charles; but the part of me that mattered, the instinctive, honest part of me, went out to meet her with open hands.

At that moment Sally's mother came up to me, gushing and bejewelled. "My naughty daughter's failing in her duties," she said. "I must make you known to everyone, Joe." Out of the corner of my eye I saw Reggie take Susan away, and the next ten minutes were a blur of new faces and half-heard names. There was a young man with a broken nose who was training to be a doctor, a sprinkling of young officers, some young-old men who were, I think, executives of Carstairs and Co., and what seemed to be a hundred girls in party dresses.

It's already difficult to remember the days of rationing, but I am sure of one thing: one was always hungry. Not hungry in the way I'd been at Stalag 1000, but hungry for profusion, hungry for more than enough, hungry for cream and pineapples and roast pork and chocolate. The Carstairs were in the business, of course; but the meal laid out in the dining-room would have been considered sumptuous even today. There was lobster, mushroom patties, anchovy rolls, chicken sandwiches, ham sandwiches, turkey sandwiches, smoked roe on ryebread, real fruit salad flavoured with sherry, meringues, apple pie, Danish Blue and Cheshire and Gorgonzola and a dozen different kinds of cake loaded with cream and chocolate and fruit and marzipan. Susan watched me eat with a pleased maternal expression. "Where does it all go?"

"No difficulty," I said with my mouth full. "A sound stomach and a pure heart."

"Our Joe has a huge appetite for everything," Anne Barlby said. "If only he were a little fatter he'd be just like Henry the Eighth."

"You're horrid," Susan said. "I like to see a man eat."

"Henry wasn't famous only for eating," Anne said.

I laughed in her face. "I haven't chopped off anyone's head yet. Or been divorced, for that matter." I smiled at Susan. "I'm single-hearted. There's only one girl for me."

"Which one?" asked Anne. "It becomes confusing."

Susan was going pink. She made me think of a kitten whom someone had kicked instead of stroking. Without having any very clear idea of what was going on, she knew I was being got at.

"I always thought you liked older women," Anne said. "More mature and soignée."

I looked at her too prominent nose and saw near the head of the table Johnnie Rogers talking animatedly with Sally; suddenly I understood. "I didn't hear you, love," I said mildly. "Not one word did I hear."

She looked at me angrily. "You've very good hearing."

"Not for anything I don't want to listen to."

Anne went off in the direction of Johnnie without saying another word. She knows too much, I thought, feeling a premonition of danger.

"You're scowling," Susan said. "Are you angry with me?"

"Good God, no. I was just thinking."

"What were you thinking about?"

"You. I'm always thinking about you."

"It doesn't seem to make you very happy. You had a horrid murderous scowl. You look awfully hard sometimes, Joe."

"I'm very weak and sentimental where you're concerned."

"What were you thinking about me?"

"I'll tell you some other time."

"Tell me now."

"It's too private. I'll tell you when we're alone."

"Oh," she said. "*Wicked*."

After supper the floor was cleared for dancing. Susan was a good dancer, precise and light and free, always as it were poised above the ground, gay with weightlessness. In the intervals we sat on the sofa and held hands. Her hands were white and a little plump, and the nails were rosy and gleaming. (I thought of Alice's, already on the verge of boniness, the index finger yellow with tobacco and the nails flecked with white.) Whenever I looked at Susan she gave me a frank full-hearted smile: no reservations, no pretence: I could sense the joyfulness kicking inside her like a child.

Halfway through the evening they put on a tango. "I can't do this one," I said to her.

"Neither can I."

"It's terribly warm in here."

"I was thinking that too."

It was cool outside and as we walked over to the summer-house we both retained the lightness of dancing in our feet; it was as if the lawn were a sprung floor. There was a full moon, softening the inflamed harshness of the red brick front; from the lounge we could hear the genteel exoticism of *Two to Tango* – like Earl Grey with gin in it – washing against the iron silence of the moors.

The night was like a scene from a musical comedy: one word, one change of lighting, and the trellises would bleed with roses and the flowerbeds draw themselves up into a pattern of tulips and pansies and aubrietia and lupins and the damp mustiness of the summer-house be overlaid by the smell of night-scented stock and the air turn warm and lazy with birdsong and the buzzing of bees.

When I took her in my arms she was trembling violently. I kissed her on her forehead. "That's a pure kiss for you," I said. I kissed her again, on the lips. "Don't be frightened, dearest."

"I'm never frightened of you."

I wanted to give her something, as one would give a child a packet of sweets when it's pleased to see you. I wanted badly to give her something worth as much as what I knew she was at that moment giving me.

"Tomorrow?" I asked. "I'll 'phone at ten."

"No."

"Why?"

"You were very wicked to Susan before. You said you'd phone and you never did. Say when and where."

"Six at the Leddersford Grand. Oh darling—" I kissed her cheeks and her chin and her nose and the smooth nape of her neck. She was still trembling.

"I wish we could stay here for always," she said.

"So do I, dearest." And so I did; perhaps if time had released me then and there I'd have been able to strangle the shabby little sense of triumph that was being born inside me, I'd have been able to accumulate enough emotional capital to match her gift. Two hours would have been enough in that summer-house on that night when we were still caught up with the dance, when the moon and the feeling of winter being dead and the first-time delight of our bodies meeting had erased all complications and commitments; but two hours weren't available. Time, like a loan from the bank, is something you're only given when you possess so much that you don't need it.

Sixteen

Susan was already there when I reached the Grand. Against the black buildings of Leddersford her face was fresh and glowing. "Hello darling." I took both her hands. "Sorry I'm late."

"You're very naughty." She squeezed my hands. "I won't go out with you again." She held out her face for a kiss. "I've been longing for that. Aren't I wicked?"

"You're the joy of my life," I said, feeling for a moment very old. I took the evening paper from my pocket. "There's a good film at the Odeon. Or a mediocre play at the Grand. Or what do you fancy?"

She looked at her feet. "Don't be angry with me. But I don't want to go to the pictures. Or the theatre."

"Of course I'm not angry. But if we're going for a walk, you'll have to tell me where. I'm a stranger here."

"Ooh," she said. "Wicked, wicked. I never said I wanted to go for a walk. There's Benton Woods though. I've a friend up there. But we needn't see her."

She took my arm, holding it tightly as we walked over to the Benton 'bus stop. Passing the warehouses with their heavy, oily but curiously non-industrial smell of raw wool and the cramped littered offices with their mahogany furniture and high stools and the Gothic Wool Exchange straight out of Doré I felt as the owners of the big cars outside, the gaffers, masters, overlords, must feel: the city was mine, a loving mother, its darkness and dirtiness was the foundation of my big house in Ilkley or Harrogate or Burley, my holiday at Biarritz or Monte Carlo, my suit from my own personal roll of cloth: Susan took all the envy out of me at that very moment, she made me rich. We walked slowly, looking in all the shop windows; I bought a pair of made-to-measure aniline calf brogues, a made-to-measure shirt in real silk, a dozen wool ties, a fur felt trilby at five guineas, a beaver shaving-brush, and a Triumph roadster. I bought Susan a big flask of Coty, a mink cape, a silver hairbrush, a nylon negligee, and a jar of crystallised ginger. Or I would have done if the shops hadn't all for some unaccountable reason been closed.

The 'bus had wooden seats; they reminded her of travelling third-class on the Continent. She chattered in her high clear voice about Rouen and Paris and Versailles and Reims and St. Malo and Dinan and Montmartre and Montparnasse and the Louvre and the Comédie-française – but I never had the feeling she was showing off, she hadn't a trace of self-consciousness; she'd been to all these places, they'd interested her very much, and she wanted to tell me all about them. Leddersford is a place where they don't like people who put on airs. To speak Standard English is in itself suspect; they call it talking well-off. And to talk about holidays abroad is one of the almost infallible marks of the stuck-up, the high-and-mighty, who are no better than they should be. All the people on the top deck had been listening to Susan; but there were no signs of resentment on their faces. Instead there was that pleased indulgent look, that wistful admiration (the princess has come amongst us, close enough for us to touch her if we dared) that I was to become accustomed to everywhere I took her. I've often thought that if I wanted to put paid to Communism once and for all, I'd have a hundred girls like Susan ride on 'buses the length and breadth of Great Britain.

"You're making me envious," I said. "I'd love to go to France before I get too old to enjoy it."

"You're not old, silly."

"I'm very old. I'm twenty-five. A genuine DOM."

"What's a DOM?"

"You're joking. Of course you know."

"Truly I don't."

"Dirty Old Man." I took out my pocket diary and scribbled for a moment.

"What are you doing?" She looked over my shoulder. "Oh Joe, you are wicked. I'll tear it out."

I put the diary away. "I'm going to make a collection of Susanisms," I said. "Last night you told me that I had a voice like treacle toffee, and my smile was awfully old and naughty. That'll do for a beginning."

"It's true though," she said. "You have a voice like treacle toffee, it's dark and deep and rich. It's lovely. I adore treacle toffee. I wish I had some now, but all my coupons are gone."

"That's *very* sad," I said. "If you were to look in my right-hand pocket you might find something . . ."

She leaned over me, her soft, orange-scented hair brushing my cheek. From the corner of my eye I caught sight of the road where Elspeth lived. That was a different body, I thought, a long time ago; the body with which, through several layers of clothing, Susan was being permitted a minimal, facetious intimacy, was younger, stronger, cleaner than the instrument of pleasure which Alice had used in Elspeth's boudoir.

Susan squealed with delight. "Darling Joekins, just what I wanted." She turned a glowing smile upon me. "Joe, will you always give me just what I want?"

"Always, darling."

She held my hand tightly the rest of the journey, only releasing it to put another toffee in her mouth.

Benton used to be a pretty little village with a definite character of its own; there was even a local cheese, the Benton Blue. Now the original village with its grey stone houses clustered round the cobbled market square has been surrounded by a sort of dermoid cyst of pebbledash and brick and concrete. But the woods are still there, though the black tarmac road which has been plunged through them has almost entirely destroyed the pleasurably frightening quietness which all woods ought to possess. Susan took my arm as we walked along the road. On either side stood dank regiments of firs; there was no-one about and it was very quiet, but not the sort of quiet I wanted. There was a stile past the plantation where the firs gave way to the real trees, the English trees with their green, locked away all winter, on the point of bursting out like birdsong. We went on into the woods until we came to a hollow in the hillside. As if in obedience to my desire for privacy, the sun began to set at the moment I put my raincoat on the ground and drew Susan down beside me.

She held me tightly as we kissed, and I thought of the difference between her and Alice. Alice held me tightly too, but she was fully aware of my body against hers; Susan held me tightly out of a kind of childish abandon. Her embrace was clumsy like a bad dancer's.

"I can't feel you," I said. I unbuttoned her coat and put my arms underneath it, stroking her warm back beneath the thin cashmere of her sweater. Her skirt had ridden above her knees; she pushed it down automatically. She was trembling as she'd done at the party; I laid my hand very lightly on her breast.

"Your heart's very loud," I said. "You're not really frightened, are you, pet?"

"A little now," she said in a low voice.

I put my hand inside the wide sleeves of her coat and stroked her arms. Her skin was so cool and smooth that I felt grubby and sausage-fingered. Then I put my fingers round her wrist, spanning it easily with little finger and thumb. "What little wrists you have."

"Now you're really frightening me," she said happily. "Just like Little Red Riding Hood and the great big 'normous wolf."

"But I *am* a wolf," I said, deepening my voice, and bit her ear.

"Oh," she said, "Susan tingle. Susan tingle up and down. Do it again."

As I took her roughly into my arms I felt loneliness come over me, real as the damp churchyard smell of the grass, melancholy as the sound of the beck in the little glen below us. I felt heavy as Sunday, as if time might drag me into a world like a bad engraving, stiff and dark and dull and lost. I pulled myself out of the picture which the loneliness had suddenly outlined – the woods at evening, the two figures for no good reason locked together, the shadows in the background that meant watchers – and rummaged round in my mind for pretty words to give Susan. "My God," I said, "you're so beautiful and sweet that I can hardly believe it. You make me think of spring flowers . . ."

"You make me think of the sea on a stormy day," she said, "I don't know why—Oh Joe I do—" She stopped suddenly. "Joe, tell me something."

"Anything you like, honey."

She stroked my hair. "It's lovely, so smooth and soft and fair." I remembered Alice advising me a long time ago to stop using hair-

oil ("Too too Palais de Danse, darling") and congratulated myself
upon having taken her advice; for Susan's hand to have encoun-
tered scented grease at this moment would have destroyed the
whole atmosphere. "Joe," she said, "you didn't think me wicked
last night, did you? Awfully forward and shameless?"

"You were lovely, darling," I said.

"I thought you mightn't like me. You seemed so cold and
scowly afterwards." She ran her finger along my forehead. "You're
an awful old scowler." She kissed my forehead. "I'll kiss the scowl
away. Don't you like me, old grumpy?"

"You've come between me and my sleep from the very first
moment I saw you," I said.

"I thought you were horrid then," she said. "You stared at me
so. And you scowled at Jack as if you wanted to kill him."

"So I did. Pure jealousy."

She put her hand on my wrist. "You've got 'normous bones. And
a great big strong neck. Were you really jealous? I've never had
anyone jealous of me before." She paused. "At least, I don't think
so."

"You've broken so many hearts that you don't know."

"Oh what fun. Am I a *femme fatale* like Alice? In *The Farm* I
mean. Very slinky and seductive?"

"Definitely not."

"You're horrid," she said, and rolled away from me. "I won't
have anything more to do with you, Joe Lampton."

"You're something much better than a *femme fatale*," I said.
"You're an enchantress. Young and fresh and fair . . . ." I remembered Eva's words. "*Comme la rose au jour de bataille.*"

"That's beautiful," she said. She repeated the words; her accent
was much better than mine. She flung her arms around my neck
and covered me with kisses. "Darling darling Joe." Then we lay
silent for a while. "Joe," she said, "what were you thinking about
at the party? You said you'd tell me when we were properly
alone."

What *had* I been thinking about? Then I remembered what I
had to accomplish. I looked at the pale oval of her face with the
large eyes now dark and serious and a scrap of poetry which Alice

had been fond of came back to me. "Tulip figure, so appealing, Oval face, so serious-eyed . . ."

"That's Betjeman," she said. "It's gorgeous. I'm not so nice as that, though."

"It was written for you," I said. "I'll call you tulip, shall I?"

She hit me on the arm. "You're maddening, Joe. Tell me now. What were you thinking about last night?"

If I did tell you, I thought, what would happen? I've got her, I took my friend's advice, she's mine and I can do what I like with her. I've beaten that bastard Wales. I'll marry her if I have to put her in the family way to do it. I'll make her daddy give me a damned good job. I'll never count pennies again. And, every now and again, sharp as toothache, the loneliness, the torment of needing the one person I didn't want to need – those were my thoughts, those and a gloating appraisement of young virginity and a maudlin pity like a paste jewel in a toad's head. I pushed my conscience away from the controls and let my intelligence take over.

"You'll be angry with me if I tell you," I said.

"I promise not to be. Cross my heart."

"I couldn't."

"You are mean," she said. I could see tears glittering in her eyes. "You promised. I wish you hadn't told me—"

I kissed her hard, putting my tongue between her lips. "I love you," I said. "I've always loved you. That's what I was thinking."

"I love you too," she said.

I inserted the correct amount of delighted incredulity into my voice. "Do you really, Susan? Honestly and truly? Oh darling, I can't believe it."

"It's true. I think I did all the time – because even when I thought you were awful I thought a lot about how awful you were. And I was going with Jack and it was most confusing."

"Were you in love with Jack?"

"Not really. I've known him a long time and Mummy likes him. He's very safe and solid."

"Am I safe and solid?"

She dropped her eyes. "You make me feel funny inside," she said. "I never felt like that before."

"You make me feel all funny inside too. You know, there's hundreds of times I've cursed you – all the time we were going out together you seemed so cold and withdrawn, so damned platonic. I just gave it up, it didn't seem any use."

"Golly. Were you blazing with pent-up desire like people in books?"

"Too true I was."

"You never tried to kiss me."

"It was futile. You always know when a woman wants to be kissed."

"You don't like to be rebuffed, do you, Joe?"

Her tone was disconcertingly shrewd.

"No. I'll be honest with you. I can't bear it. Neither could you if you were me."

"Why should it be worse for you than for me?"

I felt angry. She was lucky, she'd always been lucky, she'd never known the reality of the cold bedroom and the stuffy living-room with the blaring radio, she'd never had to worry about exams or a job or the price of new clothes, even her way of speaking with its touchingly childish affectations was a luxury no-one of the working classes could afford. I wanted to blurt all this out; but she wouldn't have understood and, in any case, I must transform myself into a different person for her. She had, I felt instinctively, a conception of Joe Lampton which I'd never to depart from in the smallest detail. Self-pity and class-consciousness weren't included in that conception. Alice would accept these things, though she'd play the devil with me for my stupidity. Alice was old enough to understand that men aren't all of a piece, old enough to take me as I was and not as she'd like me to be. I was taking Susan not as Susan, but as a Grade A. lovely, as the daughter of a factory-owner, as the means of obtaining the key to the Aladdin's cave of my ambitions; and she was taking me as the perfect lover and delightful companion, passionate and tender and exciting and infinitely wise; Susan might of course be prepared to take me with all my faults because she loved me so wholeheartedly – indeed, to behave badly might be a sure way of holding her. But I couldn't afford to take any risks.

"I'm horribly shy," I said. "I know it sounds funny, but I can never believe that any woman could possibly like me well enough to let me kiss her." I took her hand. "Darling, I know it sounds funny, but there it is. And perhaps – well, perhaps I'm a little conceited too. Masculine bumptiousness – in an odd way I think not only that I'm most unattractive but that I'm wonderful too. Too wonderful to be rebuffed." I moved away a little from her and lit a cigarette. "Oh God, I'm sick of myself. I'm afraid you've mixed yourself up with a very queer type."

As the words came from my lips I felt that they had nothing to do with me. And they hadn't: a part of me felt a great tenderness for her – she was as trustful as a baby – but the most important part of me was continuing the operation according to plan.

She kissed my hand. "They're beautiful. Square and strong."

"They're wicked hands. When they're with Susan they always want to go where they've no business to be."

"Oh, wicked Joe. Wicked hands. So warm too, warm as hot muffins. Oh, you are wonderful, you're the wonderfullest man in the whole world. Do you know, you're not queer a little bit? Most men are like that."

"Not like me."

"Silly billy, of course like you. Now you make *me* feel awfully old."

Her hands were icy. "We'd better go," I said. "You're cold."

"*Not* cold," she said. "Never cold with Joekins."

"Dearest Susan," I said. "I'll always keep you warm. But it isn't summer yet, you know."

"I'm not cold, so there."

"Don't argue. Or I'll beat you black and blue."

"I'd like that."

I helped her up to her feet. She put her cheek against mine, standing on her toes. "Joe, do you really love me?"

"You know I do."

"How much?"

"A hundred thousand pounds' worth," I said. "A hundred thousand pounds' worth."

Seventeen

Hoylake showed all his dentures in a dazzling smile. "Sit down, won't you, Joe? Cigarette?"

The slight unease which had accompanied me into his office evaporated; obviously he hadn't found out about me and Alice. I had been a little scared of that; local government officials are by no means free to behave as they like in their spare time. There's always the shadow of the Town Hall looming over one; I've known of married officials who've been told either to stop committing adultery or give in their notice. However, I didn't seriously consider the possibility of anything unpleasant happening that morning; I was in far too happy a mood, good fortune seemed to be following me like a huge affectionate dog. I'd been going out with Susan about a month now, and the memory of what had happened last night when baby-sitting at the Storrs' still left a haze of pleasure over my common-sense – a world that could hold such pleasure, I reasoned, couldn't possibly be unkind to me in the slightest way.

"It's a miserable day," I said.

Hoylake stopped doodling on his blotter and looked through the window. The sound of the rain filled the room, a sort of rhythmic silence. "The valley's a rain-trap," he said. He shuffled the papers on his desk in an undecided yet intent kind of way, as if there were some way of arranging them which would say all he had to say for him. "You've picked up the work here very quickly," he said.

"Thank you, sir."

"Six months now, isn't it?"

"That's right," I said, wondering what the devil he was trying to say.

June came in with a cup of tea. "Ah," he said, "welcome refreshment. Bring Mr. Lampton one, will you, dear?" He sipped his tea as if it tasted bitter. June came in with my own cup, a blue and white Worcester. "That's a very pretty cup," he said. "Does June especially like you?"

"It belongs to me."

"Ah. Quite the sybarite, aren't you?" He put out his cigarette and lit another. "Well," he said, clearing his throat, "I'll give you a little autobiography, Joe. I was born here in Warley. I've lived here all my life. So have all my family. I married a local girl, and I must say that I've never regretted it. I know Warley like the palm of my hand. In fact, much better, because I don't know the palm of my hand. And I know all the councillors. Especially Councillor Brown. We went to school together."

He paused. The haze in my mind cleared suddenly, and my heart started to pound uncomfortably.

"You've done remarkably well here, Joe. And I'm most gratified to see that you're acquiring the qualifications to do even better. There's plenty of room for promotion here, you know. People rarely stay for long in Warley. They move on to bigger places. They receive more salary, but it costs them far more to live; they generally are presented with the alternative of either living in a scruffy backstreet or an expensive suburb. It's much more agreeable here – you can live next door to your work and still be, as it were, in the country. You like it here, don't you?"

"Very much."

"Ah. You're a sensible young man." He cleared his throat again. "It's highly likely that you may resent what I'm going to say now. In a sense you're entitled to."

Now it comes, I thought. I kept my face still and expressionless.

"What you do in your spare time is your own business, Joe. Within limits, of course, and I needn't tell you what those limits are."

"Have there been any complaints?"

He lifted up his hand as if warding off attack. "I don't mean that at all, Joe. For Heaven's sake don't misunderstand me. Whatever the limits of – of decorum – are, you haven't, I do assure you, transgressed them."

"What's wrong, then?" I looked at him angrily, but his eyes refused to meet mine; the two holes in his skull behind his spec-

tacles were directed at me but I had the impression that his real
eyes were somewhere else, scampering round the dark cramped
office like mice.

"I'm going to tell you what is wrong. Not that there is, properly speaking, anything wrong. Let me put it this way: I'm giving
you some advice about living in Warley. I'm speaking as man to
man. For your own benefit. And because I'm your superior" –
he treated me to one of his apologetic twinkles – "you have to
listen to the old bore. Well. To continue, you have, I'm sure, some
notion of the workings of local government. The most important
cog in the machine is, theoretically, the councillor. In practice,
however, it is the senior official who runs the show. The councillor
can be removed from his post; the official, unless he is dishonest,
unbelievably dissolute, or incompetent to the point of idiocy, is
absolutely secure. No-one can touch him if he does his work properly. If he does his work as well as you do, Joe, no-one will attempt
to touch him. For their own sakes, not just for his."

The 'phone rang. "Excuse me, Joe. Hoylake speaking. Yes. Yes.
Of course. In about fifteen minutes. I'm engaged now. I'll ring you
back. Goodbye." He turned back to me. "As I was saying, for their
own sakes. The official is quite safe. But that is all. Promotion is
another thing. Promotion, whatever the head of a department
may recommend, is dependent upon a majority vote of the Establishments Committee. Then the full Council. And, you know,
councillors are like sheep. If one powerful personality declares
himself unalterably opposed to an official's promotion, the majority will follow him. They'll follow him to curry favour, or because
they're indebted to him in some way, or simply because they feel
that, since the wise Councillor So-and-So is against the man, there
must be something wrong with him. And, of course, there's always
the last resort of offering some solid inducement to anyone likely
to upset the plans of our hypothetical Councillor. . . ."

"You mean that Councillor Brown—"

He cut in quickly. "I mean nothing of the sort. I'm not discussing Councillor Brown. I said that we went to school together and
that I had more than a casual acquaintanceship with him. The only
connection you have with Councillor Brown is that you meet him

at your interview and that you've met him here once or twice."

"I remember him. A cheerful type. Overplays the part of the blunt Yorkshire business man rather."

Hoylake tittered. "Between ourselves, he does. But he's no fool. He rose from nothing, absolutely nothing. I have talked about you with him on several occasions. I said that you were a very promising young man. Highly intelligent. Intelligent enough to seize the point straightaway without any wearisome emotionalism." He offered me another cigarette. I noticed that his case was silver.

"I wouldn't know my exact intelligence rating, Mr. Hoylake," I said. "But I understand you very clearly." I forced a smile.

"Splendid, splendid. We'll say, then, that I'm talking in general terms. Imagine me, if you like, as a lecturer at a summer school . . . Councillor Brown, since you mention his name, is a very wealthy man. He has a great deal of influence. He is also a self-willed man. He is, as you know, the chairman of the Establishments Committee. He's an engineer; he likes everything about him to run with the smoothness of first-class machinery. He has his whole life, and the life of all his family, arranged in detail for the next twenty years. If anyone got in his way he'd be utterly ruthless . . ."

It was very dark in the room; Hoylake switched on his table-lamp. The little yellow puddle of light made his mahogany desk look larger, big enough for an operation-table. His skin looked dry as paper, and there were Commissar-harsh lines ruled from his nostrils to the corners of his mouth. I felt small and frightened then suddenly, refreshingly, angry.

"Perhaps I'd better apply for a job elsewhere," I said.

"Good God, my dear chap, whatever gave you that idea?" He wagged his finger playfully at me. "I'm afraid that you haven't been giving me your undivided attention. Surely I've been at great pains to emphasise – in the strongest possible terms – the excellence of your work, though, as I've also emphasised, the question of promotion doesn't arise at present. If your immediate senior, Mr. Harrod, were to obtain another post, that would be a different matter . . . That's our little secret, though, we'll just see what transpires. . . ."

I was remembering the supercilious look on Mrs. Brown's face,

the big house on Poplar Avenue blazing with light and music, Jack
Wales' shiny red M.G., his genuine Public School accent – I was
on the outside again, my grubby little face pressed against the
window, I'd lost the wherewithal to buy what I hankered for and
the shopkeeper was chasing me away.

"You haven't a girl in Warley, have you, Joe? You're not, as we
say in these parts, *courting?*"

"There's plenty of time," I said.

"Um. You're attractive to women. It's sometimes a curse. It can
lead you into awkward situations. Of course, you should really
be thinking of marriage by now. Nothing like an early marriage.
Gives a man a sense of responsibility, something concrete to work
for."

"That's very true," I said, fighting to keep the anger out of my
voice. "It also makes a man easier to handle."

"You sound a little bitter," he said reprovingly. "By the way,
you're going to the Civic Ball, aren't you?"

"I hope so," I said. "Providing that I can hire an evening suit."

"There are some very pretty girls going to the Civic Ball." He
achieved a genteel leer. "I'll introduce you to some."

"I was thinking of taking someone."

"The Spring Term ends on the fifteenth," he said. "The ball
takes place on the twenty-fifth."

"I don't know what you mean."

"Come, come." He was smiling, but not with his eyes. "I'm sure
that you do, Joe. I want you to save yourself a guinea. You don't
take a bottle of beer into a pub with you, do you?" He looked at his
empty cup. "I think I'll have some more tea."

I rose. "I'll ask June to bring you some."

"I'll 'phone for two more cups," he said. "Don't go yet, Joe. I
haven't quite finished."

I needed the second cup; my mouth was bone-dry and my
tongue seemed too big for it.

"Like Chekov, isn't it?" he said surprisingly. "We sit here drinking
tea and talking about life . . . Without an audience, unfortunately.
You do see my point, don't you?"

I laughed. It sounded hoarse and strained, and I abandoned

it half way. "I do indeed. I've enjoyed our little private talk, Mr. Hoylake. And I'll remember what you said: there are some very pretty girls going to the Civic Ball."

"That's right," he said approvingly, "that's right. I don't often say it, Joe, but you've a great future ahead of you."

"You've been a long time with Der Fuehrer," Teddy Soames said when I returned. "Hasn't been tearing you off a strip, has he?"

"Positively not," I said. "There was an atmosphere of great cordiality." I yawned; I felt so tired that I could have gone to sleep on the floor.

"Come off it," he said. "He didn't have you in there for twenty-five minutes just to be cordial. Sometimes I don't trust you, Joseph. What were you talking about?"

"Sex," I said.

Eighteen

Going home that evening I called at the chemist's for some razor blades. The owner of the shop, a tall thin man with an angry sergeant-major's face, was talking politics with a customer, a fat woolman type. The chemist knew that I worked at the Town Hall, and greeted me by name. (He greeted most of his customers by name, which was one of the reasons for his prosperity.)

"'Evening, Mr. Lampton, and how are the town's finances?"

"We're solvent," I said.

"A damned sight more than can be said for the country," said the woolman heavily.

"By God, but you never spoke a truer word, Tom." The chemist's face was nearly purple with anger. "Every damned thing rationed, not one promise kept. You might think that they were deliberately trying to ruin the business man. Where's our freedom? Winnie was right, we're under a Gestapo."

The chemist's assistant finished wrapping a large parcel for the woolman. "That's right, Mr. Robbins," he said. "And look at the income-tax . . ." He was a big man, as tall as me, on the verge of forty. I remembered him telling me once that he'd been at Robbins' for twenty years. He was obviously the unqualified general mug who did all the rough work and worked the most awkward hours. His pale face was set in a fixed smile; the habit of submissiveness had rounded what had once been a fine pair of shoulders. "You're right, Mr. Robbins," he repeated. "Dead right." His smile widened, and he nodded his head to underline the point. The other two took no notice of him at all, though they were standing cheek-by-jowl.

I left the shop feeling a bit sick. How on earth did the assistant stand it? He'd sold himself, and what price had he got? Perhaps seven pounds a week, and not even any assurance of security; he was dependent for his daily bread on one man, and that man was ignorant, ill-mannered, and mean. Then I remembered my interview with Hoylake, and wondered how much difference there was between me and the assistant. True, I had more money, better working conditions, and security; but essentially our positions were the same. My master was better-mannered than Robbins, and had less power over me; but he was still my master. My price was a shade higher, that was all.

It was still raining; I caught the 'bus at the station. It smelled of wet clothes and stale tobacco, and there wasn't a seat vacant. I went to the front of the 'bus, and whilst I was thinking about all this, didn't notice the awkwardness of my position until we were nearly at Eagle Road. By the time I'd squeezed my way out of the 'bus I was breathless and ruffled. I walked up Eagle Road, turning my collar up and holding my hat against the wind and the rain, and saw Bob Storr's Austin disappear along St. Clair Road.

After tea I rang him up. "Want a baby-sitter again tomorrow, Bob?"

"I'm not sure . . . Wait a moment, Joe." His voice was noncommittal.

"You said you did last week."

"Yes, of course. I'll have a word with Eva."

I waited, my heart beating fast with anger; I knew what was coming.

"I'm awfully sorry, old man," he said, "but Eva invited some

friends up. Between you and me, for business reasons. She's been
reading those articles on how to help your hubby to success. Personally I'd rather go out, they're crashing bores, but there it is.
Some other time, eh? The weather's getting warmer now anyway."
He laughed; I seemed to detect a gloating note. "Give my love to
Sue," he said. "And Eva sends hers. Sorry if this has messed up
your plans, Joe."

"That's all right," I said. "I hadn't really any plans."

"When I was younger, I used to go to the Folly. No-one else ever
visits the spot. Or if they do, they won't bother you." He laughed
again. "It's hell to be young and passionate in a cold climate."

"How true," I said, "how true. I'll return to the delights of economics now, Bob. Goodbye."

I replaced the 'phone and went to the window. The ground was
shiny with rain. The room was quiet. The Thompsons had gone
to the theatre and wouldn't return till late. The fire was burning
brightly and smelled faintly aromatic, as it had done the first time
I'd been in the room. The quietness hit my sense of time like a
Commando ear-box; I had to pick up the paper to reassure myself
of the date. It was as if somehow I would find myself in yesterday with the knowledge that I would have to endure the interview
with Hoylake and the 'phone call to Bob again.

I lit a cigarette and turned to Benham's Economics. Halfway
through a chapter I stopped. I wasn't taking in a single word; the
truth was that I'd already had a very stiff lesson in economics. We
shall begin by examining Joseph Lampton. Born January 1921 at
Dufton. Father John Lampton, occupation overseer. Educated
Dufton Grammar School. Junior Clerk, Treasurer's Department,
Dufton UDC, 1937. Sergeant-Observer, 1940. 1943-1945, Stalag 1000,
Bavaria. Present post, Senior Audit Clerk, Warley UDC. Salary,
APT Two. Resources, £800, from accumulated RAF pay, gratuity,
and insurance on parents. Prospects: he might be the Treasurer of
Warley one day. Shall we say a thousand a year at the age of forty
if he's very fortunate? Lampton has risen remarkably high, considering his humble beginnings; but, in our considered opinion, he
has not the capacity to succeed in our sense of the word. He lacks
the necessary background, the poise, the breeding: in short, he is

essentially vulgar, and possesses no talents which might compensate for this drawback.

We learn to our astonishment and horror that Lampton has entered upon a clandestine relationship with a young Grade Two woman. The young woman in question is of an ardent and impetuous nature and lacks the worldly experience which would enable her to deal firmly with a man of Lampton's type; it is, therefore, imperative that we intervene.

The impassable gulf between Grade Eight (at the highest) and Grade Two (at the lowest) is sufficient reason in itself for the immediate termination of the relationship. But there is yet a stronger reason: the existence of John Alexander Wales. Born at about the same time as Lampton, he has all the qualities which his rival so conspicuously lacks. He is at present studying for a science degree at Cambridge, acquiring not only the knowledge of technics which will qualify him ultimately for the position of Managing Director of Wales Enterprises Incorporated, but also the polish of manner, the habit of command, the calm superiority of bearing which are the attributes of – let us not be afraid to the use the word – a *gentleman*.

An illuminating insight into the characters of the two men may be obtained by examining the parts which they played in the Second European War. Mr. Wales had a distinguished RAF career, which was doubly distinguished by his escape from Camp 2001 in 1942. Mr. Wales is too modest to wish his exploit to be discussed, but it is sufficient to say that it reflects the greatest credit on his ingenuity, courage, and resourcefulness. It will be noted that Lampton, in the same position, made no attempt to escape, but devoted his attention to his studies, passing his main accountancy examination whilst actually a prisoner. This proves – we are anxious to be fair – that he possesses an admirable pertinacity of purpose, since it must have been extremely difficult to study under prison-camp conditions. It does not, however, say much for his manhood or patriotism.

Mr. Wales was a Squadron-Leader at the end of hostilities, and wore a DSO and bar, and also a DFC. Lampton has no decorations apart from those which all servicemen who served his length of time are given, as they say, with the rations. And Lampton was, of course, merely a Sergeant-Observer from start to finish. He is not, it may be seen, officer material. We might feel differently about him if he were.

The friendship between Mr. Wales and Miss Brown (the young woman who is entangled with Lampton) is one of long standing. Mr. Alexander Wales, the head of Wales Enterprises Incorporated, has long had a close friendship with Miss Brown's father. They have felt of late that a closer business association – possibly to the extent of a merger – might be to their mutual benefit. If Mr. Wales' son and Mr. Brown's daughter should also decide to effect what we may term a permanent merger this would, as it were, underline their parents' business relationship. Such happy coincidences are the foundation of British business, which is not, as certain people appear to believe, a jungle in which the weakest go to the wall, but simply a civilised and harmonious way of earning one's daily bread.

There is no wish to coerce the young people into marriage against their will, but it is most strongly felt by those who have their best interests at heart that they are perfectly suited to each other, and that Miss Brown's love (or what she imagines to be love) for Lampton will be of short duration. Lampton is not of her class, and the disparity is far too great to be bridged. Should he object to this, one might point out that there are many young women, perfectly respectable and of reasonable intelligence and attractiveness, whom Lampton himself would not dream of marrying – purely on social grounds. He would not demean himself by marrying a mill-hand or shop-girl; why should Miss Brown demean herself by marrying a minor municipal official?

It has come to our attention that Lampton has spent several evenings alone with Miss Brown in the house of a local business man. It is not suggested that anything beyond a few embraces has transpired; we do not believe that either of them are totally lacking in restraint or discretion. But as her grandfather used to remark: "Where a man and a woman are alone together, the Devil makes a third." Mr. Brown's business interests extend to the wool trade, and he has a great deal of influence both in Warley and Leddersford; it must be pointed out tactfully to this business man that it would be unwise to antagonise a man who can help him substantially both in business and in his ambition to occupy a place on the Warley Council.

We are not living in the Middle Ages; it would be unwise to forbid Miss Brown to see Lampton and, strictly speaking, impossible to forbid Lampton to see Miss Brown. In any case, Miss Brown is a girl of spirit and nearly twenty years old; it is not inconceivable that tactless handling of the situation might result in an elopement. It would be as well though, if Miss Brown were gently discouraged from seeing Lampton; it would be wise for her to abandon her connection with the Warley Thespians, for instance. She has been seeing Lampton on the pretext of attending meetings of the Thespians and of going out with friends of her own sex; it would be as well to reproach her gently on this score. A holiday abroad and a visit to Bond Street and the Ivy and the Savoy Grill and Goodwood would also be helpful. However, counter-measures against Lampton may safely be left in the hands of Fred Hoylake, the Warley Treasurer, a man of sterling worth, whose cousin, Mr. Squire Oldroyd, is, incidentally, a valued member of Mr. Brown's sales staff. . . .

"You fool," I said aloud to myself, "you bloody fool. Why didn't you see it before? The whole of Warley's ganged up against you." I looked at myself in the mirror above the mantelshelf. Good-looking enough, but the suit was my demob Utility. And I was wearing my shirt for the second day. I had the working-class mentality; anything was good enough for work. I might as well face facts: goodbye Susan, goodbye a big car, goodbye a big house, goodbye power, goodbye the silly handsome dreams. I looked around the room; it had never seemed so attractive. It might even be good-bye to Warley, the spindle-legged furniture, the gold-and-white paper, the hot bath at evening, the trees and the river and the moors, the winding cobbled streets of the eastern quarter with their elegiac cosiness. And goodbye to Alice. But we had already said goodbye; why did I still think of her in the present tense, why had I, in the morning, instinctively thought that Hoylake had found out about Alice, why had I felt that the dead relationship with a woman almost ten years older than myself was the most important? I could see her now, screaming at me like a fishwife, naked, with her figure beginning to submit to middle age, I could remember her tobacco-stained fingers, the upper left grinder which needed filling. And none of it made any difference.

I swore aloud to myself, using the old RAF obscenities that I'd almost forgotten the sound of. Then I went over to the telephone. I stopped with my hand on it, and returned to the armchair and Benham. At first I kept thinking of Alice with every page; I would master a concept, then it would end with her name. I didn't dare think of what she had done in London – but that was there too, like a toothache masked with aspirin. And then I stopped the attempt to suppress it and set myself the task of doing twice as much as I did normally. After a while her name came up neutral as a page number or chapter heading as I got into the rhythm of concentration.

Nineteen

"Aren't we baby-sitting?" Susan asked.

"No," I said. "They have company."

Susan's face puckered up as if she were going to cry, and she stamped her foot. "It's horrid of them, they practically *promised*."

"We won't be going there again," I said.

"What do you mean?"

"The 'bus is coming," I said. "We'll have to run for it."

We jumped on it as it was going out of the station square and sat down breathing heavily.

"Where are we going, Joety?" Susan asked.

"The Folly."

"Oo, *wicked*. It's very lonely there."

"That's why we're going there." I squeezed her hand. "Unless you'd rather go to the flicks."

"No, truly." She looked at me with shining eyes.

"It's not cold now," I said. "But tell me if you do feel chilly and we'll go home straightaway."

"I won't be cold. Cross my heart." She leaned towards me and whispered: "If you love me up, I'll be as warm as toast." Her breath smelled of toothpaste and, better than that, of youth and health. She did not simply look clean; she looked as if she had never been dirty. And the night was clean, too, with a new moon silvering the trees along Eagle Road and an energetic breeze tidying away the clouds. With Susan beside me, the happenings of yesterday seemed absurdly unreal. Then my heart stopped a beat when a middle-aged man with spectacles boarded the 'bus. But it wasn't Hoylake.

A young man and a girl of about nineteen got in at the next stop. At least, I thought that she was about nineteen; her face, like the young man's, had a settled look, as if she'd decided what was the most respectable age to be, and wasn't going to change it in a hurry. She had a round flat face with lipstick the wrong shade and her silk stockings and high heels struck an incongruously voluptuous note; it was as if she were scrubbing floors in a transparent nylon nightie. The young man had a navy-blue overcoat, gloves, and scarf, but no hat; he was following the odd working-class fashion which seemed to me now, after Alice's tuition, as queer as going out without trousers. I felt a mean complacency; with that solid mass of brilliantined hair and mass-produced face, bony, awkward, mousy, the face behind the requests on Forces Favourites, the face enjoying itself at Blackpool with an open-necked shirt spread out over its jacket, the face which Wilfred Pickles might love but which depressed me intensely – Len or Sid or Cliff or Ron – he'd never have the chance of enjoying a woman like Susan, he'd never explore in another person the passion and innocence which a hundred thousand in the bank could alone make possible.

"Why shan't we be going to Eva's again?" Susan asked.

"Don't you know?"

"Don't be so inscrutable, darling. If I knew, I wouldn't ask you."

"I don't think that your parents like me," I said. "Bob's obeying their orders."

She withdrew her hand from mine. "That's a beastly thing to say. As if they were all-powerful tyrants and Bob danced at their bidding."

"Part of it's true and you can't deny it. Your parents definitely don't approve of me."

She put her hand back. "I don't care. They can't stop us. We're not doing anything wrong."

We got off the 'bus at St. Clair Park and walked through the entrance where the great iron gates had been. They had been, Cedric once told me, the finest existing example of Georgian iron-work in England; the Council had taken them away during the war and sold them for scrap. One of the St. Clair falcons on the gate-posts was wingless, the result of a drunken soldier doing a little professional practice with a Sten gun. At the top of the drive you could see the St. Clair mansion. It wasn't large as mansions go, absolutely severe with a flat parapet line and no projections. But I caught my breath as I looked at it, remembering suddenly the Dufton art master's favourite phrase: here was frozen music. Who-ever designed the house would no more have dreamt of including the smallest false detail than I would have dreamt of presenting a balance sheet a penny in error. But it was dead. You didn't have to see the boarded-up windows, the choked-up fountains, the stag-nant ornamental ponds east and west of it, to realise that. It smelled dead, it had wanted to die.

We climbed the winding path up the hillside behind the manor. It had as many turns as a maze, and there was about the turns a slightly sinister quality, as if it wouldn't mind, given the opportu-nity, leading one into an oubliette. In the moonlight the big trees around us looked as bare as gallows, and yet at some points the bushes grew so thickly as to make the path almost impassable. When we reached the little promontory where the Folly stood, I was sweating. I put my raincoat down, and we sat on the grass in silence for a moment. Below us we could see the whole of Warley as far as Snow Park. I noticed for the first time that it was shaped like a cross, with the Market Place in the centre and T"Top in the northern upright. And I saw roads and houses which I'd never seen before – big square houses, broad straight roads, not black and grey, but all white and clean. I realised afterwards that I'd been looking at the new Council estate above the eastern quarter; in the moonlight the concrete looked like marble and the unmade road like stone.

The Folly was an artificial ruin in the Gothic style. There were three turrets, sawn off, as it were, obliquely, and far too small ever to have been much use as turrets. The tallest even had two window slits. One side of the main building had a door and an aurora of stone round it, and the other had three windows ending a little too abruptly halfway up. It was very solidly built; Cedric said that if you compared it with contemporary prints it was evident that it had survived over a hundred years on that exposed promontory absolutely unscathed.

"My great-great-great-grandpa built this," Susan said. "He was called Peregrine St. Clair and he was terribly dissipated and used to be a friend of Byron's. Mummy told me a bit about it; he had orgies here. All of Warley practically was St. Clair land and he could do just what he liked."

"What did he use to do at the orgies?"

"Wicked!" she said. "I don't really know, darling. Mummy would never be very explicit. Though actually she seems rather proud of him. He's been dead long enough to be romantic. He squandered most of the family fortune on these orgies and then my great-great-grandfather squandered the rest and was killed in the Crimea. She's rather proud of him too, he was very brave and dashing."

"Aren't there any St. Clairs in Warley?" I asked her.

"Only Mummy really. Death duties and drink finished off the St. Clairs, Mummy says. Her people used to live at Richmond – they're dead now. There was only one male St. Clair left and he was killed in the 1914 war. Most of them were killed in wars." She shivered. "I'm jolly glad I'm a girl."

"So am I," I said, and kissed her.

A cloud passed over the moon, darkening the Folly for a moment into a genuine ruin. The man who built it was dead, all the St. Clairs were dead; I was alive, and I felt that the mere fact of my survival was in itself a victory over them; and her parents, and Hoylake, and Bob, and Jack Wales; they were zombies, all of them, and only I was real.

"Would you like to come to the Civic Ball with me?" I asked.

"I'm awfully sorry," she said, "I can't."

"Why not?"

"I'm going with Jack."

"I thought you loved me. Do you prefer him? And his M.G.?"

"How can you say an awful thing like that to me?" She leapt to her feet in one movement; it was as if anger had plucked her upright. "I don't care about his silly old car. I don't care if you haven't got one, either. Mummy invited him to make up the party, she always does. We'll go in the Bentley, we won't even be alone together." She started to weep. "I don't believe that you love me at all."

She was hurt, she looked lonely and small. I felt as sorry for her at that moment as if she'd been an ordinary girl and not the daughter of Harry Brown with a hundred thousand pounds as a barrier between her and real sorrow.

"My darling," I said, "I'm sorry. I do love you, I'm just idiotically jealous." I took her hand and pulled her down beside me. "Don't cry, love, you'll make your eyes red. Cuddle up and stop crying, just to please Joe." I kissed her gently and felt her relax in my arms.

"It's horrid at home sometimes," she said between sobs. "They don't talk about you, but I know they don't think we should go about together. They say I'm too young to go about regularly with anyone, but I know that isn't the reason."

"Why don't you tell them?"

"Joe," she said, "I'm only nineteen. I'm not trained for anything. They always said there was no need."

"I can keep you."

"What if we can't get permission to marry?"

I thought of the blue budgerigar we once kept at home. I let it out of its cage and it flew into the grimy backyard; within five minutes the cat had got it. I suddenly realised that I couldn't ask her to leave home for some cheap lodgings and a soul-killing routine job in a shop or factory until she was twenty-one. Susan standing all day behind a shop counter, her face frozen into a selling smile and her feet aching, Susan in a factory taking orders from a fore-woman who would hate her fiercely because of her youth, her beauty, her accent, her obvious superiority, and who would find a thousand petty ways to make her life miserable: it would make me experience again that moment twenty years ago when I'd seen the mangled body of the budgerigar and had known, without the shadow of a doubt, that the guilt was mine.

"Don't worry, sweetheart," I said. "We'll find a way to get married."

"They generally give me what I want," she said. "At least, Daddy does. They're not unkind, Joe, truly they're not." Suddenly she threw herself on me, covering my face with kisses. "Oh God, I do love you so much, you've no idea—"

She made love strenuously; I was put in mind of a hard set of mixed tennis. When I put my hand under her blouse she moaned and shuddered convulsively, "Joe Joe Joe." She was somewhere away from me, I couldn't follow her but I knew that I should be with her. "I love you, Joe. I love you so much that I'd let you walk over me if you wanted, I'd let you tear me into bits and I wouldn't mind." She pressed my hand deep into her breast. "I want you to hurt me there. Oh God, you're so beautiful. You've lovely eyes, like Christ's—"

I felt the desire ebb out of me. The words were echoing in my ears, I wouldn't ever be able to rid myself of them. They were romantic, but what was behind them, was a passion frightening in its intensity.

"I love you," I said. "I'd like to kiss you all over, every inch of you."

"You mightn't like every inch of me," she said.

"I would." I put my hand under her skirt.

"No. Please no."

"Don't you love me?"

"I'd do anything for you. But I'm scared."

I rolled away from her. This was how it always ended, and I didn't know whether to be sorry or glad. I lit a cigarette with trembling hands.

"Don't you love me any more?" she asked in a small voice.

"My God, Susan, don't you know the facts of life yet? I love you too much, that's the trouble. Can't you see?" I held out my hand. "What do you think I'm made of, darling?"

"Rats and snails and puppy-dogs' tails," she said. "So there!"

"And you're sugar and spice and all that's nice," I said. It was futile to explain to her that it plays hell with the nerves to stop at the crucial moment; besides, I wanted to keep her within the framework of the fairy story. "Perhaps it's best to wait," I said. "But I want you properly – you know what I mean?"

"Are you sure, Joe? Quite sure."

"I love you and I want to marry you and give you children," I said. The wind blew her hair across my face, soft and black and smelling of orange-water; I wanted it to be longer, I wanted it to cover me and bury me, I wanted to sleep and not to argue, not to lie, not to promise, not to plot my future like a raid over the Ruhr.

"I want you to," she said. "I dreamt we had a baby last night. He was fair like you, and he was laughing all the time and we were very proud of him. But – oh, never mind." She stroked my hair gently.

"But what?"

"You'll think I'm silly."

"I promise I won't. Cross my heart."

"That's not a heart, Lampton," she said. "It's a swinging brick."

"It's the only one I've got." I tickled her in the ribs and she struggled squealing in my arms. "I'll tickle you until you do tell me."

"You're cruel," she said. "You're very cruel to poor Susan."

"Tell me."

"I was thinking," she said in a whisper, "that you wouldn't like me when I – when I was having the baby."

I rocked her in my arms gently. "Silly Susie. A pregnant woman is pleasing unto the Lord. I'd love you all the more, I'd be proud because it was my child."

"Oh, you are good to me," she said, half-crying. "You're so kind, I love you so much."

That was what I wanted; I applauded my own skill impersonally. The strange thing was that I meant every word of what I said; and it was easy enough to speak them with her firm young body touching mine. But the words were meant for someone else, along with the night, and the new look of Warley under the moon, and the wind, faint again now, as if the grass and the trees and the river down in the valley were breathing in my face: Susan was welcome to all of it, but I had reserved it for someone else a long time ago.

Twenty

I hired an evening suit for the Civic Ball. It didn't fit very well, and neither did the shirt I bought to go with it. But as I stood at the open door of the Albert Institute I couldn't help feeling happy. Light and music spilled out into the road, glistening on the dark leaves of the laurels in the drive; the tune was the tune which all dance bands seem to play just before one enters the dancehall, a sad, refined, rather sexy little foxtrot of no particular period. The hall was hung with balloons and festooned with coloured paper and there were flowers and ferns everywhere: the Civic Ball was the event of the year at Warley, good for two full pages in the *Courier*. There was a blue haze of tobacco smoke and a smell of perfume and powder and clean linen and women's sweat; the voices of the guests seemed to rise and fall together as if everyone were one person who'd just been assured on good authority that life on this segment of the globe was going to make sense for the next few hours – there's no doubt about it, the voice was saying calmly and vigorously, *I'm going to enjoy myself.*

Most of the councillors were there, and practically all the Town Hall staff, unfamiliar in the black-and-white of evening suits and with bosoms and arms revealed which were in most instances, I thought, looking with fascination at the tremendous mottled shelf of flesh which the Clerk's secretary carried in front of her, better hidden.

I saw June at the edge of the dance floor, talking with Teddy Soames. She was wearing an off-the-shoulder green taffeta gown; Teddy, as might be expected, wasn't looking at her face. I went towards her, but just as I was going to speak they moved off into a waltz. I tried my luck with some of the other girls but only succeeded in getting the promise of some dances later on; the Civic Ball was a programme dance, the first of its kind I'd been to. The advice which Hoylake had given me wasn't very good; it was pre-eminently a function to which one had to take a partner. Otherwise, I reflected gloomily as I made a stiff-legged circuit of the floor with a mousy-haired and bespectacled girl from the Library, one was landed with the Grade Tens. I'd have done better to have gone to some dive in Leddersford and picked up a nice broad-minded millgirl.

I went into the bar. That, I thought, as I tried to catch the waiter's eye, was another drawback to these evening-dress functions. You either paid the earth for shorts or you blew yourself up on bottled beer. As I gestured in the direction of the waiter my shirt-front bulged out; I felt a slow flush mottling my neck. It was at that moment that I saw Susan. Jack was with her in a tailored evening-suit – white tie and tails, no less. His cuff-links were of gold, naturally, and the white handkerchief in his breast pocket was of silk. He was laughing, showing his white teeth. I would have liked to have smashed them for him; except that he would have smashed mine first. Susan was wearing a silver dress which was a compromise between demureness and sophistication, showing just enough of her thin but rounded shoulders and the shape of those firm young breasts which, I remembered with rather a nasty gloating, I'd seen much more of than that rich oaf beside her.

She and Jack were part of a little circle of which Brown, his face red and beaming, was the centre. Hoylake was in it too; he was looking straight at me but gave only a brief flicker of a smile. They were at the far side of the room; I turned away from them and got my drink. There was a bad taste in my mouth, the indigestion which always attacks me when I'm angry.

I drank my beer quickly and ordered a whisky. I stood there with my back to the little circle, wondering whether to join it. I took out a cigarette, fumbled in my pockets, and asked the man next to me for a light. I caught Susan's eye; she smiled dazzlingly and, riding on its crest, I went over to the little group which, as I made the terribly long journey across the room, looked more and more impregnable and dangerous, like one of those circular iron-clads with revolving turrets which they used in the American Civil War.

"Good evening, Susan," I said.

"Hello, Joe." She hesitated perceptibly. "Have you met my mother and father?"

"How do you do, Mr. Lampton." There was real warmth in Mrs. Brown's voice. Seen at close quarters she looked even more formidable; she had a face which I felt could set like stone with the pride of caste.

"Ah've met you at t'Town Hall, lad," Brown said. He gave me a quick appraising look from brown eyes the colour of Susan's. He looked as sure of himself as Jack, but in a different way; the Yorkshire accent, which I suspected him of overdoing a bit, was one of the marks of that self-assurance. "Well, what are you drinking?"

"Scotch, please."

He snapped his fingers and a waiter came up apparently out of thin air. I glanced at Hoylake. There was for a second a sort of dry glow on his face. He made his excuses and moved off quickly; the room was crowded but he made his way through it without brushing anyone. He wasn't looking where he was going either; I remembered the old story of Queen Victoria, who always sat down immediately she felt the desire to, never for an instant bothering whether or not a chair might be there. The light winked on his black spectacles and bald head, his evening suit was the uniform of some complicated and cruel Byzantine hierarchy; the King and Queen were looking at me thoughtfully and coolly now, the servant was handing me a glass of hot amber, which the thought of drinking made my stomach twist away from in fear as if it were some potion which would force me to divulge the whole unforgivable truth, the Princess was whispering something polite and giving me a social smile as if we'd only that moment met, and the Prince from his superior height was preparing to say something gracious to the poor vulgar ex-sergeant who might perhaps be ill-at-ease among his betters.

"By the way, weren't you at Compton Bassett?" he asked.

"The Fifty-first," I said.

"A *very* great friend of mine was with that squadron. Darrow, Chick Darrow. Thoroughly decent chap, went to school with him. Went for a Burton over the Ruhr."

We noncoms used to say *got the chopper*. Going for a Burton was journalist's talk. It sickened me a bit; though I suppose that he was merely making an attempt to talk what he thought was my language. "I don't remember him."

"Oh, you must have met him. You couldn't miss old Chick. Bright red hair and a terrific baritone. Could've been professional."

"I never met him," I said, and kept saying for the next fifteen minutes during which he, assisted from time to time by Brown and his wife, played the Do You Know So and so game hard and fast from all angles, social, political, and even religious – they were *astounded* that I didn't know Canon Jones at Leddersford, he was very High of course but he was the only clergyman of any intellectual distinction whatever in the North of England . . . It's a well-known game, its object being the humiliation of those with less money than yourself; I wouldn't exactly say that they were successful in this, but I certainly paid dearly for Brown's whisky and the whisky which Jack also bought me. The extra refinement, the grace-note, was Jack's waving away of my offer to buy the drinks. ("No, no old boy, frightfully dear stuff this.")

I've never in all my life felt so completely friendless; I was at bay among the glasses of sherry and whisky, with the vicious little darts laden with the pride-paralysing curare of Do you know—? and Surely you've met—? and You must have come across—? thrown at me unceasingly. Susan said very little but I could see that she knew what was going on. She would have helped me if she could but didn't possess the necessary experience or strength of character to do so.

I'd had two pints of old at the St. Clair before I went into the dance; combined with four whiskies and my increasing irritation they made me forget my usual caution. I wasn't drunk; but I wasn't fully in control of myself. Jack asked me if I knew the Smiling Zombie's son.

"Amazing chap," he said. "Mind you, he'll kill himself in that old Alfa. Drives like a maniac. You must know him, he's always around Dufton."

"I don't know any tallymen," I said.

There was a silence.

"I don't follow you, old man."

"A tallyman sells clothes on credit," I said. "In effect it's money-lending. You buy direct from the manufacturer and sell at a retail price about fifty per cent above what I, or any other person with eyes in his head, would pay. Then you charge interest—"

"It's business," Jack cut in. "You wouldn't refuse the profits, would you?"

"It's a dirty business," I said.

Mrs. Brown's face had up to then been quite blank. It was a well-shaped face with large eyes and a pale clear skin which accentuated the soft blackness of her hair. As I spoke she admitted an expression of faint disgust to her face; she wasn't, the expression said, a friend of this vulgar person with the bulging shirt-front and the chromium cuff-links, nor did she wish to be after being a witness of the crude and ill-balanced way in which he had answered a perfectly civil remark of dear Jack's; Jack had been remarkably kind, speaking to him almost as if he were a human being, and naturally it had gone to the creature's head. She took Brown's arm.

"This is our dance, dear. Goodbye for the present, Mr. Lampton."

Brown grinned at me. "Don't worry about the way the world's run, lad. Enjoy yourself when you're young." He gave me a pat on the shoulder and moved off into the crowd. He had the same way of talking and the same Edwardian solidity as my father; I found myself wishing that I wasn't, for the sake of my self-esteem, compelled to hate him.

Twenty-one

"I must see you, Alice," I said.

"Must you really?"

"I'm sorry. I'm sorry about it all."

"It's taken you a long time to find it out."

"I can't explain over the 'phone," I said. "I wouldn't have made all that fuss but—"

"But what?"

"You meant so much to me. I was so happy with you . . ." The words wouldn't come out of the stable from which they'd pranced so readily to take Susan into a world of fantasy; I knew they were there, they were the groomed and saddled horses waiting to take us away from lies and loneliness, from the humiliation of the hired evening suit and the whiskies flung at me like hot pennies. But it wasn't the time yet.

"I might have found someone else," she said.

"Oh God, no." But I wasn't really frightened; I was sure she'd sensed the unspoken words too.

"I haven't. I love the cool way you assume that I've just been sitting here waiting for you to crook your little finger. You take too much for granted."

"All right then. I suppose I was a fool to expect you to forgive me—"

"Wait. I'll be at the St. Clair. About nine. I must go now. George is coming down."

"But it's past ten," I said stupidly.

She laughed. "You're incredible, darling. Goodbye."

She hung up before I had the chance to answer and I went back to the Town Hall, nearly walking under a 'bus; everything was tickety-boo again and I was so happy that I moved in a trance; simply to hear her slightly husky voice again had lifted all the worries from my shoulders, made what had happened at the Civic Ball trivial.

I bumped into June when I was running along the long corridor into the Treasurer's. Unthinkingly I put my hands out to her waist and kissed her soft cheek with its lovely golden down. I didn't kiss her but all women; I know they're stupid and unaccountable, ruled by the moon one and all, poor bitches, but there's a physical goodness about them as sacred as milk – there's no such thing as a bad woman, because their soft complexities are what give us life.

She put her hand to her cheek. "Summer is here," she said.

"It's always summer wherever you are," I said.

I saw her lips tremble and her face go dreamy. For a second I saw the truth. She was a good girl, a virgin – you can always tell – and I'd seen her mother once, a decent plump woman with a cheerful face who, June had once told me, had taught her everything about housekeeping from baking to brewing. In a healthier kind of society she'd have worn a special headdress or hair-style or a flower behind her ear to indicate that she was looking for a husband; and in a healthier kind of society all the young men would have been pursuing her – hotly and fiercely but with honourable intentions. There was an honest nourishing happiness emanating from her; if women were like food she'd be like good dripping with its mixture of salty richness and almost sweet blandness; if the image seems ludicrous, put your nose near a bowl of fresh beef dripping; it has a smell which is homely and warm as a clean kitchen but is also as exciting and poetic as the flowers and grass the beasts feed upon.

I realised all this but I went on running past her, not looking back. Before Christmas it would have been possible for me to look back; before Christmas I could have courted June. Nothing else would have done, and I'm always glad that I realised this. She's been married happily now this past four years – or at least she's not unhappy that I know of. But I somehow feel that I hurt her. It must have seemed that she was offering me a good home-cooked dinner and that I was rejecting it in favour of a slice of chalky shop bread spread with factory-made meat paste – I feel a sense of waste whenever I think of June. I'm sure that we choose our own destinies; but I can't help feeling that once one's chosen a certain track there's remarkably little opportunity of changing it.

But there was no room in my head for such thoughts that morning; all that mattered was that soon I'd be with Alice and the celibacy of two months would be broken. My desire to be with her again was mostly on this account; after all, one can't be expected to lead a normal sex-life for a long period and then suddenly be deprived of it and not suffer. I don't mean that I wanted her only as a body; the main reason for my celibacy was that she had spoiled me for the dancehall pickup and the pub flopsie, for the bit of fun, the quick nibble; there are a thousand synonyms for the sort of thing I mean, and their flat nastiness reflects the disgust which any man one stage above the apes is bound to feel when he unites with a woman whom he despises. But all the humiliation I'd suffered since we'd quarrelled – from Hoylake, from the Storrs, from

Jack Wales, from the Browns – dissolved in my memory beside the image of Alice in my arms again, of grown-up love instead of the frustrating teenage games I'd been playing with Susan.

I went up to Gilden in the afternoon and took in money for rent and rates and paid out money for wages for about three hours; it was fortunate that this job – which was being palmed off on to me more and more often – was the sort which could be performed in his sleep by an idiot child. Even then, I generally enjoyed it; Gilden was, as I've said before, a typical moorland village, its inhabitants incredibly inbred, and it was always interesting to see the twelve basic faces – there had only really been twelve families there since the Conquest – popping up with slight variations due to sex and age.

That afternoon each of the faces before me was a blank. There was only one face that I wanted to see, only one voice that I wanted to hear, only one body that I wanted to touch. I was once extravagant with my cigarette ration at Stalag 1000 and spent three days without tobacco; it was like that but worse, a brackish wanting, a roughness inside, a black uneasiness; the blank faces before me were prisoners' faces, the long oak table and the heavy ledgers and the official notices and the official buff and olive walls of the front room of the village Institute were the barbed wire and machine-gun towers and the Alsatians which everyone said were trained to go for your genitals first.

When we met at the St. Clair it wasn't at all as I imagined it would be. We were alone in the Snug; I kissed her briefly on the cheek. She put her hand out to my face and gulped back a tear: it was a noisy snuffle, without grace or artifice, and I found my guts dissolving with pity.

"I'm so sorry, darling. I didn't mean it, I never meant to hurt you."

"I'm making a show of myself. I was going to be very sensible!"

"For Christ's sake no. Let's get out of here and then we can talk."

Once she was in the car she let herself go; the tears poured down her cheeks unceasingly, leaving two parallel streaks in her makeup. I drove as fast as I dared to Sparrow Hill, nearly knocking down a cyclist at the top of St. Clair Road; I saw his white face as he wobbled into the gutter, shaking his fist at us.

Lying under the beeches in the gentle darkness I didn't speak. She kept on crying, burying her face in my chest; there was a dark patch of moisture on my shirt.

"It doesn't matter now," I said, when at last she'd dried her eyes. "There's no need to cry. You know why I made such a fuss, don't you?"

"I'm glad you did," she said. "It was horrible when you looked at me as if I were dirt, but I'm glad you cared."

"I love you."

"I'm old and I look terrible. You can't possibly."

She did look terrible, every year of her age even in the darkness; but the words were out now, our journey had begun. It wasn't a romantic feeling: I had no illusions about her or myself. When we were together I wasn't lonely, when we were apart I was lonely. It was as simple as that.

"Don't you love me?" I asked her.

"Of course I do, you fool. What do you think I was crying for?"

She took my hand and put it inside her blouse. "There, honey," she whispered. "Like some animal returning home."

There was a smell of summer around us, of new green and moist earth; the air up there on the moors was good and clean and sharp, there was no smoke and dirt to make your lungs feel as if they were stuffed with cotton wool – we were part of that, but not violently, we were one happy person, one reality. I wanted to take her then, not because the act itself mattered, but because I wanted to be close to her, to give her something of myself. I put my hand upon her knee. She pushed it away.

"Not now."

"I'm sorry."

"Me too. I wasn't going to come tonight, I always look awful and feel worse – you know how it is."

"Fortunately no." We began to laugh.

"I needed to see you so badly but I hate inflicting myself on you when . . ."

"You couldn't ever inflict yourself upon me. I love you just as much now as when you're well."

"Would you sleep with me, though? Would you share a bed with me?"

"Why not? You need company when you're feeling ill and miserable."

She started to cry again. "Oh God, you're so *normal*. I do love you for that, I do love you, I do love you—" She spoke the next words in a whisper. "I'm so happy with you that I wish I could die now. *I wish that I could die now.*"

Twenty-two

The next two months were – at least, when I was with Alice – entirely happy. We stopped being lovers; we became husband and wife. Of course I always gave her what in our private language we described as a fine piece of china; but that was almost incidental now. The security, the calm, the matter-of-fact tenderness which came from her – that is what was important; that, and talking to each other and having no dangerous corners or forbidden subjects. We never hid anything from one another, we really talked; our words were something more than animal noises or counters in a social or financial or sexual game.

I continued to take Susan out after the Civic Ball. I had no hope now of marrying her; but I saw no point in letting her go. She was my weekly shilling on the pools, my selection at random with no hope of winning. And I suppose that to run two women at once rather tickled my vanity; and to take her out at all was still a satisfactory way of spitting in the eye of Jack Wales and the rest of them.

I didn't really enjoy making love to Susan now. Once she was wound up, so to speak, she never stopped. Even when we were on a 'bus or in the street she wanted to hold hands or for me to put my arm around her waist. And when she thought no-one was looking she'd take my hand and press it against her breast. Once the novelty had worn off, it was wearisome. It hadn't the proper end; no matter how deep our intimacies – and in some ways I knew her body better than Alice's – she still stopped short at the crucial moment. If Alice hadn't been my mistress, I'm certain that I would have forced her to give me what I wanted. As it was, she was the sweetmeat I toyed with after the main course – delicious, pure, light with youth's spun sugar, but unimportant, neither real nor nourishing.

There was a compensation: with Susan I recaptured my youth. I joined the RAF when I was nineteen and grew up far too quickly. At an age when a kiss should have been Technicolored excitement, not seriously in one's inmost thoughts to be connected with the acrid physical tumults of adolescence, I was in a field near Cardington with the WAAF's red cookhouse hands expertly unbuttoning me: ("Ee, Ah doan't think tha's done this often afore, luv".) I recaptured my youth, that is as far as it could be recaptured. The sky didn't seem on the point of exploding, I didn't have that feeling of nearly dying with joy at discovering how wonderful female bodies are – the children's games we played were full of magic only if one believed in magic.

It seems surprising now that I should have got away with it for so long. Alice knew that I was going about with Susan; but she didn't to outward appearances let it bother her.

"She's a baby," she said to me once. "You'll soon tire of her. Try not to hurt her, that's all, darling."

At the time her attitude puzzled me. It doesn't now. She was sure that Susan wouldn't marry me, and she was sure that she could hold me. She wasn't going to waste her strength in fits of jealousy; she would simply wait for the inevitable break-up. It happened rather differently than she had anticipated, however.

The last evening under the old dispensation I remember as one remembers the party on the eve of the mutiny, the play seen a couple of hours before the earthquake. It was a warm evening and I was lying in the bed too lazy to put my clothes on; Alice came into the room wearing a black taffeta dress. She rustled down beside me.

"Do my buttons up at the back, honey."

I did as she asked, my eyes half-closed, feeling with every tiny gold button snapped into place that I too was being fastened closer and closer to her.

"You'd better dress," she said. "Elspeth'll be here before we know where we are."

"Alice dress me."

"You sensual old ram, you," she said happily. "Would you really let me?"

"Why do you think I asked you?" I put my arm around her; the smooth roughness of the taffeta against my bare skin made me shiver with pleasure. "Come on. I want to be cherished and made much of."

She dressed me with a nurse's efficiency. I closed my eyes, smelling the goodness of her sweat and the sunshine-in-the-breakfast-room smell of her lavender-water.

"I like being looked after," I said.

She looked pale and her mouth was set tightly. "I can't find your socks."

"I feel as if you'd left your hands all over me. It's wonderful—"

Her face wrinkled up and she slumped across the bed, weeping noisily.

"I want to look after you all the time, Joe. I want to do everything for you and cook for you and mend your socks and clean your shoes and dress you if you want dressing and have your children—"

"I want it too."

Her face was across my feet. The words were muffled; I couldn't be sure what she said. "I'm too old for you. It's too late." I felt the warm moisture of her tears on my feet.

"Let's go away together," I said. "I'm sick of meeting you like this. I want to sleep with you – remember?"

"This is tearing me up inside." Moving up beside me, she pressed my hand fiercely into her belly. "I'm empty. I lie awake at nights aching with emptiness. I wake up and I'm alone and I walk round Warley and I'm alone and I talk with people and I'm alone and I look at his face when I'm home and it's dead – when he smiles or laughs or looks thoughtful it's as if different strings were being pulled or different lights had been ordered—" She giggled, clasping my hand and driving her nails deep into it. She drew blood, then released her hold, looking at me wildly. "I'm hysterical, aren't I?"

I shook her gently. "You find my socks and make me some tea. I love you."

"Yes. Yes I will." She retrieved the socks from under the dressing-table and brought them over to me. "I've washed your feet with my tears," she said. She brushed them lightly with her hair. "Washed your feet with my tears and dried them with my hair."

She put on my socks for me and laced my shoes. Then she went out of the room. She stopped at the door as if she'd been hit or as if a hundred-mile-an-hour gale had sprung up and she were bracing herself against it. Then she put her hand to her belly very slowly. "Give me my bag, Joe."

I ran across to her. "What is it, dearest?"

"Nothing at all." Her face was tense with fear as if the gale, inch by inch, were driving her over the edge of the cliff. She swallowed two tablets from the bag and I felt her body relax. "Don't look so worried, Joe. It's only an illness peculiar to women. I won't die."

"But you only—"

"There's more than one kind, precious. Just you sit down and wait for the tea." She kissed me on the forehead. "I do love you, Joe."

I sat on the pink-and-flame chintz bedspread, surrounded by the photographs and the glass menagerie and the scent-sprays and the pot-pourri vases and the flowers and the copies of *The Stage* and *Theatre Arts*, feeling empty myself, knowing in a flash what it was to be Alice; it was as if I myself had that pain in my belly, as if, by an effort of will, we'd changed bodies.

After supper I left the flat before her as usual. Striding along in the dim corridor with its silence as different from real silence as a barbitone trance from natural sleep I thought suddenly: There's no need for me to leave her. Going down the spiral staircase I kept hearing her words: *I want to do everything for you, I want to have your children*. It was possible, it was real; I could be with her all the time, we could become as firmly rooted and as good as my father and my mother. We could enter into marriage, not just acquire a licence for sexual intercourse – I was old enough to cease chasing phantoms, to enjoy Now in its true colours, not spoilt by the silly iridescence of dreams.

As I came out into the street I felt a tap on my shoulder. I wheeled round. It was Eva Storr.

"You look guilty," she said. "What are you doing so far from home?"

"What are *you* doing, my sweet?"

Standing there with her plump little body brushing mine and her round black eyes staring at me, she reminded me of a bird. But birds not only sing and dance across the sky, they swoop down to their victim from a thousand feet, and they peck dead men's eyes out – or living men's if they dare.

"I've been seeing an old friend," she said. "All above board."

"Female of course?"

"I went to school with her."

"All right. I believe you." I took her arm. "Going on the 'bus?" I wanted to get her away quickly; the Fiat was parked nearby.

"I've no option. Bob couldn't fiddle any extra petrol this month."

"Do you good to be among the common people."

She pushed away my arm. "Wrong way round." She put her arm in mine. "There, I'm not so affectionate as Susan, but I'll do for tonight, won't I? God help us if anyone's watching. You'd be surprised if you knew how many Warley people come to Leddersford."

I was armoured against her now. As we walked down the drive I said, in what can only be described as a bitchy snarl: "Your chastity's too well-known, darling."

She didn't take away her arm. "You're being sarcastic."

"Oh no. I *respect* you, Mrs. Storr."

She appeared to disregard this. "You haven't told me whom you've been visiting."

"An old friend."

"Man or woman?"

"That's telling." There wasn't anything else I could say; I contemplated the invention of an old RAF friend, but lies are always dangerous. And I didn't dare mention Elspeth's name.

"Look," I said, pointing to the west. The sun was setting, going down like a battleship, its flaring red extinguishing itself in the black sea of Leddersford. The great bulk of the mansion began to erupt little yellow lights and I could hear the soft clicks of drawing curtains. "A good sunset always gives me the hell of a kick," I said.

"Does it?" Eva put her head on my shoulder for a second. "If your friend's male you should tell him not to use lavender-water," she said.

Twenty-three

And that was why, only three days later, I found myself staring at a letter from Susan.

I don't want to see you ever again. I didn't listen when people told me about you and her but now I know that all the time we've been going together you've been making love to her. I'll be going abroad soon so it's no use your writing or telephoning. You've been very bad to me and what hurts most is that you were telling lies all the time. I expect you thought that I was too young and silly to make you happy. Perhaps I was; but now I feel grown-up. I hope you will be happy and get all the things you want so much. I don't feel angry with you, only sad and hurt, as if someone I loved had died.

It was a nicely-expressed letter, all things considered; the first I'd had from her or any other woman. In a way, it was a relief; I wasn't obliged any more to spend even that figurative shilling; all my physical and emotional capital could go to Alice. The affair was neatly rounded off – it was rather flattering, too, that I should be the reason of her sadness. *As if someone I loved had died* – I made a mental note of the phrase. It conveyed the fact that she had loved me, that everything was over, and that she was most distressed about it, without descending to abuse or threats of suicide. It was a Grade Two letter; a woman of my own grade could never – even if she'd got round to writing a letter – have achieved that innocent, dignified, *elegiac* note.

Smiling, I opened Charles' letter.

I'm settling down happily in London, though so far I've been unable to find one of the rich old sugar-mammies with whom, I'd been given to understand, the place abounded. However, I'm now entangled with the Children's Librarian, a delicious little Grade 5 – if not 4 – intelligent (at least, she agrees with everything I say) untampered-with I'll take my oath, and, to my great surprise and joy, with a daddy who is a MANAGING DIRECTOR. *Mind you, it's a small firm, and daddy has three sons – big boozy clots who are all continually wasting the Old Man's substance: one's at Oxford, another's a writer and gets far too generous an allowance, and the eldest is in the business and draws far too big a salary. No-one gives a thought to poor little Julia – but she has in me a devoted defender, you may be sure.*

But that isn't what I wanted to ask you about. Before the dark night of matrimony descends upon us – or at any rate, upon me – how about this holiday in Dorset? I've got the offer of a cottage at Cumley, which is at the head of a little cove near Lulworth. Roy Maidstone will share expenses with us and we can have a fortnight's fishing, swimming, drinking, and, I hope, sinful goings-on with the local wenches who, everyone says, are stupid, loving, and passionate, and smell of hay and honeysuckle.

The only snag is that the place is only available from the 20th of June to the 11th July, and Roy and I can't get down until the 24th. It's only four days we shan't be getting our money's worth for but it niggles me rather. You said you could get away on the 20th – so if you'd like to go on ahead of us and draw up a list of likely virgins and places of historical interest and so on, the picturesque little residence is all yours. Or you can stay at my digs – it's up to you . . .

I smiled again. Alice and I had been making vague plans to go away together even if only for one night. She was going to visit an old friend in London in July. George was going to the Continent on business—

"You've let your tea go cold, Joe," Mrs. Thompson said.

"I'm thinking about my holidays."

She gave me a fresh cup of tea. "Everything fixed?"

"Yes," I said. "It's odd, but whenever you want something you get it."

A change came over the happy composure of her face. I'd seen something like it before: Aunt Emily had looked like that at my parents' inquest. It was an old face looking at me, knowing too much about love, proper human love as prosaic as wet Mondays and as necessary as wages, knowing too much about the pain which announces itself in accents as matter-of-fact as the policeman giving evidence; Mrs. Thompson at that moment knew all about me, saw through the flesh of my words and into the skull beneath.

"You always get what you want when you're young," she said. "The whole world's in a conspiracy to give you things . . ."

Then she was herself again, and I was out of that courtroom in 1943 with its smell of damp wool and dried ink and stone floors and the coroner listening to Aunt Emily with a bored look on his fat face, and back in the front room with the sun sparkling on the polished oak table and Eagle Road outside as bright and bouncing as a newly-bathed baby.

When I reached the office it was full of people shaking Tom Harrod's hand. Tom was the Chief Audit Clerk, spectacled and bald and in his early thirties, with the typical sedentary worker's stoop and pasty face; I suppose that he had all the normal human attributes, but to me it always seemed that he'd been included with a new consignment of office equipment or given at Christmas instead of a desk diary or inkstand.

I joined the crowd. "Congratulations. You'll make a good Deputy Treasurer. When are you leaving for the South?"

"Steady on," he said. "I haven't resigned yet." He put his hand on Teddy's shoulder. "I expect you'll be able to carry on without me."

Teddy looked smug. It didn't suit him. When Tom had gone and we were left alone together, he said: "Are you applying, Joe?"

"You don't get Grade Four until you're too old to enjoy it," I said. "Besides, it's not worth the extra responsibility."

"I think I'll have a bash just the same," he said.

"You stand a better chance than me anyway. You've been here longer." He had been there longer than me; but he wasn't as good as me and he knew it. "They'll put you on Grade Three at first," I said. "There's something about Four which terrifies them."

"Every little helps," Teddy said. "You know I'm going steady with June?"

"You couldn't do better." I had a sudden sense of loss, and then a feeling of barriers being raised between me and the rest of the world. "I wish you luck, Teddy. With both her and the job."

"You're sure that you don't mind about me applying?"

"Why the hell should I?"

"I'd be your senior."

"Tom never bothered me much."

"I had the buzz that Hoylake's reorganising."

"I knew that a long time ago," I said. I looked at the rows of files, the red and black inkwells that the office-boy should have cleaned out yesterday, the tin lid used as an ashtray in which my cigarette was smouldering, the calculating machine and the typewriter, the calendar with the picture of the girl like Susan, the basket full of accounts at my desk, and each became part of a dreadfully cosy desert – though at least, I thought as I turned away from the calendar, I was no longer deceived by the mirage.

"I knew a long time ago," I repeated. I dropped my hand heavily on Teddy's shoulder and squeezed it in mock friendliness until he winced with pain. "You go right ahead, Teddy."

Twenty-four

When we reached Wool, Alice was asleep on my shoulder. It was almost too hot; we'd had the window open all the way but it only had the effect of stirring the air like porridge without bringing any fresh oxygen in. I shook Alice gently and she came to wakefulness slowly, smiling happily at me as her eyes opened. She was wearing a blue dirndl skirt and a white blouse; I helped her to her feet, my hand touching with gratitude the good heaviness of her breast.

"Four days," she said, when we were at last in the taxi. "Four whole days. I don't know how I managed to wait for so long—" She kissed me, regardless of the crowd of holidaymakers around the station. "Look," she said as the car snaked through the lushly green lanes, "there's Tess of the D'Urbervilles' mansion. I once was cast as Tess in an awful rep. production and I swotted up everything about her. This is the country for passion, darling."

I bit her ear gently. "Is that a promise?"

"Anything you want," she said in a whisper. "You can beat me if you like."

"That depends upon your cooking."

"There's a caseful of food. Our larder's bare now."

I whispered something mildly improper into her ear and to my surprise she blushed, then giggled like a schoolgirl.

"Oh, you *are* a one, Mr. L, reely there's no 'olding you once your passions are aflame. Don't never leave a gal alone for one minute, you don't."

"Aye, lass," I said. "T'truth is, Ah'm *insattible*. Tha's let thisen in for a rough time, Ah'm telling tha straight."

She put her finger on her lips, looking in the direction of the driver, "Hasn't it been hellish waiting, though?"

"God, yes. Until I saw you at Waterloo I didn't believe we'd ever manage it. It doesn't seem quite real even now."

"We'll make it real." We sat in silence then, holding hands until the taxi pulled up at the cottage.

It was limewashed and thatch-roofed, with two front doors next to each other; it had originally been two cottages and its owners had converted it. Standing at the bottom of a steep lane off the main road amongst a wilderness of elders and blackberry bushes it had a strange atmosphere of self-willed isolation. From beyond the little rise in front I could hear the faint muttering of the sea.

When I'd paid the taxi-driver he drove up the lane at break-neck pace; the taxi was an old high-built Minerva and lurched all over the place, its springs squealing. "You'd think the place was haunted," I said.

"It probably is. We'll haunt it after we're gone, shall we?"

"We're not going to die yet," I said, scooping her off her feet and carrying her over the threshold. I dropped her on the sofa in the living-room and stood over her, feeling a little dizzy.

"You've done it now," she said. "You're compromised."

"I don't care," I said. "Have you realised, darling, we're *alone*? We needn't worry about Elspeth coming in unexpectedly, or Eva spying on us. I don't have to leave you at ten o'clock, and I can give you some fine china anytime I like."

"What's wrong with right now?" She pulled me down beside her. I accompanied her almost immediately into an agony of pleasure; we sank into a different dimension from which we emerged shaking and frightened – it was as if we'd been fused together, melting into each other like amœbæ but violently, like cars crashing head-on.

"Christ," she said, "that was almost too wonderful." The word didn't sound like a blasphemy, any more than it had done when we were making love. She had said it again and again then, in a breathless amazement; it was the first time I'd heard her use the word.

Before tea we washed in the kitchen. It was small and stone-flagged and cool; the sink was shallow and the water splashed up from the stone. The water was icy cold; Alice, stripped to the waist, shivered as drops ran down her back. The window was small and covered in dust; in the half-light her skin seemed almost luminous. Free, at that moment, from the desire to enter her body, I saw its beauty impersonally, as an arrangement of colour and light, a satisfying theorem of lines which curved generously, which gave, gave, gave to the air, to the cold stinging water, to me: a woman's body always wants to live, all of it, and a man's is always deathwards inclined – as long as Alice was there I wouldn't die, it was like having my father and mother alive again, it was the end of being afraid and alone.

She turned to me and put her arms around my neck. "I've never let any man see me washing before," she said. "I've always been fussy about it – they only were allowed to see me at my best, made-up, bathed, my hair just so. But you – if it gave you pleasure you could watch me doing anything. I don't care how you see me, as long as you do see me. I love you, Joe, I love you properly, like a wife. I'd like us to love each other so much that there'd be no need for us to say it. But I want to say it all the time."

"I love you, I love you like a husband. I'd die for you."

"Don't talk about death."

"I'll live for you, then. I'll make you the most-loved woman in the whole world."

"No. Just the woman *you* love most." She sighed. "I could stay here for ever."

My eyes prickled with tears. We're all imprisoned within that selfish dwarf I – we love someone and we grow so quickly into human beings that it hurts.

"It's real now," I said. "The whole earth's solid."

She pressed herself harder against me. "Do you like the way I feel? Do you like these? Or are they too old?"

"They're perfect. The only ones my head's happy in between." But as I said it I found myself wishing for a second that they were younger.

We had a big tea of American canned sausage and dried eggs and tinned fruit and then went down to Cumley. Or, rather, up; the village was about a mile from the sea and the cottage was at the head of Cumley Cove. It was six o'clock when we reached the village, and a little cooler; after we'd ordered bread and milk at the village stores, we sat on the village green under the shade of a big oak, letting the quietness come to us and stay with us, nuzzling our hands gentle as a spaniel.

She'd changed into a low-cut silk dress with a pattern of turquoise and flame and gold, each colour running softly into the other; it had a dark plum-cake richness and against it her pale honey hair and skin, already beginning to tan, looked smoothly exotic. A farm labourer going home, well-wrapped up against a temperature of seventy in the shade, bade us good evening, his pale eyes wandering ruminatively over her body.

"Pullover, waistcoat, flannel shirt, corduroys, and probably ankle-length woollen underwear," she said. "It makes me sweat just to look at him."

"I used to work stripped to the waist in Germany," I said. "I nearly went mad with sunburn and I caught cold every time the wind changed."

"Clever Dick," she said. "Think yer knows every think, doncha?"

"I don't even know where I am. No mountains, no mill-chimneys, no black buildings – it's positively decadent."

"You wouldn't exactly call Warley heavily industrialised."

"Yes, but industry's there in the background. This is different." I looked at the cottages nearby, dazzling white or fresh biscuit, with their low thatched roofs and air of conscious charm, and then across at the church in weathered grey stone. The whole place seemed to smell of milk and hay and clean summer dust; and it had about it a drowsy tolerant sensuousness. A Dales village on an evening like this would have taken the sun like a palatable medicine, a necessity which happened to be enjoyable: Cumley relaxed into a shameless abandonment.

"It *is* different," she said. "It's an older world. It's so different that it's foreign. It belongs to the farmers and the gentry. I suppose they're mostly stinkers, but at least a manure heap smells more wholesome than a woolcombing shed. It's more English than the North – my God, listen to me talking!"

"You needn't stop." I always liked to hear her; she could talk about impersonal things without turning the conversation into a lecture.

We'd been there about an hour when two girls passed us, followed by two youths. One of the girls caught my eye. She looked about fifteen, with a flat impassive face and black hair. She was wearing a skimpy print dress and I could see the shape of her legs through it.

"Good evening," she said. "Have you the time, please?"

Before I could look at my watch Alice gave her the necessary information quickly and curtly. The girl continued to look at me, her eyes running up and down my body as mine had hers.

"Thank you, sir," she said. "Proper warm weather, isn't it?" Then she turned and went off down the lane, swaying her hips slightly. I heard them giggling as they disappeared from view in the direction of the woods which stood west of the village.

"I need a drink," Alice said. She glanced towards the woods. "*She* doesn't."

"I love you," I said. "I'm not interested in little girls. Particularly not in jail-bait like that one."

"You'll be here after I'm gone," she said. "Will you promise me something – now, stone-cold sober in broad daylight? Don't sleep with her. Anyone else, darling, but not her."

"Of course not. I'll be in no condition to."

She giggled, and the strain passed from her face. We walked on to the pub with our arms round each other's waists; never before had I felt so free, so free of tension and worry and shame. The pub, an old building with low ceilings and oak beams and thick walls and mullioned windows, was an agreeable place to sit in, listening to the warm burr of Dorset and drinking a brown ale which, unlike most Southern beers had a good malty taste. When we reached the third round, I offered Alice a cigarette.

"No, darling."

"I have plenty."

"I don't want one. I don't believe I'll ever want one again. I have you and tonight and another three days and we have a house and plenty to eat and drink and my nerves aren't on edge. It's not important enough for me to think about and yet it is, because it's a symbol. You have one if you want, dearest. But if my nerves need soothing I'll—" She whispered in my ear.

I felt as if I'd been taken by the scruff of the neck and dropped through a sky of hands and each hand Alice's, slowing me down gradually until I was down in the pub again, dizzy with exhilaration, looking into Alice's dark blue eyes. I couldn't say anything; the moment was too enormous. I had discovered what love was like, I had discovered not, as before, its likeness to other people's but what made it different from other people's. When I looked at her I knew that here was all the love I'd ever get; I'd drawn my ration. It would have been better if she'd been ten years younger and had money of her own, just as life would be more agreeable if the rivers ran beer and the trees grew ham sandwiches. I was past being sensible.

The notion that there is only one woman to suit a man may appear foolishly romantic. All I know is this: there wasn't any other woman with whom I could be happy. There wasn't any obsessive compulsion towards each other, nor was our love efficient, an exact matching of virtues and defects. When I say that she suited me I use the word in the Yorkshire sense too, meaning pleased with, delighted about: *Ah'm right suited wi' thee, lass* was a statement I made entirely without facetiousness, it expressed something I couldn't say in any other language.

That night, and the nights that followed, I learned all about a woman's body and my own – all that I'll ever know, for now as far as I'm concerned, there are no more women, only friendly strangers with the appearance and functions of women. Whenever I make love now I feel as if I were one of the characters in a magazine advertisement. You know the kind – a big room and everything in it brand new and lithographer's sunbeams pouring through the window. The girl in the bed is, as they put it in the song, as pink and as soft as a nursery. She looks scarcely old enough to be married, but she has a wedding-ring to prove it. The husband generally has a smooth monkeyish face with round eyes and a long upper lip and a few wrinkles on his forehead. The last items are, together with his crew cut, simple ways of indicating sex. They both look very clean – but too clean, as if they were made of something hard and shiny that could be washed down like bathroom tiles. They need more sleep in their eyes, they need at least a little rumpling and staleness, just as the room needs at least a small crack in the plaster and a set of false teeth in a glass, and the sunbeams a suggestion of that dust which, whether we came from it or not, we all eat a peck of before we die. My wife and I aren't exact facsimiles of that couple, of course, but we belong to the same world; and what happens two or three times a week between the fine linen sheets in the front bedroom of our cosy little cottage off Linnet Road is, I feel sure, exactly what has just happened to the couple in the advertisement. Not that I don't enjoy it; it's decent and wholesome and satisfying. But what Alice and I enjoyed together was something no-one else could enjoy. There was no restraint, no shame, no normal or abnormal in that cramped double bed in the room with the dormer window or lying naked in the little cove nearby or running through the honeysuckle-heavy woods and the sunken lanes overgrown with trees and bushes into dark hot tunnels. We stopped smoking: it was part of the heightened perception we shared those four days. Anything that would have dulled that perception or have smothered even the smallest fragment of time was unthinkable. For, although we'd planned a lifetime together, we instinctively behaved as if we were meeting for the last time.

Twenty-five

She cried all the way into Dorchester. I held her tightly, her face against mine; I remember the smell of her hair, brine and olives and sweat. We hardly spoke; I kept staring outside at the rolling downs, at the wheat that seemed to have the dark glitter of pyrites, at the stretches of heath as theatrically bleak as the farmland was theatrically opulent, taking in great gulps of scenery like brandy against my mounting guilt and emptiness.

As we walked into the station she said suddenly: "I wish you'd kill me." The words were made shocking by her matter-of-fact tone.

"*Kill* you?"

"If you wanted to now, I'd let you." Her colour was patchy under the tan. "You've made me so happy that I can't imagine living for one second without you. I can't really imagine the moment when I'll be alone in the compartment . . . I suppose people who are going to be hanged don't really believe it until they're standing on the trap—"

"Hush now, silly. You'll see me again. You'll see me again often. For the rest of our lives, remember?"

"Do you love me? Even now, you don't have to lie about it. Do you really want me to divorce him?" Her eyes were ugly with weeping, her clothes had lost their bandbox appearance; I suddenly remembered the cool well-dressed Alice I'd met that first evening at the Thespians, and felt like a murderer.

"I swear it." I looked straight into her eyes. "I do love you, Alice. I'll love you till the day I die. You're my wife now. There'll never be anyone else. I'll be with you every inch of the journey."

"There's nothing more I can say to you, Joe." She started to make up her face briskly and expertly. "Do something for me before the train comes, will you, darling? Get me some cigarettes and some matches. And walk away when I board the train. Walk away and don't look back. And think of me all the time. Keep on thinking of me."

After I'd seen her off on the London platform of the odd little station – far too clean and green and white, not like a real railway station at all – I went into a hotel for a drink, having an hour to kill before Charles and Roy came. Under the blazing sun the whole town seemed dedicated to pleasure. It wasn't the pleasure of Blackpool or Margate or Scarborough, a happiness set apart from the workaday. It was a highlighting of a pattern of living that was already crackling with comfort like a five-pound note: the people round me in the thickly carpeted hotel bar were enjoying themselves because for a while they hadn't to worry about briefs and contracts and reports, not because they were drinking shorts before a slap-up lunch. The de-luxe bar and the iced Pimm's and the light worsted suit and silk tie and Panama hat were part of my holiday, just as the taxi to and from Cumley had been; but such things were no treat – only necessities – to the higher grades. I finished the Pimm's and beckoned to the white-jacketed waiter; he came over immediately, so I knew that he'd accepted me as being the kind of customer the management liked. If you want to discover which grade people think you belong to, go to any cocktail bar when it's crowded and make a note of how quickly you're served.

I met Charles and Roy after lunch. Charles was wearing biscuit-coloured linen slacks, white and brown shoes, a bright red shirt, and a white cap with a green visor. Beneath the cap his face was brick-red. Roy, a tall and stooping young man who worked at the library in the borough adjacent to Charles, was wearing blue suède shoes, blue linen slacks, an orange T-shirt, and white sunglasses. Both were smoking cigars.

"My God," I said, "you look like mad film directors."

"That's the idea," Charles said. "A dozen former virgins are now awaiting contracts."

"It's easy," Roy said. "You just say Now be nice to me and I'll be nice to you, little girl." He scrutinised me slowly and shook his head. He had a Lancashire comedian's face, long and immobile, with deep furrows that gave the impression of a sardonic amiability. "You look tired, Joseph. No doubt you have been working your fingers to the bone preparing our little home for us."

"It's not his fingers he's been working to the bone," Charles said. "Examine that natty suit, the dazzling white shirt and, by God, the Panama. Observe the bags under his eyes, the look of lascivious satisfaction – he hasn't been thinking of us at all these last four days, Roy. Do you know why he's got those knife-edge creases in his pants? Because today's the first time he's worn any since he came to Dorset."

"You've not even admired our passion wagon yet," Roy said.

It was a prewar Hudson Terraplane with a gangsterish raffishness about it. "We hired it from Roy's uncle at cut rates," Charles said. "You know, the jovial type you met in the Smoke at Christmas."

"Not so bloody jovial," Roy said. "She's killed three men. Numky thought he was very clever when he bought her cheap and patched her up, but he can't sell her. Mean old blighter, the bloodstains are still on the front seat."

Charles clapped me on the back and thrust a cigar in my mouth. "There now, picture of the perfect English gent. Well-fed, slightly drunk, and in the last stage of sexual exhaustion." He looked at his watch. "Quick one before they close, or a slow wallow at the cottage?"

"The cottage," I said. I sat beside him in front, and Roy stretched himself out across the back seat.

"I'm engaged, did you know?" Charles scratched the side of his nose, a trick of his when he was embarrassed.

"It wouldn't be Julia?"

"That's right. She's a good girl. You really must meet her."

"It'll make her discontented. Mind you, I'm glad you've decided to settle down. You're too old for sleeping around. You've not kept your looks as well as I have. She's Grade One now?"

"All the grades rolled into one. Never a dull moment."

I had a feeling of change, a change as inevitable and natural as the seasons, a tide that I should be moving with but wasn't.

"I've been earmarked for matrimony too," Roy said.

"Congratulations." A thought struck me. "You're not inviting them to the cottage, are you?"

"Calm yourself, boy. Mine is in Ireland and Roy's in Scotland."

"Our mothers-in-law don't trust us," Roy said.

"No wonder," Charles said, taking the gap between a farm-wagon and an approaching motor-bike at fifty. "Lucy was one of Roy's juniors. A sweet little girl of sixteen when first she came—"

"Slow down," I said, "or I'll ruin the upholstery too. My God, what must you have been like on a jeep?"

"I was there with Errol Flynn on the day of victory. Driving over a causeway of Jap corpses. Mountbatten and Slim and the rest followed at a respectful distance. Beautiful Burmese girls smothered us with kisses and flowers and the Warner Brothers hovered overhead singing Te Deums . . ."

The motor-bike cut in on us, scraping the front wing with a fraction of an inch to spare. Charles shook his fist at him.

"You stupid bastard!" he yelled.

"I'll take over," I said. "Whenever you're at the wheel you forget that you're no longer in the glamorous East where you can mow 'em down in their hundreds and be let off with a caution."

"Caution be damned," Charles said. He stopped the car and moved over to make way for me. "A coolie cost me a hundred chips once."

"Imperialist brute," Roy said. "Men like you lost us the Empire." I started the car with a jerk, but I soon got the hang of it. The steering was low-geared and more than a trifle soggy but the engine had plenty of power and I found that I was enjoying myself. Charles and Roy started to sing In Mobile, and I took my cigar out of my mouth and joined in the chorus.

In Mobile, in Mobile
Here's a health to the drinking classes in Mobile
When they've finished with their glasses—

I looked at the cigar and remembered that I'd given up smoking. The guilt began to work inside me again; but when we'd finished the song I put the cigar back in my mouth. It was too good to waste.

Charles slapped me on the back. "Those sensitive features are set in a mask of pain. A tear quivers in those bloodshot blue eyes. Does our little ditty arouse memories of the time when you were an inordinate user of Brylcreem and never wore an overcoat even on the coldest days?"

"He's been like this all the way from London," Roy said. "He's grooming himself for Chief; he'll make some poor little squirt writhe under a flow of sarcasm one of these days."

"It might be you," Charles said. "After the usual remarks about the necessity for senior members of my staff setting an example etcetera, I shall get down to cases. *Maidstone*, I shall say, belching slightly after my lunch at the Savoy Grill, *Maidstone, I can hardly believe it possible that a man occupying so high a position is unaware of the existence of the age of consent. It is of no avail to asseverate that the juvenile issues have considerably increased. . . ."*

I slowed down going past the village green. "There's a toothsome juvenile for you," I said. It was the black-haired girl who'd asked me the time on my first day in Cumley.

"Oh my," Roy said, "strap me to the mast, said Ulysses. Almost worth ten years hard, isn't she?"

The girl was sitting on the grass at the roadside reading a magazine. She was wearing slacks and a tight, red jersey. She looked up as we passed.

"She's smiling at you," Roy said. "Charles and I will testify on your behalf. Say that everything went black."

"They're like little apples," Charles said wistfully. "It's bloody unfair; the precise age at which that type is worth having is the age when an asinine law says they're inviolate. That girl has now reached her peak. From now on she'll decline rapidly."

I thought of Alice's face raddled by tears and the tired droop of her shoulders as she turned away from me at the station; I felt angry with the girl for being young and unbroken and angry with myself for looking at her.

"You're growing old," I said. "Little girls in cinemas are the next stage."

"Doubtless, doubtless," Charles said. "When I was her age, I wouldn't look at a woman under thirty. Now I won't look at any woman over" – he looked at me sharply – "twenty. Twenty-one at the outside."

"You're a couple of worn-out old lechers," Roy said. "Let's have a bathe before tea and wash away these unclean thoughts. Which is the best place, Joe?"

We were passing the lane which led to the cove where Alice and I had been that morning. It was the best place to swim from; all the other stretches of beach nearby were shingly and exposed. But I couldn't, just then, tolerate the thought of anyone else disturbing my memories of what had taken place there less than four hours since. The cove was our own in a way that, I don't know why, the cottage wasn't.

"It's half a mile farther," I said as I drove past the lane.

"Hurry up," said Charles impatiently. "The road's clear."

I put my foot down and drew up a moment later in a flurry of dust on the narrow road by the headland north of Cumley. There was a path leading down to the beach and Charles and Roy snatched up their bathing trunks and started running down it.

"Aren't you coming, Joe?" Roy asked. "There's a spare costume somewhere."

"No, thanks," I said. "I've already bathed."

They went whooping down the path like schoolboys and in scarcely ten minutes I heard them swearing as their bare feet hit the shingles and then there was a sound of splashing. I took another cigar from the box in the back seat, pierced it, lit it carefully, and tried to think about nothing at all, stroking the worn bakelite of the steering-wheel for comfort.

Twenty-six

It was a good holiday that we had, though. We started each day with strong tea and rum, bathed before breakfast – they discovered our cove for themselves the second day – and ate huge meals. We saw all the sights – the Cerne Giant, Corfe Castle, Cloudshill, and the rest. We also drank a lot of beer; but I suppose that the food and sunshine and fresh air kept us sober. At any rate, the one day that it rained was the day that we got really stinkingly sozzled, starting at the village pub at lunchtime, carrying on in the cottage with bottled beer in the afternoon, and driving out to a roadhouse near Bournemouth in the evening. I don't believe that I've ever drunk so much before: one always tends to exaggerate the amount, but totting it up afterwards we all agreed that it couldn't have been less than twenty pints and half a bottle of gin apiece.

I don't quite know how I drove the car back. Normally we'd have left it and taken a taxi, but Roy hit a Territorial officer in the Gents' and it seemed best to remove ourselves quickly. Roy, a quiet type normally, seemed to become, as Charles said, all Id when he'd had one over the eight. Charles had a rough time with him in the back seat; he was trying for some reason to take off his clothes and he only stopped the attempt when Charles hit him on the jaw. Then he became normal, if you can call alternate fits of weeping and blasphemy normal. I was in that final stage where the mind grasps fully the fact of being drunk, orders the limbs and senses to behave themselves, and finds them obeying seconds too late. The night was steaming with heat like a great animal; you could see it rising from the ground. And the roads were slippery; twice the car shimmied into a long skid the worst part of which was that though I knew I ought to care whether or not I came out of it alive, I didn't give a damn. I was, in a crazy way, enjoying it.

When we came into Cumley the rain had stopped. There was a smell of wet grass and night-scented stock, and the moon was out, cold and faraway as an owl's hoot.

"God is dead!" Roy suddenly yelled. Then he started blubbering again. "There were two officers. I've just remembered. I hit the wrong one. God forgive me."

"The final stage," Charles said. "Maudlin remorse."

"I wouldn't want to appear inquisitive," I said, "but why did you sock him?"

"He had the M.C.," Roy said.

"You've got the D.T.'s," I said. "That's no reason to bash the poor devil. They won't give *you* a medal just because you bust his nose."

"Isn't he a card?" Charles said. "A genuine schizo once he's tiddly. He's brooding because he thinks he deserved a medal and they passed him over. Why, damn it all, I'm the one who ought to have done the bashing. I've killed forty Japs at least, not to mention that Wog I ran over in Calcutta. What thanks have I received for it, what recognition of my devotion to duty and disregard for danger? None at all. Am I bitter? No. Only glad that forty Japs are dead instead of me."

"You don't understand," Roy said. "I was a sergeant. If I'd done whatever it was that that captain had done, they wouldn't have given me an M.C. It would have been an M.M."

"Different brands of courage," Charles said. "Serge and barathea. Don't let it bother you, Sergeant."

"He worries too much," I said.

"That's better than not worrying at all," Charles said, and hiccuped. "What is worrying our friend is unimportant, and his action was childish and futile, even if he'd hit the right person. What matters is that he felt something was wrong and he did something about it."

The car skidded again turning into the lane to the cottage and I was too busy wrenching it into control to answer him. Roy had passed out cold by the time we reached the cottage; when we'd unloosened his collar and put him to bed on the sofa downstairs, Charles returned to the attack.

"You want some supper?" he asked.

"I'm going to bed. The floor won't keep still."

"You'd better eat something, then you won't get alcoholic poisoning."

He went into the kitchen, tripping up twice over his own feet, and came back in a surprisingly short time with a pot of tea and a plate of corned beef sandwiches.

He pulled up a chair opposite me, sitting astride it. "You're not going to marry Alice," he said. He took a huge bite from his sandwich. "Though I'm grateful to her for leaving all this lovely grub behind."

"Who says I'm not going to marry her?"

"I do." He took off his spectacles. Deprived of them, his eyes seemed paler and larger and colder; his round red face wasn't jolly any longer.

"Get this straight," I said. "I love Alice. She loves me. I'm happy with her. Not just in bed either."

"Love? That's a funny word to use. What would your Aunt Emily say if you went to her and said that you loved a married woman ten years older than yourself?" He took a gulp of tea.

"She'd vomit, she really would."

"You can't possibly understand. Her husband doesn't come into it. He doesn't love her and she doesn't love him."

"No," Charles said. "Of course not. But he keeps her. You said that she had no money of her own. All that tinned stuff in the larder, that bottle of whisky, that silver cigarette-case she gave you – it all came from him."

"My God," I said disgustedly, "don't turn moral on me. He can well afford it."

"That's not the point, you fool. If she'd do it to him, she'd do it to you."

I rose quickly. "I ought to hit you." I felt sick and murderous; the blood was drumming in my ears and there was a nasty sugary taste in my mouth.

Charles smiled. "Don't, Joe. It wouldn't help, believe me. Besides, you know perfectly well that it's true."

I didn't answer him, but walked round the room as if taking an inventory for the bailiffs: Windsor chairs, horsehair sofa, scrubbed deal table, a radio with a separate receiver and amplifier, a big gramophone cabinet, a glass-fronted bookcase.

"Who owns this place?" I asked.

"An actor. Friend of Roy's. He's working for once, so he thought he might as well sublet the place. Why do you ask?"

"I wondered. It has an odd feeling at times. Cold."

"It's supposed to be haunted. This is the Black Magic area. Not that you'll have noticed. You'll have been too much under her spell."

I poured myself a cup of tea and lifted it to my lips with both hands. Roy began to snore, his snortings and rumblings competing with the steady hiss of the Aladdin lamp.

"A man of twenty-six can marry a girl of sixteen," Charles said. "The only reaction will be one of envy. Look at all these society weddings: grooms of thirty and thirty-five and brides of nineteen and under. And all these elderly film stars buy dewy-eyed young brides, too. Sometimes a man marries an older woman for her money – people call him nasty names but as long as he's got the money why should he care? In our class we marry women of our own age, which I suppose is the most decent arrangement. But you want to make the worst of both worlds. You want to marry an older woman who hasn't any money. It would be bad enough if she were unmarried; but in addition to everything else you'll be dragged through the midden of the Divorce Courts."

"*He* has a mistress," I said. "They only live together for the sake of appearances."

"God give me patience! He has a lot more money than you, chum, and he's a lot brighter. *He* won't be caught out whatever he does. Did you enjoy your nude bathing with her, by the way?"

"I never told you that."

"You haven't told me much at all. That's why I know that you're serious about her. I was given a full report of your activities on the beach, right down to the last sigh. In the village pub yesterday. Such an ancient gaffer he was too. *Her only had a red bathing-cap on*, he said. *Her even took that off.* You certainly cheered his declining years; he went blue in the face with excitement when he remembered it."

"Apart from making me feel mucky all over," I said slowly, "what does all this add up to?"

"You're very dense tonight. If Mr. Aisgill wanted a divorce, he could afford detectives to trace you here. That would be enough in itself, but for good measure they'd ferret out the old boy too. Can't you imagine it? Can't you imagine the story in the Sunday papers? Face facts, Joe. You couldn't bear to be shown up like that. You don't belong to the class that thrives on scandal. You'd have your heart broken." He looked away from me and said in a low voice, "And you'd break the hearts of a lot of other people. People who don't wish you anything but good."

I tried to think of Alice just as the person I loved, the one with whom I could be kind and tender and silly, the one whom I was certain of to the last breath, the one who'd tear her heart out for me to eat if I wanted it; but all I could remember was the lifted skirt on the sofa where Roy now lay snoring, the soft naked body on the beach where we'd bathed that morning; I could only remember pleasure, easy pleasure, and that wasn't enough to set against his words.

"And what about Susan?" he asked.

"That's all over. You know perfectly well that it's all over."

"I don't. You've made no attempt to get her back."

"It wouldn't be any use." I yawned. "I'm tired." I got up and stretched myself. "The floor's steady. We've drunk ourselves sober."

"Never mind that. Look, Joe, I don't often ask you a favour. This isn't for me, either. It's for you. Promise me to write to Susan."

Twenty-seven

"Gosh, isn't it hot?" Susan said.

We were lying in a clearing in the bracken above the Folly; the afternoon sun beat down upon us like a pleasurable *peine forte et dure*.

"*You* shouldn't feel hot," I said, looking at her off-the-shoulder blouse and cotton skirt. "You've nothing on."

"*Wicked!*" she said, and pulled up the blouse till it covered her shoulders. "Happy now? Joety happy now his Susan back?"

I pulled her blouse off her shoulders again. I kissed each shoulder gently. "Happy now. Only happy now I'm with you."

Women over thirty look younger at dusk or by candlelight; a girl of nineteen looks younger, childish almost, in the hard glare of the midday sun: at that moment Susan looked no more than fourteen. Her lipstick had been kissed away, her powder had disappeared; her lips were still red, her skin flawless.

"It was a *lovely* letter," she said. "Oh Joe, I was so miserable until I got it. It was the best surprise I've ever had in my whole life."

Charles had helped me to write it, after a long argument, in the course of which he'd called me, among other things, a sex-besotted moron and an unsuccessful gigolo. "There now," he'd said when I signed it, "that should bring the silly bitch running back with the lovelight in her eyes. You can always depend upon your Uncle Charles."

Indeed I could; and there was Susan to prove it. I'd been back from Dorset a week and she'd only just returned from Cannes; she'd 'phoned me the minute she'd read the letter. The sour smoky smell of the bracken caught at my throat; I raised myself on my elbow and looked down at Warley in the valley below. I could see it all: the Town Hall with the baskets of flowers above the entrance, the boats on the river at Snow Park, the yellow 'buses crawling out of the station, the big black finger of Tebbut's Mills in Sebastopol Street, the pulse of traffic in Market Street with its shops whose names I could recite in a litany – Wintrip the jeweller with the beautiful gold and silver watches that made my own seem cheap, Finlay the tailor with the Daks and the Vantella shirts and the Jaeger dressing-gowns, Priestley the grocer with its smell of cheese and roasting coffee, Robbins the chemist with the bottles of Lenthéric after-shave lotion and the beaver shaving-brushes – I loved it all, right down to the red-brick front of the Christadelphian reading-room and the posters outside the Coliseum and Royal cinemas, I couldn't leave it. And if I married Alice I'd be forced to leave it. You can only love a town if it loves you, and Warley would never love a co-respondent. I had to love Warley properly too, I had to take all she could give me; it was too late to enjoy merely her warm friendship, a life with a Grade Six girl perhaps, a life spent in, if I were lucky, one of the concrete boxes of houses on the new Council estate. People could be happy in those little houses with their tiny gardens and one bathroom and no garage. They could be happy on my present income, even on a lot less. But it wasn't for me; if the worst came to the worst, I would accept it sooner than not live in Warley at all, but I had to force the town into granting me the ultimate intimacy, the power and privilege and luxury which emanated from T'Top.

"Joe," said Susan. "You're very naughty. You're not listening."

"I am, honey," I said. "It wasn't a lovely letter, though. I was too agitated when I wrote it. I was frightened that you'd recognise the writing and throw it away. I haven't had a happy moment since you told me it was all over between us."

"You promised me never to see Alice again. Have you told her?"

"You know she's in hospital. She's very ill too."

Susan's face was set very hard; she didn't look like a school-girl now, but more like one of those female magistrates who are always sending someone to jail without the option so that no-one will be able to accuse them of womanly soft-heartedness.

"You must tell her now." She looked like her mother: the soft curves of her face seemed to change to straight lines and her mouth became tight and disciplined – not exactly cruel, but set in an expression of judgement.

Alice had come home the day before me and had been taken to hospital in the middle of the night. I never did find out what the illness was; it wasn't cancer but it was some kind of internal swelling that was quite serious – serious enough for an operation – but not serious enough for the doctors to give her the dope necessary to keep away the pain. She was waiting for the operation now, and wasn't allowed any visitors except for family. I hadn't written her because she'd sent me a note saying that it was wisest not to; but my conscience troubled me about it because I knew that she didn't really expect me to take her at her word.

"Do you hear me, Joe?" Susan's voice had a shrill note. "Tell her now. She's not going to die. If you don't write to her straightaway I really have finished with you this time. I mean it."

"Shut up. I'll do what I promised – I'll finish the affair once and for all. When she comes out of hospital. And face to face. Not by letter. That's cowardly."

Susan stood up. "You're absolutely hateful and despicable. You won't do anything I ask you to, and now you're going back to this – this old woman just because she's supposed to be ill. I wish I'd never met you. You've spoilt France for me and now that I'm happy again you're doing *this*. I hate you, I hate you, I hate you—" She burst into tears. "I'm going. I don't want to see you again. You never loved me—"

I took hold of her roughly, then slapped her hard on the face. She gave a little cry of surprise, then flew at me with her nails. I held her off easily.

"You're not going," I said. "And I'm not going to do what you asked me either. I love you, you silly bitch, and I'm the one who says what's to be done. Now and in the future."

"Let me go," she said. "I'll scream for help. You can't make me stay against my will." She started to struggle. Her black hair was dishevelled and her brown eyes were gleaming with anger, changed into a tigerish topaz. I shook her as hard as I could. I'd done it in play before, when she'd asked me to hurt her, please hurt her; but this time I was in brutal earnest, and when I'd finished she was breathless and half-fainting. Then I kissed her, biting her lip till I tasted blood. Her arms tightened round my neck and she let herself fall to the ground. This time she did not play the frightened virgin; this time I had no scruples, no horizon but the hot lunacy of my own instincts.

"You hurt me," she said when I came to my senses afterwards, my whole body empty and exhausted. "You hurt me and you took all my clothes – look, I'm bleeding here – and here – and here. Oh Joe, I love you with all of me now, every little bit of me is yours. You won't need *her* any more, will you?"

She laughed. It was a low gurgling laugh. It was full of physical contentment. "Tell her when she comes out of hospital if you like, darling. You won't need her any more, I know that." She smiled at me; the smile radiated an almost savage well-being.

"I won't need her any more," I repeated dully. There was a taste of blood in my mouth and my hand was bleeding where she'd scratched it. The sun was hurting my eyes now, and the bracken round the clearing seemed actually to be growing taller and closing in on me.

Twenty-eight

It was almost two months before Alice came out of hospital. The day before I had a 'phone call from Brown at the Town Hall. He rang me direct, with none of the usual secretary nonsense. "Mr. Lampton? Lunch at t'Con Club. Leddersford. One."

"Are you sure it's me you want?" I asked.

"Of course I'm sure. It's important, too. See you're there on the dot."

His tone annoyed me. It was a grey drizzling September morning, muggy and cold by turns; my in-basket was full, and after I'd cleared it I had to see our junior, Raymond, about the shortages in the petty cash. Now that Raymond is a solid citizen occupying my old job, it seems hard to believe what he was like then: a skinny little boy with a white pimply face, and a shiny blue serge suit with frayed turnups and shirts that were never quite clean and never quite dirty. He was cleaning the inkwells when Brown rang and singing "Onward, Christian Soldiers" in a quavering voice, trying to keep his spirits up, I suppose.

"Are you having a prayer meeting?" Brown asked. "I can hardly hear myself speak." I noticed that he'd dropped his Yorkshire accent.

I covered the mouthpiece. "Shut up, Ray, I'm busy. What was it you wanted to see me about, Mr. Brown?"

"I can't tell you over the 'phone, and even if I could, I haven't the time." He hung up.

I lit a cigarette; it didn't taste very good. I hadn't really enjoyed tobacco since my return from Dorset. I've been lucky to avoid this till now, I thought: Hoylake, having failed to scare me off Susan, has handed the job over to Brown who, in some unpleasantly direct way, is going to kick me in the guts. A man with only a few hundred in the bank – and lucky to have that – is powerless against a man with a hundred thousand. I would be forced to leave Warley. Already I had a premonition of my future status at the Town Hall whenever I saw Teddy swelling visibly with his promotion (he'd been given APT Four, too). I'd been with Susan last night; she'd been silent and tearful and distrait and wouldn't tell me what was wrong with her. I knew now. Daddy had put his foot down, she was sprinting towards the already rising drawbridge and the slowly closing portcullis. And Jack Wales would be home at Christmas – what chance had the swineherd against the Prince? Now it had come, it was actually a relief: there was nowhere I could retreat to, no need to be pleasant to anyone, I could afford the luxury of speaking my mind.

I looked at Ray, his hands red and blue with ink, his lower lip trembling. He'd noticed me spending much more time than usual over the petty cash books, and he knew what was coming. I had it in my power to alter his whole life: he came from a poor family, and I knew just what happened to people who were sacked from local government. The Efficient Zombie had a junior sacked once for exactly the same offence as Ray's, and he'd ended up as a labourer. The reference system, unless you're very lucky or very rich or very talented, can be your implacable enemy for the rest of your life if you do one thing out of line. Ray was in the dock, all five foot four of him: I was the judge and the jury. One word from me to Hoylake, and out he went.

"Bring me the cashbox and the stamp-book and the petty cash book," I said. He took them out of the safe and came over to my desk with them, dragging his feet in their down-at-heel shoes.

"I went over these this morning, Ray," I said. "There seem to be some discrepancies."

He looked at me dumbly.

"Errors," I said. "Errors that should have been revealed by a surplus but weren't. Fifteen shillings over the last fortnight. Have you got that fifteen shillings?"

He shook his head. The tears were coming to his eyes.

"All right, then. Maybe I've made a mistake. We'll go over the books together."

He stood over me whilst my finger traced down the rows of figures, his red-and-blue hand with the bitten fingernails following mine. It was that, and those down-at-heel shoes, that sickened me: I saw myself through his eyes, old and sleek and all-powerful. I shut the books with a bang.

"You damned idiot, what did you do it for? You knew you'd be found out."

"I don't know," he said tearfully. I did, though. His elementary school pals would be earning five or six pounds a week whilst he had only two. He'd been trying to keep up with the Joneses, the poor little devil.

"Stop snivelling," I said. "You're in a mess, and crying isn't going to help you one little bit. Have you got that fifteen shillings?"

He shook his head. "No. I'm very sorry, Mr. Lampton, I won't ever do it again, I swear. Please don't tell on me, please."

I took a ten-shilling note and two half-crowns from my pocket and put them in the cashbox.

His face brightened a little. "You're not going to tell on me, Mr. Lampton?"

"What the bloody hell do you think I'm doing this for?"

He grabbed my hand and started shaking it. "Thank you, sir, thank you. I'll pay back every penny, I swear I will—"

"No," I said. Fifteen shillings was to him as impossible a sum to find as fifteen hundred. "No, you fool. Just don't do it again, that's all. I'll fix it this time; but if ever I catch you again, even if it's only a ha'penny, then you go to Mr. Hoylake straightaway. Now get out and wash your face."

After he'd gone I wondered if I hadn't gone soft in the head. I had in a sense compounded a felony, and if he were to steal anything again it would go hard with me. But I couldn't have done otherwise; I could remember the time when I was desperately in need of fifteen shillings myself, watching the Dufton yobs peacocking it in new suits and their wallets stuffed with notes when I scarcely had the price of a Woodbine. And perhaps, I thought superstitiously, if I were merciful with Raymond, Brown would be merciful with me.

The Leddersford Conservative Club was a large Italianate building in the centre of the city. The stone had been a light biscuit colour originally – sometimes I wonder if all nineteenth-century architects weren't a bit wrong in the head – and a hundred years of smoke had given it an unhealthy mottled appearance. The carpet inside the foyer was plum-coloured and ankle-deep, the furniture was heavy and dark and Victorian, and everything that could be polished, right down to the stair-rods, gave off a bright glow. It smelled of cigars and whisky and sirloin, and over it hung a brutally heavy quiet. There were a great many pictures of Conservative notabilities: they shared a sort of mean sagacity of expression, with watchful eyes and mouths like spring-traps, clamped hard on the thick juicy steak of success.

I felt a cold excitement. This was the place where the money grew. A lot of rich people patronised expensive hotels and road-houses and restaurants too; but you could never be really sure of their grade, because you only needed the price of a drink or a meal and a collar and tie to be admitted. The Leddersford Conservative Club, with its ten-guinea annual subscription plus incidentals (Put me down for a hundred, Tom, if the Party doesn't get it the Inland Revenue will) was for rich men only. Here was the place where decisions were taken, deals made between soup and sweet; here was the place where the right word or smile or gesture could trans-port one into a higher grade overnight. Here was the centre of the country I'd so long tried to conquer; here magic worked, here the smelly swineherd became the prince who wore a clean shirt every day.

I gave my name to the commissionaire. "Mr. Lampton? Yes, sir, Mr. Brown has a luncheon appointment with you. He's been unavoidably delayed, but he asked you to wait in the bar." He looked at me a trifle doubtfully; not having had time to change, I was wearing my light grey suit and brown shoes, my former Sunday best. The shoes were still good but much too heavy for the suit, and the suit was too tight and too short in the jacket. Third-rate tailors always make clothes too small. I saw or fancied that I saw, a look of contempt in the commissionaire's eye, so I put back the shilling I was going to give him into my pocket. (It was fortunate that I did; afterwards I found out that you never tip club servants.)

The bar was crowded with business men slaving to help the export drive. An attempt had been made to modernise it; the carpet was a glaring zigzag of blue and green and yellow and the bar was topped with some kind of plastic and faced with what appeared to be black glass. There wasn't any sign that it was a stamping-ground reserved for the higher grades, unless you counted the picture of Churchill above the bar – a picture which you could find in most pubs anyway. And by no means all of them spoke Stan-dard English. Leddersford's main manufacture is textiles, and most of its ruling class receive their higher education at the Technical College, where to some extent they're forced to rub shoulders with the common people and consequently pick up some traces of a Northern accent. What marked the users of the bar as being rich was their size. In Dufton or even Warley, I was thought of as being a big man; but here there were at least two dozen men as big as me, and two dozen more who were both taller and broader. And one of them, standing near me, was at least six foot four and as broad-shouldered as a gorilla – it would be genuine bone and muscle too, there'd be no padding in *that* suit. He could have broken my back across his knee without putting himself out of breath and doubtless would have done if he'd been given half a chance, to judge from the way he was scowling at me. Then the scowl changed into a social smile, and I saw that it was Jack Wales.

"How are you, old man?"

"Very fit," I said. "Had a good holiday in Dorset. *You* seem to be bursting with health, I must say."

"Been to Majorca. Cambridge seems a bit damp and chilly after it. I'm just returning there – I made a flying visit to Warley. Papa's rather off-colour. Works too hard."

"I'm sorry to hear that," I said, wondering maliciously whether it was gout, prostate trouble, or high blood pressure that was making Wales Senior ill.

"He's all right now," he said. He smiled at me. "My father puts in a sixteen-hour day, you know. Drink, old man?"

"Whisky."

"Have a double. Then you don't have to catch the waiter's eye twice."

"You shouldn't have any trouble that way."

"Whatsay? Oh, see what you mean. My height's a curse, actually. Can't get away with anything . . . What brings you here anyway? Thought you were a red-hot Labour man. Seen the light, eh?" He gave one of his hearty false laughs.

"I'm meeting Mr. Brown."

"Susan's father?"

"Uhuh."

"Nice chap. Don't let him overpower you, though. Stick out for the highest figure the traffic will bear – I suppose it's a job you're discussing?"

"Could be," I said. There wasn't anything else that I could say.

"You're cagey," he said. "Wise man." He looked at the gold watch that seemed effeminately small on his huge hairy wrist. "Well, I must push off." He finished his whisky.

"Another?"

"No thanks, old man. In any case, you can't buy one; club rule." He clicked his finger at the waiter. "Double whisky for Mr. Lampton, Henry." He gave the waiter a note, and shovelled the change into his pocket without bothering to count it. "Goodbye for now, Joe."

"Goodbye, Jack." Three double whiskies would add up to fifteen shillings, the lack of which had nearly condemned poor snivelling little Raymond to the equivalent of a life in the galleys. Not that I enjoyed the whisky any the less.

I saw Brown enter the room. He came straight over to me.

"Seem to have made yourself at home, young man. Think I'll have one of those whiskies whilst there's still some left." He crooked his finger and the waiter glided over to him.

"I'm very annoyed with you, young man," he said. He had very heavy black eyebrows and in conjunction with his grey hair and red face they were a little alarming; compressed over his deep-set eyes the effect was that of a hanging judge, a jolly old *bon viveur* sentencing some poor devil of a labourer or a clerk to death by dislocation of the neck as an aperitif to a good dinnah with a bottle of the best – the *very* best, waitah – port.

He took out a gold cigarette-case and offered me one.

"No, thanks."

"You're sensible. Bad habit before meals. It's the only thing you are sensible about; in all other respects you've been a bloody fool."

I felt myself going red in the face. "If that's all you wanted to see me about, there's no point in me staying."

"Don't be any dafter than you can help. I've a proposition for you. Anyway—" he gave me one of his unexpectedly charming smiles, the hanging judge becoming a Santa Claus who would send absolutely every item on the list – "you might as well have lunch first. Not that you'll have a very good one; this place has gone down the hill since rationing started."

"No-one here seems to be starving."

"Never said they were. Just that you couldn't get a decent meal here any more. This the first time you've been to this club?"

"This or any Conservative club," I said. "My father'd turn in his grave if he could see me."

"So would mine," he said, and winked. "So would mine, lad. But we're not bound by our fathers."

I looked at him coldly. The bluff friendliness approach no doubt came automatically; the fustian glove on the steel fist which, any moment now, I was going to be given a mouthful of. Why didn't he get it over with?

A waiter approached us and, with much bowing and scraping, led us to a table in the dining-room. This was in the same style as the foyer; the linen was blindingly white and sailcloth-stiff and the cutlery heavy enough to be silver. It wasn't a room that any moderately good hotel couldn't duplicate; but there wasn't one chip, one scratch, one speck of dust anywhere, and you had the feeling that the waiters would, without flicking an eyelash, bring you anything that you wanted the way you wanted it, even, if you really insisted, their own ears and eyes, braised in sherry.

I was taking the first spoonful of game soup when Brown said casually: "I'm thinking of setting you up in business."

I nearly choked. "Are you serious?"

He scowled. "I didn't bring you here to play jokes. You heard what I said. You can name your figure." He leaned forward, his hands gripping the table. His nails were white at the top with pressure. "You're a clever young man. You don't want to stay at the Town Hall all your life, do you? Now's the time when accountants can do well for themselves. Supposing I lend you what's necessary to buy a partnership somewhere? I won't sell you a pup; and I'll even send business your way."

"There's a catch somewhere," I said.

"There is. I'll make you a rich man – a damned sight better off than you'll ever be in local government – on one condition." He paused; suddenly he looked old and sick. "Just one condition: you never see Susan again or communicate with her in any way."

"I'm to leave Warley too, I take it?"

"Yes, you're to leave Warley too." He wiped his forehead with a white silk handkerchief. "There's no need for you to think twice about it, is there? There's nothing for you if you don't take the offer. In fact, I'll go out of my way to make things unpleasant for you."

There was a roaring in my ears; I wanted to knock over the table and hit him until my arm had no more strength in it, then give him the boot give him the boot give him the boot – I drew a deep breath. "No. Definitely no. If you were a younger man, I'd knock you down, by God I would!" To my horror, I found my accent growing broader. "Ah reckon nowt to your bloody rotten offer. Ah'll dig ditches afore Ah'll be bought—" My voice stopped shaking as I regained my self-control. "Listen. You wouldn't understand, but I love Susan."

"I wouldn't understand," he said, dragging out the words. "I wouldn't understand about love."

"I'm not in love with her," I said. "I *love* her. She's absolutely the best girl I've ever met. I wanted to marry her the first moment I saw her; I didn't know who she was then, and I didn't care. Damn it, I'll bring it before the magistrates. She can stay at my home if you throw her out. The magistrates won't refuse us permission to marry, and even if they do, I'll kick up the hell of a row—"

"You'll do no such thing, Joe," he said quietly.

"Why won't I?"

"Because you're marrying her. With my consent. Right quick."

I looked at him with my mouth open.

He'd regained his normal floridity now, and was actually smiling. I could only gape at him.

"Finish your soup," he said. "There's many folk 'ud be glad of that and you're letting it grow cold."

I spooned it up obediently as a child. He looked at me with a bristling kindliness.

"Why did you make me that offer?" I asked.

"I wanted to be sure you were right for her. Mind you, it would have been a good investment anyway. You're a bright lad."

I remembered something that Reggie had said on the evening of the Carstairs' party. "You've done this before, haven't you?"

"She was only sixteen," he said, almost apologetically. "He was a clerk at the works. Fancied himself as a writer. And a fortune-hunter. I got him a job with an advertising firm. It wasn't anything – just calf-love. He caved in straightaway. If you just spoke rough to that chap, he was licking your boots the next moment. But that's of no importance. The first thing is to fix the wedding date."

"You've been against us marrying right from the start," I said, "and now you want us to get married quickly . . . I still can't see why."

"The reason's very simple. Yes, I'm glad you've the grace to blush."

"But why didn't she tell me?"

Brown looked at the chicken the waiter had just brought him. "Chicken again," he grumbled. "I'll be turning into one soon. Well, Joe, she didn't tell you because she didn't want you to wed her just out of a sense of duty. And I didn't tell you because I didn't want you to wed her as a financial proposition. And why the hell should I present you with a gun to hold at my head?"

My respect for him increased. And then I was seized with the fact of sharing life, all life, of being in the main current – everyone talks about the joys of motherhood, but they say very little about the joys of fatherhood, when you feel an immense animal tenderness towards a woman; the Bible puts it exactly right when it talks of your bowels yearning towards someone.

"You mean that you'd let her have the baby and say nothing to me?"

"I'd sooner have that happen than have her miserable for the rest of her life."

"Susan with my son," I said, and smiled. I was dizzy with happiness. It was a happiness as wholesome as honey on the comb, I was a man at last. Instead of having the book snatched from me halfway I was reading in to the next chapter.

"You've nothing to grin about," Brown said roughly. "This isn't the way I'd planned to have my daughter wed." His eyes turned opaque as mercury and his voice had a knuckleduster menace. "Some fathers have sent their daughters away to – nursing homes. It's not too late for that."

"She wouldn't consent," I said in agony. "You couldn't do it either, you couldn't murder your grandchild. I can't believe that anyone would be so rotten. I'll take her away with me tonight, I swear I will."

"You don't know what I can do," he said. "I can get my story in first, and I can handle her better than you can."

"You try it. You try it. I'll take the matter to the police before I let you do it."

"I believe you would." He seemed pleased about it. "I really believe you would. You're an awkward customer, aren't you?"

"Being decent isn't the same thing as being awkward."

"True enough. I've no intentions of sending Susan away, in any case."

"Then what did you give me such a fright for?"

"Wanted to see what you were made of," he said with his mouth full.

"I suppose that's why you warned me off Susan, too?"

"I never warned you off Susan," he said, helping himself to roast potatoes. "My wife had a word with Hoylake at a Church social and he took it upon himself to tell you to keep away from her. That is, as much as he ever tells anyone anything. Proper Town Hall type, that chap."

"Why didn't you say something to me?"

"Why should I? If you had owt about you, I knew you'd damn my eyes and go ahead. If you were gutless, you'd let yourself be frightened off by a few vague threats, and everyone'd be saved a lot of bother. The point is, lad, that a man in my position can't get to know a man in your position very well. So I let you sweat it out."

"Jack Wales didn't have to sweat it out," I said sulkily.

Brown chuckled. "You should have seen to it that your parents had more brass. I didn't make the world."

There was now the luxury of confirming the details of my good fortunes, of admiring the pretty colours of the cheque. "There's one thing I don't understand," I said. "I thought that you had it all fixed between him and Susan. There was talk of a merger. . . ."

"There was nothing fixed and the merger had nowt to do with

it. I'm not a sort of king, I don't give my daughter away to seal a bargain."

"Will this mess up the merger?"

"You've some peculiar notions about business, young man. I never for one moment thought seriously about joining forces with Wales. For one thing, I've been boss of my own works too long to relish being just another co-director; and for another, I don't like the way they're going. They're making money hand-over-fist, but anyone capable of counting up to ten can do that nowadays . . . However, I didn't bring you here to talk about the Wales family. I want you to leave the Town Hall as soon as you can."

"I've not qualified as a cost accountant yet, you know. I've only got the C.S.—"

He silenced me with a wave of his hand. "I judge people by what they do, not by little bits of paper. I've no time to go into much detail now, but what I need, and need damned quick, is someone to reorganise the office. There's the hell of a lot too much paper; it started during the war, when we took everyone we could get hold of, thinking we could always find use for them. I'm an engineer, I'm not interested in the administrative side. But I know what we can and what we can't afford."

"So I'm to be an efficiency expert?"

"Not quite. Don't like those chaps anyway; there's bad blood wherever they are. Alterations have to be made which are best made by a new man. That's all."

"I've a wife and family to support," I said. "How much salary?"

"Thousand to begin with. Nowt at all if you don't make a success of it. You can have one of the firm's cars; there's depots at Leeds and Wakefield you'll be visiting a good deal."

"It's too good to be true," I said, trying to look keen and modest and boyish. "I can't thank you enough."

"There's just one matter to be cleared up," he said. "And if you don't, then it's all off. You've been too bloody long about it already." He scowled. "God, you have a nerve. Whenever I think about it, I could break your neck."

He fell silent again; after a minute I couldn't take it any longer.

"If you tell me what's wrong, I can do something about it," I said. "I can't read your mind."

"Leave off Alice Aisgill. Now. I'm not having my daughter hurt any more. And I'm not having my son-in-law in the divorce courts either. Not on account of an old whore like her."

"I've finished with her. There's no need for you to use that word."

He watched me through narrowed eyes. "I use words that fit, Joe. You weren't the first young man she's slept with. She's notorious for it—" I suddenly remembered, down to the last intonation, Eva's crack about Young Woodley – "there's not many likely lads haven't had a bit there. She has a pal, some old tottie that lends her a flat . . . Jack Wales. . . ."

On a trip over Cologne the bomb-aimer got a faceful of flak. I say a faceful because that takes the curse off it somehow; it was actually a bit of metal about two inches square that scooped out his eyes and most of his nose. He grunted when it happened, then he said: "Oh no. Oh no."

That is what I said when Brown spoke Jack Wales' name and, pressing his advantage home, went on to give chapter and verse.

There was a handshake, there was talk of a contract, there was tolerance – *I've been young and daft myself* – there was praise – *You're the sort of young man we want. There's always room at the top* – there was sternness – *See her tomorrow and get it done with, I'll not have it put off any more* – there was brandy and a cigar, there was a lift back to Warley in the Bentley; and I said yes to everything quite convincingly, to judge from Brown's satisfied expression; but inside, like that sergeant until the morphine silenced him, all that I could say, again and again and again, was the equivalent of those two syllables of shocked incredulity.

Twenty-nine

The month was September, the time was eight o'clock, the weather was unsettled, with a sky mottled with indigo, copper, and tinges of oxblood red. The place was Elspeth's flat, the exact point of space from where I told her it was all over was the brown stain on the carpet in the lounge, just by the door into the corridor. I knew that stain well; I'd spilt some cherry brandy there one night before Christmas. By the time I'd finished telling Alice that I didn't love her, I could have drawn a coloured map of it and its surroundings, correct down to the last scroll on the silly little gilt chair next it.

I couldn't bring myself to look at her and I didn't want to come close to her. I did look at her, of course; she was wearing a black silk dress and a pearl necklace and a sapphire on her right hand which I'd not seen before. Her hands were clenched by her side, and the rouge which she had so carefully applied stood out in two patches on her cheeks. She wasn't wearing her usual lavender but something strong and musky with an animal smell in the background like a newly-bathed tiger if anyone were ever to bathe a tiger.

"So you've finished with me, Joe?" Her lips scarcely moved and she was breathing very quickly.

"I love Susan."

"That's very sensible of you."

"There's no need to be bitter."

"I'm not bitter. Only surprised. How quickly you've changed. How long is it since you—?"

She described everything we'd done together in Dorset, using the simplest Anglo-Saxon words and talking with a cool, dry detachment.

"It hasn't left any mark on you, has it? It was only our bodies that did these things – your young one and my – my *old* one that's well past its best. Why don't you say it, Joe? I'm thirty-four and she's nineteen – you want someone young and strong and healthy. I don't mind, I should have expected it anyway, but why in God's name can't you be honest?"

"It isn't like that," I said wearily. "I did love you, but I can't now. Let's leave it at that."

I couldn't tell her about Jack Wales; it didn't seem important any longer. The knowledge that once she'd made love with him, him of all the people in the world, here on the very bed where I'd lain with her, had come between me and sleep all night; but now that I was with her it didn't matter, it was as dead as yesterday's newspaper. That she had let him make love to her had proved only her contempt for him; she'd used him in an idle hour – as a man might take a quick whisky when tired and depressed – and forgotten him. He was a trivial detail of a past era, dead millions of seconds Before Joe, just as my own dreary copulations in Dufton and Lincolnshire and Germany had been Before Alice.

"It wasn't wise for us to go on," I said. "It would have blown up in our faces anyway. Eva's found out about us, and it's only a matter of time before George does. He's too crafty to be found out himself – I'm going in no mucky divorce courts, and that's flat. And I'm not going to be thrown out of Warley either. What would we live on?"

Her mouth twisted. "You're a timid soul, aren't you?"

"I know which side my bread is buttered on," I said.

She slumped ungracefully into the nearest chair, shading her eyes as if against some arc-lamp of interrogation.

"There's something else," she said. "Why are you holding it back? Scared of hurting me?"

"I hate hurting you." My head began to throb; it wasn't aching but it felt as if a big hammer inside it were stopping just short of the threshold of pain. I wanted to escape from the stuffy little room with its smell of scent and ill-health, I wanted to be in Warley. Alice didn't belong to Warley. I couldn't have both her and Warley: that was what it all boiled down to. I knew that I couldn't explain this to her, but I was forced to try.

"I'm engaged to Susan," I said. "I'm going to work for her father. But that isn't the reason that we've got to call it a day. It's impossible for us to love each other in Warley, and I can't love anyone anywhere else – can't you see?"

"No," she said. "I wish you wouldn't lie to me. It's perfectly simple and understandable and I wish you luck. You needn't dress it up with all this nonsense. Places don't matter." She rose and came over to me. I put my arms around her waist automatically. The hammer inside my head broke into the threshold of pain; it was a crackling neuralgic ache, but it had no effect upon the tenderness and happiness that visited me when I touched her.

"There *is* something else," she said. "Please tell me, Joe. That's all I ask." She looked at me as pleadingly as a German child. Belsen or no Belsen, you gave those skinny little brats your chocolate ration; truth or no truth, I had to give Alice her self-respect. Susan wasn't the real reason for me ending our affaire; but to have made it clear to her that I was leaving her for Warley would have damaged her pride past endurance. So I told her what was, with her body touching mine, a lie; though it wouldn't have been a lie the day before.

"I heard that Jack Wales was your lover once," I said. She stiffened in my arms. "I couldn't bear that. Not him. Anyone else, but not him. Is it true?"

If she'd denied it, I think that I would have taken her back. It was like the pound-note I'd dropped on the floor after our quarrel in the winter; honour, like freedom, is a luxury for those with independent incomes, but there is a limit to dishonour, a sort of Plimsoll line of decency which marks the difference between manhood and swinishness.

"You hate Jack," she said. "I'm sorry about that. You needn't, because he doesn't hate you."

"He doesn't know I'm alive."

"He didn't when we first met. You hadn't come to Warley then. But he likes you."

"You've been with him – lately?"

She unloosened herself from me and went over to the sideboard. "I think we both need a gin." Her voice was calm. "I went with him twice. Once in his car, if you really want to torture yourself, and once here. He took me home from the Thespian Ball the first time." She handed me a drink. "There's only lime-juice."

"I don't want anything." I took it at a gulp, and coughed. "What about the second time?"

"That was after we quarrelled. The night after. I ran across him in a hotel bar."

"Why didn't you tell me?"

"It didn't seem important. I never asked you about your past – or your present, for that matter. We had an agreement about it, in case you've forgotten."

There was a heavy silence in the room, as if some had seeped in from the long grey corridors outside. There suddenly was nothing left to say. She was standing with her back to me at the sideboard; the sun had gone down and I couldn't see her very well, but I think that she had begun to cry.

"Goodbye, Alice," I said. "Thank you for everything."

She didn't answer, and I went out very quietly, as from a sickroom.

Thirty

D rinking my morning tea at the Town Hall the next day I felt very pleased with myself. In the first place, the tea was fresh and strong, with three lumps of sugar and just the amount of milk that I like; I suppose that Ray, who was looking at me with an expression of rapt devotion, had seen to that. My inkwells were clean, and there was a new box of paper-clips and a snowy-white sheet of blotting-paper. He'd even torn off the old pages from the calendar. All accountants, even toughs like me, have a bit of the old maid in them; a neat and tidy desk gives me the same satisfaction as a clean shirt and underwear.

The Town Hall atmosphere seemed all the more pleasant to me because I was going to leave it. I could see the machinery of local government as it really is, appreciate its blend of efficiency and cosiness; I hear a lot of nasty things said about municipal bureaucrats nowadays, but if every business were run as smoothly as even the most slatternly little urban district, then Americans would come over here to learn the technique of greater productivity instead of it being the other way about. I reflected on this, making a neat little speech for the NALGO conference, and when the delegates had finished applauding me – only through sheer exhaustion did they stop – I took out my good news of yesterday, adding to it the fact that I'd parted from Alice with at least a sufficiency of dignity and a minimum of pain, and unfolded it slowly, admiring its glittering colour and intricate pattern an item at a time.

I'd just finished furnishing a house in St. Clair Road, and was driving to the Civic Ball in a new Riley, Susan by my side in a scarlet dress that would make all the other men sick with lust for her and murderous with envy of me, when Teddy Soames entered.

"Heard that you had lunch with Brown on Wednesday," he said. "Leaving us for the lush pastures of private enterprise?"

"Eventually."

"Mention me, will you? I can fiddle an expense account as well as the next man."

"All that I know about fiddling I learned from Mr. Edward Soames, Chief Audit Clerk, Warley UDC – will that do?"

"Just the job. Well, Lampton, we'll get our money's worth out of you before you go – glance through these accounts, will you?"

The tone was supposed to be one of mock severity, but it came out vicious. I grinned and tugged my forelock.

"Yes, Master. Right away."

He gave me the folder of accounts and a cigarette. "I'll expect a box of Havanas in return." He frowned at me. "You don't seem bothered about Alice Aisgill," he said. "Or hadn't you heard?"

"What about her?"

"She's dead."

O merciful God, I thought, she's committed suicide and left a note blaming me. That's finished it. That's finished me in every possible way. Teddy's eyes were a pale blue, as if all the colour had been drained from them; they were probing my face now.

"She was a friend of yours, wasn't she?"

"A very good friend," I said. "How did she die?"

"Ran her car into a wall on Warley Moor. She'd been drinking all night at the Clarendon and the St. Clair. They wouldn't serve her any more at the St. Clair."

"He let her drive home, though," I said. "And he took her money for booze so that she could kill herself." It was hardly fair to blame poor old Bert; but I had to say something.

"She must have been going at the hell of a pace," Teddy said. "They say that the car's bent like that" – he cupped his hand – "and there's blood all over the road. It wasn't till this morning that they found her."

"Where exactly was it?"

"Corby Lane. You know, right up in the north, above Sparrow Hill. It's the last place that God made. What she was doing there at that time I can't imagine."

"Me neither," I said; but I could. I could imagine everything that had happened to Alice after I'd left her. She'd stayed in the flat the duration of two more double gins. Then everything in the room – the little gilt clock, the Dresden shepherdesses and Italian goat-boys, the photos of dead names of yesterday, the flounces and the gilt, the bright chintz curtains, the glass I'd drunk from – had gathered together and attacked her, trivial individually but as deadly collectively as those little South American fish which gnaw swimmers to the bone in five minutes. So she'd run out of the flat and into the Fiat; but once in Warley (she didn't know she reached there, there was a blank until she found herself waiting at the lights in Market Street repeating my name under her breath) she didn't know what to do with herself. She turned up St. Clair Road with the idea of going home. Home would be an abstract notion – Father, Mother, safety, hugs, and hot milk and a roaring fire and all the trouble and grief forgotten in the morning. But as she'd gone past Eagle Road (Joe lives there) she'd recovered her bearings. Home was the house where she lived with a husband she didn't love; she was fleeing towards an electric radiator and George's cold tolerance, she was too old for hot milk, there were no hugs going, even if she wanted any from him, and it would all be even more unbearable tomorrow. She'd reversed at Calder Crescent or Wyndham Terrace and gone to the Clarendon. Probably she'd used the Snug, where she was less likely to see anyone she knew – the Thespians always used the Lounge. If she needed company, if she were able to persuade herself that she didn't care about me ditching her, she could move out of the Snug and return to the main stream, return to, perhaps not happiness, but a sort of emotional limbo. When she heard their voices from the Lounge at about nine-fifteen, she discovered that she didn't want to see anyone whom she knew or who knew me. She slipped out of the back door. To the double gins which she'd had at the flat would have been added three or four more. She still wouldn't want to go home. There was only the St. Clair. The gins rolled their sleeves up and got to work on her: you must eliminate

him from your system, they said. Eliminate, obliterate, expunge.
You've been to the St. Clair often with him? Very well, then, walk
straight in and sit where you used to sit with him. Spit in his eye—

Or had she gone there in an attempt to recapture the decent and
wholesome happiness we shared once when I was nearly a year
younger and fully ten years more innocent? More gins had been
called upon to assist her nearer towards whichever stage of illusion
she wished for, and then she'd started to sing or to swear or to fall
flat upon her face or all three, and Bert, who kept a respectable
house, had persuaded her to leave. She drove up St. Clair Road
again, then along the narrow switchback of Sparrow Hill Road;
but she couldn't exorcise my presence by stopping at the old brickworks. And she still couldn't go home. If she pressed the accelerator
down still harder, she could travel out of herself – I was beside her
in the car now, she was approaching that double bend which only
a racing-car could take at over twenty—

"What a damned awful way to die," Teddy said.

"I expected it," Joe Lampton said soberly. "She drove like a
maniac. It doesn't make it any the less tragic, though." I didn't like
Joe Lampton. He was a sensible young accountant with a neatly-
pressed blue suit and a stiff white collar. He always said and did
the correct thing and never embarrassed anyone with an unseemly
display of emotion. Why, he even made a roll in the hay with a
pretty little teenager pay dividends. I hated Joe Lampton, but he
looked and sounded very sure of himself sitting at my desk in my
skin; he'd come to stay, this was no flying visit.

"Alice wasn't perfect," Joe Lampton said. "But who is? She was
a jolly good sort, and I'm going to miss her very much." He shook
his handsome dignified head slowly. That meant that a moral exor-
dium was on the way. "I enjoy a drink myself, but no-one in charge
of a car should be allowed into a pub. It's lucky she killed only
herself. My God, only yesterday she was alive and cheerful, and
then, all in a second—"

"A second?" Teddy said. "She was still alive when the ambulance
came. She didn't die till eight o'clock."

"Jesus Christ," I said. "Jesus Christ." I turned on Teddy fiercely.
"Who told you? Who told you?"

"My cousin works at Warley Hospital," he said. "Turned me up a bit when I heard about it. She was crawling round the road when a farm-labourer found her. She was scalped and the steering-column—"

I half-ran out of the office and went into the lavatory. But the w.c. door was locked, and it was nearly ten minutes before it opened and one of the Health Department juniors came out looking sheepish and leaving the compartment full of tobacco smoke. I locked the door and sat on the w.c. seat with my head between my hands, those gentle loving hands that had so often caressed what was, because of the treachery in the brain in the head between the hands, a lump of raw meat with the bones sticking through.

At twelve o'clock I told Teddy that I was sick. I don't know what I did till then; I hope that I had at least the decency to make a lot of mistakes checking the accounts. I stood about at the station end of Market Street for about ten minutes, then caught a 'bus to Leddersford. I couldn't eat any lunch, and I couldn't stay in Warley, and I couldn't face the Thompsons. They were sure to talk about her, and then Joe Lampton would take possession of me again. Joe Lampton Export Model Mark Ia warranted free of dust, flaws, cracks, dust or pity; as long as I was in the 'bus I was safe. I tried to make my mind a blank as it speeded up on the main road; a stationer's, a draper's, a tobacconist's, a cricket-field, a little girl pulled along by an Alsatian, an old woman wincing away from the Alsatian, who only wanted to lick her face anyway. Then there were fields and cows and narrow roads wriggling like tapeworms into the new Council estate. But Alice had been killed, and what I saw was the components of a huge machine that now only functioned out of bravado: it had been designed and manufactured for one purpose, to kill Alice. That purpose was accomplished; it should have been allowed to run down and then stop, the driver asleep at the wheel, the passengers sitting docilely with their mouths wide open, waiting for the 'bus to fly away, the estate left unfinished, the shops shuttered and overrun with rats, the unmilked cows lowing in agony with swollen udders, the dogs and cats running wild and bloody-mouthed, and then a great storm to scour the whole dirty earth down to clean rock and flame. I licked my dry lips, looking round the 'bus at the other passengers, sleek, rosy, whole, stinking of food and tobacco and sleep; I closed my eyes as a big sickness came over me. I was cold and trembling and on the point of vomiting, but it was more than that. It was an attack of the truth: I saw quite clearly that there were no dreams and no mercy left in the world, nothing but a storm of violence.

I sat with my hands clasped tightly, waiting for the next blow. It didn't come; so when the 'bus reached Leddersford I went into the first pub that I saw.

It was an old building with an atmosphere of damp plaster and dusty plush; the front door opened directly into the saloon bar. As I opened it, the noise and light from the street outside was cut off. There were a lot of people at the bar, talking in subdued voices. I ordered a rum and a half of bitter, and stood at the bar staring at the pictures which were hung round the walls and on the staircase leading to the Ladies'; they were all battle-scenes, rather pleasant coloured prints with energetic marionettes waving swords with red paint on the tips, firing muskets which each discharged one round puff of white smoke, planting their standards on little cone-shaped hills above the perfectly flat battlefield, advancing relentlessly in perfect parade-ground formation and, occasionally, dying very stiffly with their left hand clutching their bosoms and their right hand beckoning their comrades on to victory. The beer tasted like water after the rum, and for a moment I was nauseated, and couldn't face the idea of having another drink. Then I felt the first tiny glow of warmth in my belly and ordered another; the glow increased until, at the fourth or the fifth, a slatternly happiness sidled up to me: I had eight hundred in the bank, I was going to be an executive with an expense account, I was going to marry the boss's daughter, I was clever and virile and handsome, a Prince Charming from Dufton, every obstacle had been magically cleared from my path—

Every obstacle? That meant Alice. That wasn't magic. How long must she have crawled round in her own blood in the dark? Where was I now? There was Dufton, there was Cardington, there was Compton Bassett, there was Cologne and Hamburg and Essen from the air, there was the wine-growing country of Bavaria, there was Berlin and the pale schoolgirls and their mothers. Five Woodbines for the mother, ten for the daughter. And Dufton again, then Warley, only a year ago. I should have stayed in the place where I was born, and then Alice would be walking round Warley now with her hair shining in the sun or lying on the divan at home reading a play for the Selection Committee or eating chicken and salad if it were the season for salad. I put my hand to my head.

"You ill?" the landlord asked. He had a doughy, expressionless face and a gratingly heavy voice. Up to that moment he'd been talking about football to a knot of his cronies. Now, the wheels of whatever passed for his intelligence creaking, he turned his attention to me. I took my hand away from my head and ordered a brandy. He didn't move to serve me.

"I said, Are – you – ill?"

"Uh?"

"Are you ill?"

"Of course not. I asked for a brandy."

Everybody had stopped talking and were devouring me with glittering eyes, hoping that there'd be a fight and that I'd get my face bashed in; there was nothing personal about it, it's simply that, at any given moment, the majority of people are bored stiff. I glanced round the room and saw that it wasn't a pub for casuals; it was a betting-slip and pansy pub (there were three of them next to me now, standing out like sore teeth amongst the surrounding roughs).

"You've had enough," the landlord repeated. I scowled at him. There was no reason why I shouldn't have walked out; but my feet seemed bolted to the floor.

"I'll buy you one, dear," one of the pansies said. He had dyed hair of a metallic yellow and smelled of geraniums. "I think you're awfully mean, Ronnie." He smiled at me, showing a mouthful of blindingly white false teeth. "You're not doing anything wrong, are you, dear?"

"You'll get yourself into trouble," the landlord said.

"Yes, *please*," the pansy said, and they all giggled in unison. I let him buy me a double brandy, and then asked him what he'd have. It was tonic-and-lemon; pansies only use pubs for picking up boy friends. They don't booze themselves, any more than you or I would if surrounded by bedworthy women who might be had for the price of a few drinks.

"My name's George," he said. "What's yours, handsome?"

I gave him the name of the Superintendent Methodist Minister of Warley, who'd Struck Out Fearlessly Against Immorality (meaning sex) in last week's *Clarion*.

"Lancelot," he said. "I shall call you Lance. It suits you. Isn't it a funny thing, how you can tell just what a boy's like from his first name? Will you have another brandy, Lance?"

I went on drinking at his expense until five minutes to three, then slipped out on the pretence of a visit to the Gent's. Then I bought some peppermints at a chemist's and sat in a news theatre until half-past five. Joseph Lampton was doing the sensible thing, keeping out of harm's way until the rum and the beer and the brandy settled down; and Joseph Lampton was keeping a barrier of warmth and darkness and coloured shadows between himself and pain. I came out into the acid daylight with that headachy feeling that matinees always induce; but I'd stopped thinking about Alice and I was walking steadily.

I went into a café and ate a plateful of fish-and-chips, bread and butter, two queer-tasting cream cakes (that was the time that confectioners were using blood plasma and liquid paraffin) and a strawberry ice. Then I drank a pot of mahogany-coloured Indian tea. When I'd finished my third cigarette and there wasn't a drop of tea left in the pot I looked at my watch and saw that it was half-past six. So I paid the bill and strolled out into the street; I was pretty well in control of myself by then, and it occurred to me that my becoming hopelessly drunk wasn't going to help anyone, least of all Alice. I'd go home – for Warley, after all, *was* my home, I'd chosen it myself – and go to bed with a hot-water bottle and a couple of aspirins. I wasn't Alice's keeper; let George take over whatever guilt there was to bear. Then I saw Elspeth.

She stood in my path, a henna-haired, tightly corseted old woman swaying slightly on her three-inch heels. I had never seen her look such a wreck; her face was so bedizened with powder, rouge, and lipstick, all in shades meant for the stage, that only her red-rimmed eyes were human.

"You pig," she said. "You low rotten pimp. You murdering little—" she glared up at me – "ponce. Are you happy now, you bastard? Got rid of her nicely, didn't you?"

"Let me go," I said. "I didn't want her to die."

She spat in my face.

"You can't punish me any more," I said. "I'll punish myself. Now for Christ's sake leave me alone. Leave us both alone." Her face changed; tears began to furrow the makeup. She put her skinny hand on mine; it was dry and hot. "I 'phoned this morning and they told me," she said. "I knew what had happened. Oh Joe, how could you do it? She loved you so much, Joe, how could you do it?"

I shook off her hand and walked off quickly. She made no attempt to follow me, but stood looking sadly at me, like a young wife watching a troopship leave harbour. I half-ran through the maze of side-streets off the city centre, making my way to the working-class quarter round Birmingham Road. Birmingham Road, if you keep on for about a hundred and fifty miles, does eventually take you to Birmingham; that was another reason for me wanting to become really drunk. All the voyages of the heart ended in a strange city with all the pubs and the shops shut and not a penny in your pocket and the train home cancelled without notice, cancelled for a million years – *Leave us alone*, I'd said to Elspeth; but who was *us?* Myself and a corpse, a corpse that would soon be in the hands of the undertaker – a little rouge, a little wax, careful needlework, white silk bandages over the places past repair, and we wouldn't be ashamed to face anyone. I was the better-looking corpse; they wouldn't need to bury me for a long time yet.

It was the trams and warehouses which forced the drill against the decay inside me. Each time a tram ground and swayed past me, missing unconcerned pedestrians by inches, I saw Alice under the wheels, bloody and screaming; and I wanted to be there with her, to have the guilt slashed away, to stop the traffic, to make all the bovine pay-night faces sick with horror. I didn't mind the other traffic, I don't know why; and I don't know why I thought of such an irrelevant kind of death. Nor why I daren't look at the warehouses. There was one with a new sign – Umpelby and Dickinson, Tops and Noils, Est. 1855 – that still gives me bad dreams. It had sixty-three dirty windows and four of the raised letters on those adjacent the main office were missing. Umpelb and D kinso are the three most terrible words that I have ever seen. I think now that I was frightened because the warehouses didn't care about what had happened to Alice; but why did I hate the innocent friendly trams?

I went on for about a mile, going farther and farther from the main road, but still with the sound of the trams grinding in my ears. It was a fine evening for the time of the year, with an unseasonable soapy warmth trickling along the mean little streets; most of the house doors were open and people were standing inside them, just standing, saying nothing, looking at the black millstone grit and the chimneys and the dejected little shops. It was Friday and soon they'd go out and get drunk. At this moment they were pretending that it was Monday or even Thursday and they hadn't any money and they'd be forced to sit in the living-room amongst the drying nappies looking at their wife's pasty face and varicose legs and hating the guts of the bastard in the next street who'd won a cool hundred on a five-shilling accumulator; then they'd stop pretending and gloat over their spending-money, at least three quid—

I stopped and leaned against a lamp-post because I couldn't go on any longer. I should have gone into the country. You can walk in the country without wanting to vomit, and you're not hurt because the trees and the grass and the water don't care because you can't expect them to, they were never concerned with love; but the city should be full of love, and never is.

A policeman walked past, and gave me a hard inquiring look. Five minutes later he walked past again; so there was nothing else to do but go into the nearest pub. I went into the Bar first, where the customers mostly seemed to be Irish navvies; even when they weren't talking, they gave an impression of animated violence. I was out of place there, as they would have been out of place at the Clarendon, and they knew it. I sensed their resentment with a deep enjoyment. It was what I needed, as satisfyingly acrid as cheap shag; I took half my pint of bitter at one gulp, looking with a derisive pity at the stupid faces around me – the faces of, if they were lucky, my future lorry-drivers and labourers and warehousemen.

I drank another pint. It changed taste several times: bitter, scented, sour, watery, sweet, brackish. My head was full of an oily fog that forced its way up through my throat, the pressure increasing until it seeped into my eyes, and the chairs and the mirrors and the faces and the rows of bottles behind the bar blurred together into a kind of pavane on the slowly heaving floor. The bar had a brass rail, and I clung to it tightly, taking deep breath after deep breath until the floor, under protest like a whipped animal, stayed quiet.

After two rums I moved into the Lounge next door. There were no vacant seats in the Bar and my legs were aching, but that wasn't the reason for my going there. The true reason was sitting alone near the entrance; as soon as I saw her I discovered that she was the one thing necessary to round the evening off, the one drug that I hadn't tried.

She was about twenty, with frizzy blonde hair and small bones; she wasn't bad-looking, but her face had a quality of inadequacy, as if there hadn't been enough flesh available to make a good job of her femininity. When she saw me looking at her, she smiled. I didn't like it very much when she smiled; the pale flesh seemed as though it were going to split. But one hasn't to be too choosy about pick-ups; they're not so easy to come by in peacetime as the respectable would suppose. And there was something about her that suddenly prodded to life a side of me that I thought had been dead for years, a lust that was more than half curiosity, a sly, sniggering desire to see what she was like under her clothes.

I sat down beside her. "I'm not squeezing you, am I?"

She giggled. "There's plenty of room."

I offered her a cigarette.

"Thank you very much," she said. "Oh, what a lovely case." She stroked the silver, her long thin fingers with their too-curved red nails brushing mine. "You don't come from round here, do you?"

"Dufton. I'm a traveller."

"What in?"

"Ladies' underwear," I said. When she laughed I noticed that her upper teeth were scored horizontally with a brown line of decay.

"You're a devil," she said. "Will you give me a free sample?"

"If you're a good girl," I said. "Will you have a drink with me?"

"IPA, please."

"You don't want beer," I said. "How about something short? I've sold thousands of pairs of knickers this week."

"You're cheeky," she said; but she had a gin-and-it and another and another and then a brandy, and soon we were touching each other lightly all the time, coming closer and closer together and yet farther and farther apart; we were, I saw in a moment of clarity before brandy and lust close over my head, only touching ourselves. But at least I wasn't thinking of Alice. She wasn't crawling round Corby Lane now with her scalp in tatters over her face. She hadn't been born, there had never been any such person; and there was no Joe Lampton, only a commercial traveller from Dufton having a jolly evening with a hot piece of stuff.

I think that it was about half-past eight when I was aware of a nasty silence over the room. I looked up; a young man was standing scowling over us. He had the sort of face that one's always seeing in the yellow press – staring-eyed, mousy, the features cramped and shapeless and the mouth loose. He was wearing a light blue double-breasted suit that was so dashingly draped as to look décolleté and he had a blue rayon tie of an oddly slimy-looking texture. At that moment he was enjoying what a thousand films and magazines had assured him to be righteous anger: His Girl had been Untrue.

"Come along," he said to her. "Come along, Mavis."

"Oh go away," she said. "We were all right until you came."

She took out her compact and began to powder her nose. He grabbed her hands. "Bloody well stop that," he said. "I couldn't help being late, see? I was working over."

I'd been measuring him up, wondering whether or not to leave her to him. I wasn't so drunk that I wanted to be beaten up in a Birmingham Road pub. But he was no Garth: he was as tall as me, but his shoulders were all padding and he had a look of softness about him; he was the type whose bones never seem to harden.

"Leave her alone," I said.

"Who the hell are you?"

"Jack Wales."

"Never heard of you."

"I don't expect that you have." I stood up. "You heard what I said." My hand groped about on the table independently of me until it found an empty beer-glass. There wasn't a sound in the room. There was a decently dowdy-looking middle-aged couple at the next table who looked frightened. The man was small and skinny and the woman had pale horn-rimmed spectacles and a little button of a mouth. I remember feeling rather sorry for them, and an anger as smooth and cold and potentially as jagged and murderous as the beer-glass started to grow inside me.

"Take your hands off her." I lifted the beer-glass as if to strike it against the table. His hand loosened and she pulled her wrist away. The compact dropped, and a little cloud of powder floated up from it. He turned and went out without a word. The ordinary noises of the pub began again, the incident obliterated as quickly as it had begun.

"He's not my boy friend really, Jack," she said. "I'm sick of him. Thinks he owns me just because I've been out with him a time or two."

"He's introduced us, anyway," I said. "Mavis. It suits you, darling." She stroked my hand. "You say that nicely," she said.

"It's easy to say things nicely to you."

"You're the best-looking boy I've ever met. And you have lovely clothes." She felt the texture of my suit. It was new, a mid-grey hopsack made from a roll of cloth that Alice had given me five months ago. "I work in a mill, I know good cloth."

"If you like it, Mavis, I'll never wear anything else," I said. My words were beginning to slur. "I feel so happy with you, you're so gentle and bright and beautiful—" I went into the old routine, mixing scraps of poetry, names of songs, bits of autobiography, binding it all with the golden syrup of flattery. It wasn't necessary, I well knew; a skinful of shorts, a thousand lungfuls of nicotine, and ordinary good manners, were enough to get me what I wanted; but I had to have my sex dressed up now, I was forced to tone down the raw rhythms of copulation, to make the inevitable five or ten minutes of shuddering lunacy a little more civilised, to give sex a nodding acquaintance with kindness and tenderness.

"Let me buy the drinks," she said after we'd had two more.

"That's all right," I said.

"You've spent pounds, I know you have. I'm not one of those girls who's just out for what she can get, Jack. If I like a boy, I don't care if he can only afford tea. I earn good money. I took home six pounds last week."

I felt the tears coming to my eyes. "Six pounds," I said. "That's very good money, Mavis. You'll be able to save for your bottom drawer."

"You've got to find the chap first," she said. She fumbled in her handbag. It was a large one of black patent leather, with diamanté initials. There was the usual litter of powder and lipstick and cotton-wool and handkerchiefs and cigarettes and matches and photos inside it. She slid a ten-shilling note into my hand. "This is on me, love," she said. The warm Northern voice and the sight of the open handbag gave me an intolerable feeling of loneliness. I wanted to put my head between the sharp little breasts and shut out the cruel world in which every action had consequences.

I ordered a bottle of IPA and a gin-and-it. Time was beginning to move too quickly, to slither helplessly away; each minute I looked at my watch it was ten minutes later; I knew that I'd only that minute met Mavis, but that minute was anything up to a year ago; as I drank the sharp summer-smelling beer the floor started to move again. Then every impression possible for one man to undergo all gathered together from nowhere like a crowd at the scene of an accident and yelled to be let in: time dancing, time with clay on its hobnailed boots, the new taste of the beer and the old taste of brandy and rum and fish and cornflour and tobacco and soot and wool scourings and Mavis' sweat that had something not quite healthy about it and her powder and lipstick – chalk, orris-root, pear-drops – and the hot hand of brandy steadying me again and just as it seemed that there wasn't to be any other place in the world but the long room with the green *art moderne* chairs and glass-topped tables, we were out in the street with our arms round each other's waists and turning in and out of narrow streets

and alleys and courts and patches of waste ground and over a footbridge with engines clanging together aimlessly in the cold below
as if slapping themselves to keep warm and then we were in a
corner of a woodyard in a little cave of piled timber; I took myself
away from my body, which performed all the actions she expected
from it. She clung to it after the scalding trembling moment of
fusion as if it were human, kissing its drunken face and putting its
hands against her breasts.

There were houses very near on the dirt road at the top of the
woodyard; I could hear voices and music and smell cooking. All
around were the lights of the city; Birmingham Road rises from
the centre of Leddersford and we were on a little plateau about
halfway up; there was no open country to be seen, not one acre
where there wasn't a human being, two hundred thousand separate lonelinesses, two hundred thousand different deaths. And all
the darkness the lights had done away with, all the emptiness of
fields and woods long since built over, suddenly swept over me,
leaving no pain, no happiness, no despair, no hope, but simply
nothingness, the ghost in the peepshow vanishing into the blank
wall and no pennies left to bring him out again.

"You've lovely soft hands," Mavis said. "Like a woman's."

"They're not – not lovely," I said with difficulty. "Cruel. Cruel
hands."

"You're drunk, love."

"Never feltfeltbetter." I'd returned to my body, I realised with
horror, and didn't know what to do with it.

"You're a funny boy," she said.

I fumbled for my cigarette-case. It was empty. She brought out
a packet of Players and lit two. "Keep these," she said. We smoked
in silence for a while. I was trying to will myself into sobriety, but
it was useless. I honestly couldn't even remember where I lived,
and I literally truly Fowler's English Usage didn't know whether I
was awake or dreaming.

"Jack, do you like me?"

"From the veryfirstmomentthat – that I saw you." I made another
effort. "You'reverysweet. Like you verymuchveryverymuch."

The lights started to wheel around and there was a clanging

sound in my ears. "Those bloody engines," I said. "Those bloody engines. Why can't they stop?"

She must have half-carried me away; I don't know how she managed it. We stopped outside a terrace house eventually; I was trying to keep myself upright, and not succeeding very well. Finally I propped myself against the garden railings.

"Are you all right now, Jack?"

"Fine," I said. "Fine."

"You turn left and keep straight on – have you enough for a taxi?"

I pulled out a fistful of notes.

"You be careful," she said. A light came on above us, and I heard a man's voice growling her name. "Oh God," she said, "they've woken up." She kissed me. "Goodbye, Jack. It's been lovely, really it has." She ran into the house.

I walked away, weaving my body from side to side in a pattern of movement which I felt to be not only graceful and harmonious but so exquisitely funny that I had to laugh.

A hand on my shoulder broke the laugh in half and started the Unarmed Combat reflexes working. The gears were stiff, but any second now, I thought with joy, pain and humiliation would move forward to crush the stupid bodies of the two men who faced me.

One of them was Mavis' ex-lover. I didn't know the other, but he was the one who had me worried the most. He seemed quite sober and his shoulders were broader than mine.

"This is the —" Mavis' ex-lover said. "Full of brandy and conceit, the bloody bastard—" He swore at me monotonously; the words depressed me more than they annoyed me. "She's *my* woman, see? We don't like strangers muscling in, see?" His hand tightened on my shoulder. "You're going to be bloody sorry you came round these parts, chum."

"Shove off," I said.

"*You're* shoving off. But not before—" He struck out with his fist; I sidestepped, but not quickly enough, and he hit my cheekbone, cutting it with something (a ring, I realised afterwards). But I thought it was a razor, so I hit him in the Adam's apple. He gave a sound halfway between a baby's gurgle and a death-rattle and staggered away from me, his hands to his throat.

"You dirty bastard," his friend said, and tried to kick me in the groin. More by good luck than good management I turned sideways; but not properly as the PT Sergeant had taught me; his foot landed home on my thigh and I lost my balance and went down with him on top of me. We rolled about on the pavement like quarrelling children; I was trying to keep him off and he, I think, had no idea in his head that wasn't based upon making me suffer as much as his friend (whom I could still hear choking with agony) had been made to suffer by me. He got both hands around my throat and began to squeeze; a black and red stream of pain spread like lava behind my eyes. My hands had lost their strength and I couldn't move my legs and I could taste blood from my cut cheek and smell his hair-oil and the laundered stiffness of his shirt and orange and fish and dog from the gutter; the lamp-posts shot up suddenly to a hundred times their height like bean-flowers in educational films, taking the buildings with them in elongated smudges of yellow light; and then I remembered another of the PT Sergeant's maxims, and I spat in his face. He recoiled instinctively, his hold relaxing for a second; then I remembered a lot more things and within thirty seconds he was in an untidy heap in the pavement and I was running as fast as I could down the street.

My luck was in that night; I didn't see one policeman, and I heard no pursuing footsteps. After I'd been running for about ten minutes I came to the main road and caught a tram to the city centre. My hands and face were bleeding when I mounted it, and I saw from my reflection in the lighted window that my suit had big splotches of dirt and blood on the jacket, and that not one button on my fly was fastened. Fortunately there were a lot of other drunks on board, so I was not as conspicuous as I might have been. I was squeezed up against a woman who seemed the only sober person on the tram, white-haired, with an old-fashioned thick wedding ring, who kept looking at me with a disgusted expression. The words of a Salvation Army hymn erupted to the surface of my mind and, without knowing it, I started to sing under my breath – *The old rugged cross the old rugged cross I will CLING to the old rugged cross*— The disgust on her face deepened to contempt. She looked so clean and motherly, her blue boxcloth coat showing a vee of crisply starched white blouse, that I found tears coming to my eyes. I was grateful to her for noticing me, for caring enough to be disgusted.

The lights and the noise and the cars and the 'buses and the trams and the people in the centre of the city were too much for me. I was nearly run over twice, and I was just as frightened of the people as I was of the traffic. It seemed to me as if they too were made of metal and rubber, as if they too were capable of mangling me in a second and speeding away not knowing and not caring that they'd killed me.

The Warley 'bus station was away from the city centre. I couldn't remember the way, and I couldn't remember the time of the last 'bus. I lit a cigarette which tasted of Mavis' powder and stood, or rather swayed, outside a milk bar near the railway station. I wondered if the police had picked up the two yobs; I'd probably hurt them badly. I thought of the first one's hands, red and scarred, with black ridged nails, clutching his throat, and the limp body of the other with his nice clean collar and new rayon tie spoiled, and I felt a deep shame, as if I'd hit a child.

I walked around until I found a taxi-rank. It took a great deal of finding; having visited Leddersford a few times, I kept a mental street map of the place, which normally I could unfold in a second. That night it had been turned upside down and all the streets had changed their names; I went up one street and found myself in Birmingham Road again, and twice I re-passed the milk bar from where I'd set off. When I saw the row of taxis at the other side of the road, I paused for a second to see if it were safe to cross.

Then I found myself falling. There was a kind of exhilaration about it; I imagined a mattress below me to break my fall, to bounce away from, higher and higher into the sky. . . . There was only the pavement, the cold stone that I wanted to lie upon, to kiss, to sleep with my face against. I struggled up to my feet when I heard a car stop beside me, holding on to a lamp-standard. If it were the police, there was nothing left but to face them; I was too tired and confused to run away, and I knew that if I tried to cross the road by myself I should be killed. I braced myself for the official questions, staring at the dark green standard.

"Time for you to come home, Joe." I turned. It was Bob Storr.

"I have no home."

"Yes, you have. We've all been worrying about you." He took my arm. Eva came out of the car and took my other arm; as soon as she came, I let myself be taken quietly, but I still insisted that I had no home. I sat in the back with her; I was trembling with cold, and she put a rug over my knees.

"My God," she said, "what have you been up to? There've been search-parties out all over Yorkshire for you. The Thompsons are nearly off their heads with worry . . ."

"Susan," I said. "What about Susan?"

"You *are* pie-eyed, aren't you?" Eva said. "She went to London for a wedding-dress this morning. Had you forgotten?"

"Leave him alone," Bob said. "He's had enough for one day."

"I murdered Alice," I said, and began to cry.

"Don't talk rubbish," Bob said.

"Everyone knows that I killed her. The Thompsons too."

"The Thompsons knew that she was your mistress," Bob said. "They had a son themselves and they know what young men are like. They don't blame you. Nobody does."

The car was climbing the eastern heights of the city now, away from the smoke and the dirt and the black fingernails scrabbling the pavement and the sad, lost faces that had tried to keep up with me; the engine purred smoothly, as it would have done if Alice had been beside me instead of Eva, as it would have done if Bob had suddenly grown talons and horns, as it would have done if the world were due to end in five minutes.

I went on crying, as if the tears would blur the image of Alice crawling round Corby Road on her hands and knees, as if they would drown her first shrill screams and her last delirious moans. "Oh God," I said, "I did kill her. I wasn't there, but I killed her."

Eva drew my head on to her breast. "Poor darling, you mustn't take on so. You don't see it now, but it was all for the best. She'd have ruined your whole life. Nobody blames you, love. Nobody blames you."

I pulled myself away from her abruptly. "Oh my God," I said, "that's the trouble."

ALSO AVAILABLE FROM VALANCOURT BOOKS

MICHAEL ARLEN	Hell! said the Duchess
R. C. ASHBY (RUBY FERGUSON)	He Arrived at Dusk
FRANK BAKER	The Birds
CHARLES BEAUMONT	The Hunger and Other Stories
DAVID BENEDICTUS	The Fourth of June
CHARLES BIRKIN	The Smell of Evil
JOHN BLACKBURN	A Scent of New-Mown Hay
	Broken Boy
	Blue Octavo
	The Flame and the Wind
	Nothing but the Night
	Bury Him Darkly
	Our Lady of Pain
THOMAS BLACKBURN	The Feast of the Wolf
JOHN BRAINE	Room at the Top
	The Vodi
R. CHETWYND-HAYES	The Monster Club
BASIL COPPER	The Great White Space
	Necropolis
HUNTER DAVIES	Body Charge
JENNIFER DAWSON	The Ha-Ha
BARRY ENGLAND	Figures in a Landscape
RONALD FRASER	Flower Phantoms
GILLIAN FREEMAN	The Liberty Man
	The Leather Boys
	The Leader
STEPHEN GILBERT	The Landslide
	The Burnaby Experiments
	Ratman's Notebooks
MARTYN GOFF	The Plaster Fabric
	The Youngest Director
STEPHEN GREGORY	The Cormorant
THOMAS HINDE	Mr. Nicholas
	The Day the Call Came
CLAUDE HOUGHTON	I Am Jonathan Scrivener
	This Was Ivor Trent
GERALD KERSH	Nightshade and Damnations
	Fowlers End
	Night and the City

FRANCIS KING	Never Again
	An Air That Kills
	The Dark Glasses
C.H.B. KITCHIN	Ten Pollitt Place
	The Book of Life
HILDA LEWIS	The Witch and the Priest
JOHN LODWICK	Brother Death
KENNETH MARTIN	Aubade
MICHAEL NELSON	Knock or Ring
	A Room in Chelsea Square
BEVERLEY NICHOLS	Crazy Pavements
J.B. PRIESTLEY	Benighted
	The Doomsday Men
	The Other Place
	The Magicians
	The Shapes of Sleep
	Saturn Over the Water
	The Thirty-First of June
	Salt is Leaving
PETER PRINCE	Play Things
PIERS PAUL READ	Monk Dawson
FORREST REID	Following Darkness
	The Spring Song
	Brian Westby
	Denis Bracknel
GEORGE SIMS	The Last Best Friend
	Sleep No More
ANDREW SINCLAIR	The Raker
	The Facts in the Case of E. A. Poe
COLIN SPENCER	Panic
DAVID STOREY	Radcliffe
	Pasmore
	Saville
RUSSELL THORNDIKE	The Slype
	The Master of the Macabre
JOHN WAIN	Hurry on Down
	The Smaller Sky
KEITH WATERHOUSE	There is a Happy Land
	Billy Liar
COLIN WILSON	Ritual in the Dark
	Man Without a Shadow
	The Philosopher's Stone
	The God of the Labyrinth

CPSIA information can be obtained
at www.ICGtesting.com
Printed in the USA
BVHW081443190822
644666BV00003B/55